BLOOD BOUND

Beshadowed
Darkness Unknown
Blood Bound
Shadows Awoken
Everdark Cursed

Published by Fairies and Fantasy Pty Ltd 2021
ISBN: 978-1-922390-20-2 (paperback)
ISBN: 978-1-922390-21-9 (hardcover)

www.selinafenech.com

BLOOD BOUND

SELINA A. FENECH

BOOK TWO OF

BESHADOWED

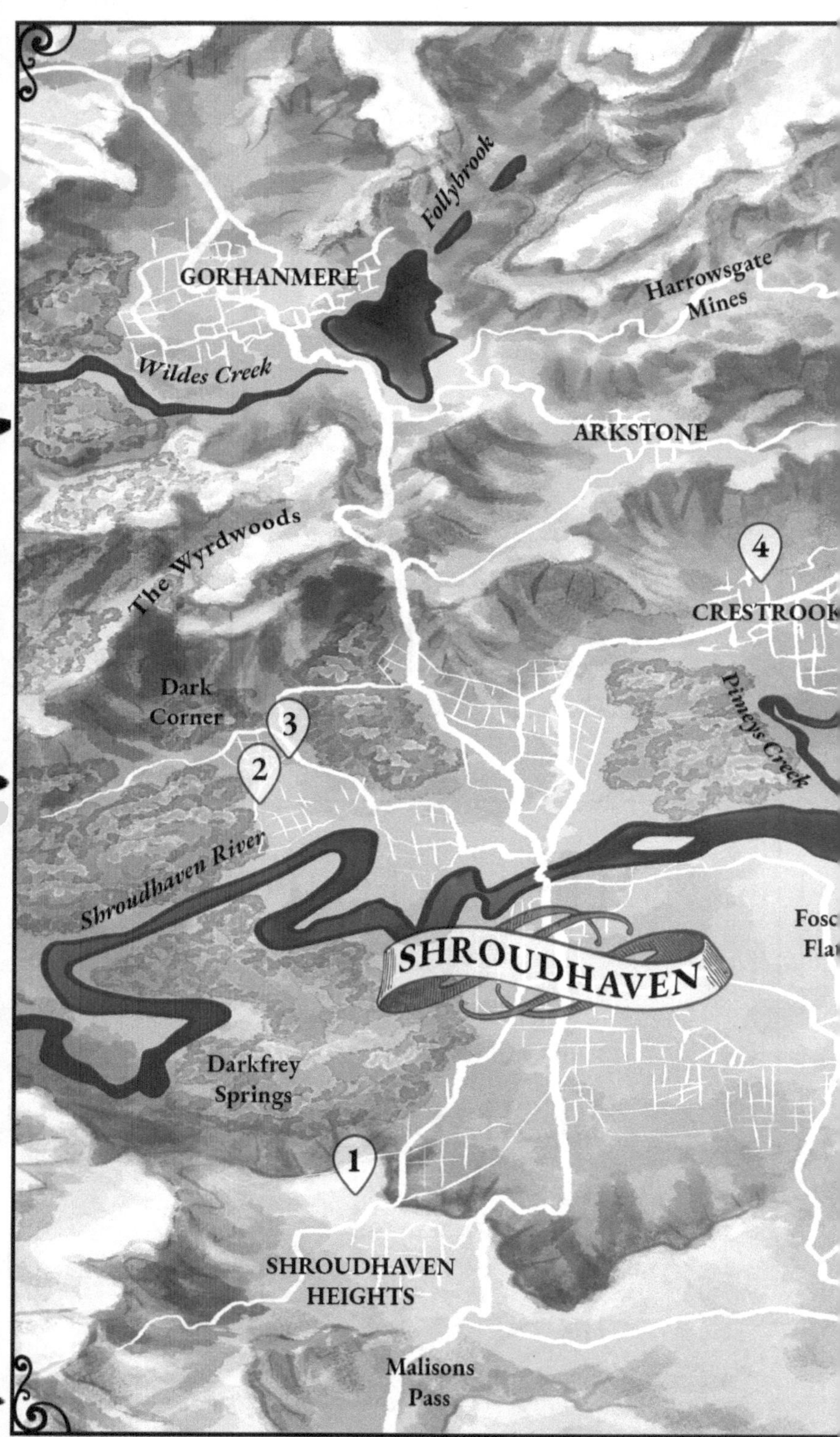

Follybrook
GORHANMERE
Harrowsgate
Mines
Wildes Creek
ARKSTONE
The Wyrdwoods
4
CRESTROOK
Dark
Corner
3
2
Pinney's Creek
Shroudhaven River
Fosc
Fla
SHROUDHAVEN
Darkfrey
Springs
1
SHROUDHAVEN
HEIGHTS
Malisons
Pass

Wolfgrounds
Bright Corner
HARTLEYDALE
6
Terras Beach
meys eak
CRYBELS COVE
IRESTON
Myrkur Lake
Bakers Marsh
Sanctuary Point
CARNOCK ISLAND
5

KEY
1. DARKFREY ESTATE
2. BODERLETH ANTIQUES
3. HOWELL HOUSE
4. CRESTROOK UNIVERSITY
5. CARNOCK LIGHTHOUSE
6. ROOKS HOTEL

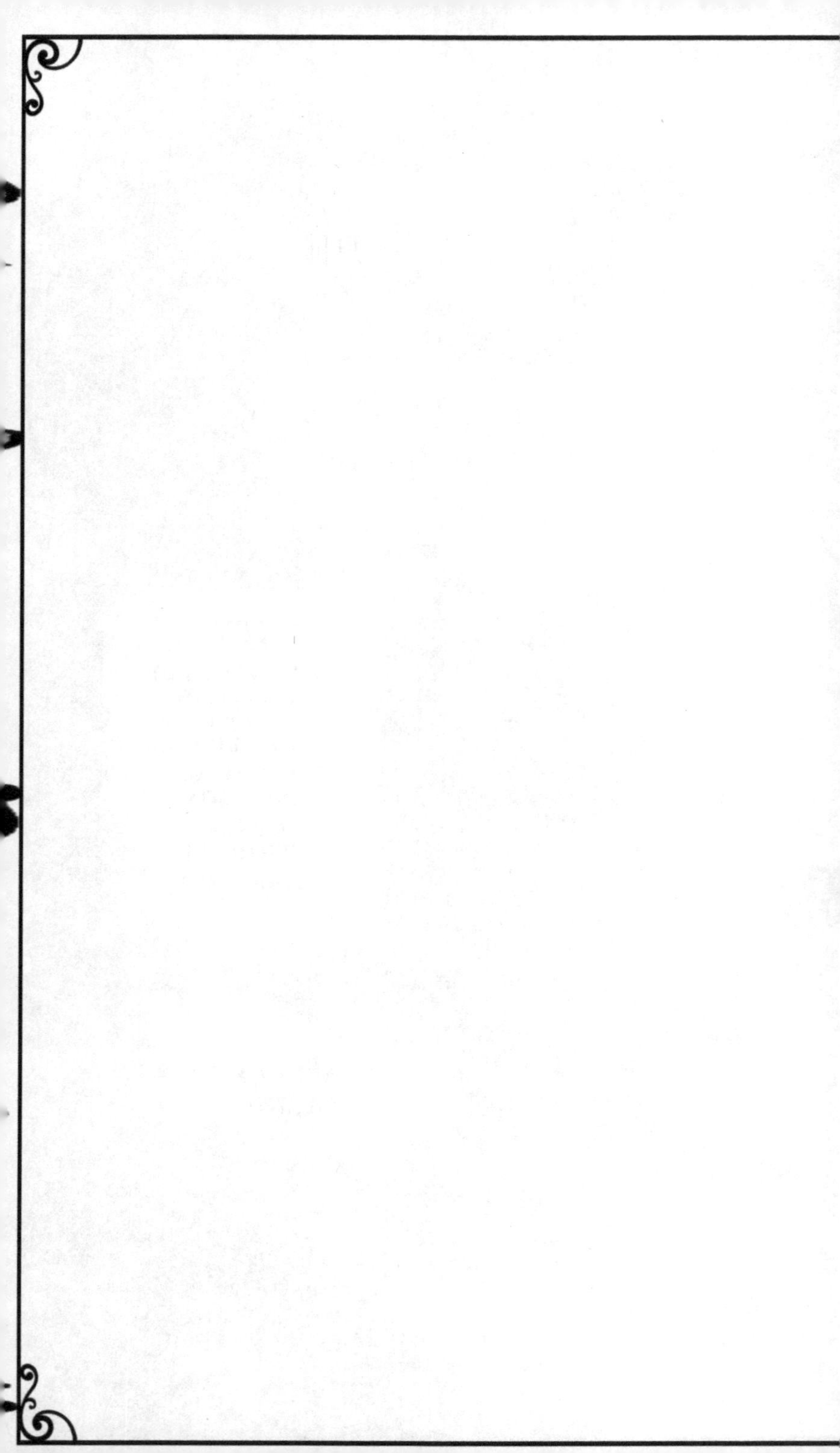

CHAPTER ONE

When Everly used to daydream about having Rylan Howell in her bed, this was never how she'd imagined it.

She used to fantasize about his warm green gaze on her, heavy with love. His body would fit against hers like they were meant to be together, like she'd always believed they were. It was an ever-present yearning. A dream she couldn't shake.

They *definitely* wouldn't have been in the childhood home of her nightmares. In the town shrouded in mist and loss, haunted by the specter of her father's death and memories of a mother who liked whiskey and one-night stands more than her own daughter.

And Rylan would also have been conscious.

"Yep. That's probably the biggest difference." Everly

halted just inside the door and stared at Rylan's still figure lying on the single bed in her childhood bedroom.

No change. She hadn't expected there to be, but she'd hoped. Every moment of the last week, she'd hoped to walk in and find Rylan awake, alert, back to himself. She'd been certain that now he was safe, he'd come out of his supernatural stasis. But as time wore on, it became obvious that something else was wrong.

Now, instead of hoping his eyes would spontaneously open, Everly wondered about the long-term effects of this state on his mind and body.

This can't last forever. He can't last forever, like this.

Everly ventured farther into the room, her steps hesitant. She lifted his wrist. The skin was cool and firm to her touch, almost corpse-like. But his pulse was still there.

It tapped a slow and lazy beat, as though holding onto life was an afterthought for his body. As if some automatic, paranormal process of regeneration brought on by his shadyr powers kept him alive, rather than a mind fighting to live.

If it weren't for his semi-shifted form, giving him the semblance of a vampire, it might almost seem like he was sleeping. His head was tilted ever so slightly toward the door, and his expression was blank and unbothered. Pale, unblemished skin showed no visible injuries, no bruises to indicate that not long ago he'd been flayed open by a vasmire and left to die.

"Are you even in there at all?" Everly squeezed his cold hand.

The one place Rylan seemed most alive was in her dreams. He still appeared to Everly nightly, a conscious prisoner in her dreamscapes. How he ended up there, how to get him out again, and whether that would bring his body back to life, were all questions no one had been able to answer. Everly was sure most of her friends didn't even believe that he was there.

Harper appeared in the doorway with a clattering of beaded bracelets. She peered around the scratched wooden trim with all the panache of a celebrity posing for a headshot.

"Hey, you ready? Callan's pacing out front. He wants to get there ASAP so we don't miss our chance."

Of course, Everly's best friend had chosen to wear a glittery pink plaid flannel over high-waisted, stonewashed denim shorts to go hunting for vasmires. As far as Everly knew, Harper Bells had never appeared before a living soul without a full face of makeup and attire fit for a fashion model.

"Yeah, good to go. Just wanted to check Rylan before we left." Under Harper's gaze, Everly quickly removed her hand from Rylan's.

She zipped up her faded red bomber jacket. Maybe

not the height of fashion, but as comfortable to wear as her own skin.

Also doesn't show up bloodstains too much, Everly thought, her anxious mind serving her up visions of the risks they were about to face.

Harper's nose wrinkled, and she cut her gaze across the shelves at the back of the room where the rotting vasmire parts lay in transparent plastic crates. One bloated, gray tentacle had slipped over the edge, leaking fluids onto the hardwood floor.

"I kind of hoped they would stop smelling after a while," Harper said.

"I think when they stop smelling, they'd be so rotted away they wouldn't be helpful to Rylan anymore."

"Great, great, so no chance of our place not smelling like dumpster vomit anytime soon then?"

Everly tensed.

Harper lifted a hand to her mouth. "It's not that I *don't* think he's going to wake up soon. And I'm totally supportive of him and his monster-gore life-support being here however long is needed. I'm cool. I'll just get a peg or something."

She pinched the bridge of her nose and offered Everly a smile.

Everly slid past her through the doorway, grabbing her by the elbow. "Come on, let's go. You don't want to spend too long in there. You know what Callan said."

Harper sighed, blowing an errant chunk of her long, dark hair from her eyes. "Yeah, yeah. 'Even deteriorating eidolghast bits could cause a beshadowing effect on humans.' Blah, blah, supernatural woo-woo, blah. I don't see you avoiding the room though."

Everly turned away and took the lead as they headed down the narrow staircase. "I'm ... different."

"Sure thing, Sparkles, but we don't know what you are or that you can't get beshadowed."

"But keeping you safe is my responsibility."

"Babe, I know that's coming from a place of love, but I'm my own grown-ass woman and can keep myself safe, thanks very much."

Everly grimaced. She knew Harper Bells was the highest of all high achievers, able to excel at anything she set her mind to. But this wasn't contouring or kickboxing or becoming a successful online influencer.

Harper seemed to be approaching the deadly supernatural side of Shroudhaven with the same enthusiasm she did any new pet project, and Everly didn't like that at all.

"And how are you supposed to do your next photo shoot if you've lost your mind because a monster's rotting corpse has turned you into a mindless zombie?"

Harper gasped in a way that made Everly turn back to face her. Lips trembling, Harper reached out and took

Everly's hands and held them up to her heart.

"Promise me, if it comes to that, *promise me* ... you'll take lots of photos and upload them to my socials for me? Because a mindless zombie photo shoot sounds *amazing*. What a way to go."

Everly chuckled and shook her hands out of her friend's grasp. "You're such a goof."

Harper blew her a kiss. Everly couldn't stay mad at her, and couldn't control her. But she would do everything she could to keep Harper safe.

Stepping off the staircase into the downstairs hallway, Everly took a moment to admire how hard they'd worked to clean the place up.

A week and a half ago, they'd hardly been able to navigate the house, it had been so full of her mother's garbage. And *rats*. The plan had been to clean all evidence of her mother's hoarding tendencies and destroy any remnants of the substance abuse that killed her, then sell the place off to the first interested buyer.

Now ... Everly sighed and turned to leave out the back door. Now their stay was indefinite. Something Harper seemed far happier about than Everly was.

Everly worked at braiding her pale gray hair out of her face as they headed past the jungle of a backyard, and up the side path that led to the front of the house.

The last vestiges of the evening sun still colored the

horizon rosy, but the shadows in Shroudhaven had always seemed darker than most, so the glow barely touched the street. Fog had already crept in off the water, shifting and morphing through the cool evening like ghosts.

Everly shuddered, glancing at the cluster of semi-dead rosebushes where she'd been knocked unconscious the night Rylan was hurt. She vividly remembered the "sculpture" she'd crashed into, and the sensation that all of the black pieces that had broken beneath her had been bones.

Except the pieces had all been gone the next day.

More questions than answers, Everly thought, tugging her jacket tighter against the cold night.

Callan Howell waited on the sidewalk beside Harper's vintage Volkswagen campervan, his nebulous gaze staring into the darkness down the block. Everly could see nothing but blurry shadows, but she knew he had a shadyr's near-perfect night vision, so if anything came at them from the dark, he'd be able to see it. If he didn't sense it first.

He shook his long dark hair back, and it settled around his face in messy layers as he turned his gaze on her. He was like a ganglier version of Rylan, but smiled in a way his brother never did. Especially when he looked at Harper.

Everly hadn't seen Rylan happy since they were kids. Since his father died, and he'd taken the entire weight of it upon himself. Something Everly thought she could relate to, but it had only driven them apart.

"Got you a present," Callan said to Harper, hefting a shiny new axe off the ground beside him and presenting it to her.

Harper took it reverentially, inspecting the chrome-bright sharp edge.

"It's beautiful," she gushed. "And it matches my nails!"

"What? Nothing for me?" Everly said it teasingly but she wished she had some kind of weapon too.

The shadyrs' shifted forms came with inbuilt, natural weapons that she and Harper didn't have. Everly had her dragon, but she couldn't control it. And when it was out of control, it did terrible things. Like taking Nell's husband's life.

She still hadn't shared that secret with the others. How could she tell them what a monster she really was?

Before Callan could reply, a lazy drawl declared, "Don't worry, sexy. I'll protect those sweet curves of yours."

Denny's head poked out from around the back of the campervan door, and he made a clear show of looking her and Harper up and down.

Everly rolled her eyes and kept her gaze firmly trained on Callan, who took the opportunity to mouth an apology.

A step behind Denny came Cherry, who slapped the leering man on the back of the head. "Can you stop being the walking embodiment of sexual harassment for even five minutes?"

Denny rubbed his blond curls where he was hit. "You're just sour 'cause you're no good with the ladies."

"I'm *gay*, you complete waste of sentience."

"Whatever."

"Does he have to come along?" Harper grunted, resting her new axe up on her shoulder.

A smaller figure lurking in the shadows behind Cherry huffed in monotone. "How funny. I was going to ask the same thing about you two blivs."

Tammy leaned her petite, goth-styled self on the back of the campervan. In the faint glow of the streetlamps, her skin had the eerie pallor of a shadyr in vampire form. At sixteen, she was the youngest of the group, and still hadn't mastered keeping control over her form. Even the presence of the rotting parts in the room upstairs had changed her.

Harper jangled the keys to the campervan and headed to the driver's seat. "I've got the only vehicle that can fit all of us, and our potential booty of monster parts. You're welcome."

Tammy unfolded her arms, revealing her ink black hands. She droned, "Not like it matters if you get killed anyway, or if you get us all killed. Makes no difference to me. All got to die one day."

With a lazy eye roll, she flicked her hood up over her buzz-cut head and climbed into the van.

"She's so cheery and sweet," Everly whispered to Callan.

He shrugged, casting a frown in Tammy's direction.

Everly had started making her way to the front passenger seat when Cherry jumped into her path.

He grabbed the door handle. "I call shotgun. Sorry. I get carsick in back."

Everly held up both palms.

"No worries," she said, then went around to the side door, ignoring Denny's leering gaze as she hopped up the shallow steps and into the camper.

Tammy was already perched up on the back bed area, beneath which Harper kept most of her portable photoshoot belongings and wardrobe overflow. The girl looked uncomfortable being the only one stuck in shifted form. Her skin resembled smooth, pale marble, and her fangs had elongated enough to dent her lower lip. She sat so statue-still, she looked dead.

With her lip curling involuntarily in disgust, Everly took a seat on the bench beside Denny.

Callan entered the van last, tugging the door shut behind him.

He slapped his hand against the wall and called, "Hit it, Harper."

He slouched back against the side of the van, clinging to the railing next to the staircase as the van lurched forward. In front, Cherry gave Harper directions between their

gossiping in hushed whispers.

Everly frowned as they drove away from Boderleth Antiques, and Rylan.

"Don't worry." Callan nodded as though he understood her expression. "Mom and Rush are on their way to keep an eye on him while we're gone."

It wasn't only monsters from the Everdark that were a threat in Shroudhaven. Someone had tried to kill Rylan, and might still want him dead.

Callan's gaze swept the world outside. Everly had a feeling those shadyr eyes missed nothing. It was still new to her—the idea that the two boys she'd grown up with lived in a completely different world than she'd ever known.

The knowledge that Callan, Rylan, and their mom Lian were all shapeshifting monster hunters who could take on different classical creature forms, like vampire or werewolf, to fight extra-dimensional demons called eidolghasts, was still taking some getting used to.

There was a woosh of black smokey shadows and sparks as Tammy shifted back into her human form.

"There you go, managed to change back already." Callan smiled encouragingly at the silent girl.

The streetlights flashed by as Harper picked up speed, illuminating Tammy's scowling face in harsh relief.

There was a hint of pink on her cheeks, and she ducked her head farther into her hooded jacket. "Don't treat me like a baby."

Tammy had kept her distance from everyone and had barely spoken during the time they'd been in the same spaces. Everly really wasn't sure what to think of her, except that she clearly had a problem with the world at large and acted like every minute she was alive was a hardship.

Everly knew she had some history of losing someone, and the weird magical side-effect of random teleportation that the same event had left her with. The details were sketchy, but the deep hurt the girl held was palpable.

Beneath Tammy's black lace and leather shirt, the high-tech body armor Everly had seen on other shadyrs showed through. Everly glanced at Callan and Denny and could just make out the form of their armor underneath their shirts and jackets, too.

The Darkfrey shadyrs all wore the same stuff, and Everly realized that the Howell team must have taken theirs with them when they either left or were cast out from the Darkfrey estate. She wondered whether they had any spare sets.

Harper should really be wearing something more protective. But this mission was a rush job, and they hadn't had long to prepare.

Denny lurched off the bench and started poking around some storage crates at the back of the van. "There's got to be some booze stashed in here. Where are we headed again?"

"Rooks Hotel," Callan said. "Our inside at Darkfrey Estate says they've had a report of weirdness happening at the hotel, likely vasmire related. Only just came in, so hopefully we'll get there before the Darkfrey team does."

Cherry hissed a sigh, and his face appeared in the space between the two front seats, bright red hair haloed by the glow of the headlights passing on the other side of the road. "If *the Darkfreys* would just help us out properly, we wouldn't need to go hunting. It's not like their cleanup crews haven't picked up a dead vasmire this week. You know they would have."

Callan grunted his assent, then returned to staring out the window.

"Honestly, I'm getting a little bit sick of *the Darkfrey's* attitude," Cherry grumbled to Harper.

"Aw, no don't say that," Harper cooed.

Her voice lowered again, whispering between them. Their private conversation was quickly interrupted.

"Denny Sketchman!" Harper snapped. "Put that dress back where you found it!"

He lifted the glittery material to his nose and took a deep breath. "But it smells like you."

Callan stepped away from the wall with preternatural quickness and snatched the dress from Denny's hands.

He tossed it through the aisle into Cherry's lap. "Sit down, Denny."

The burly blond muttered curses under his breath, but he obeyed.

Rooks Hotel.

Everly remembered the place from her childhood as a dashing red brick Colonial that sat outside of the downtown area, a little more off the beaten path than most places in Shroudhaven. She could still picture the giant white letters that spelled out the name across the top of the building.

Two chimneys, she thought, as she recalled her younger self thinking the place had horns. It had always had a stellar reputation for customer service and cleanliness, and an old-world charm that wasn't out of place in a town like Shroudhaven.

But when Harper pulled up outside the hotel, and the team disembarked from the van, Everly stared up at a building she didn't even recognize.

Gone were the bright red bricks—they'd turned dull gray, as if the entire building had been covered in ash. The white letters were still in place, but the *S* in *Rooks* had turned sideways, and the *T* in *Hotel* had fallen away entirely.

"What on earth happened here?" Everly asked under her breath as she stopped on the sidewalk beside Callan.

His expression turned hard as he gazed up at the roof. Everly followed his line of sight to see a foggy mist rising from both chimneys. Not smoke. Something else, something heavier.

Something otherworldly.

Callan's starry gaze was haunted as he murmured, "A beshadowing. The worst I've ever seen."

Chapter Two

A low, inhuman moan echoed out of Rooks Hotel, making the hairs on Everly's neck stand on end.

"A beshadowing? What exactly does that mean? What are we going to find in there?" she asked.

Callan waved them all forwards again. "Could be anything. Things get weird. We've seen stuff that would make the best horror movie director weep."

Everly distanced herself from Callan as he led them up the wide front sidewalk to the hotel. If he needed to transform in a hurry, she didn't want to be caught at his heels. The memory of the first time she'd seen him in shadyr form as a monstrous, werewolf-like beast still sent a pang of fear through her.

Faux torches shone from regular intervals along the facade of Rooks Hotel, and the flickering lightbulbs inside that mimicked flames hardly shed any light on the cracked sidewalk.

The glow of a single streetlamp set several yards down the road was nearly swallowed by the fog. Beyond it, Everly could barely make out the half-empty parking lot.

Enough cars squatted low in the shadows to indicate that the building was occupied, but when she traced her gaze up the outside of the hotel, she noted that all the curtains and blinds were closed, and none of the rooms appeared to be lit from within.

Creepy.

Her heart thumped a skittish pulse. The whole situation felt wrong in a way that made her skin crawl. More than the discolored bricks, broken letters, and mist rising from the chimneys. More than knowing they were purposefully walking into a fight with a supernatural monster. The wrongness went deeper.

To the dragon, stirring in her chest.

Shivering despite her jacket, Everly shoved that thought away. She couldn't deal with the dragon right now, or even think about the light that somehow lived inside her and wanted to consume everything it came into contact with.

Just focus on fixing one disaster at a time, she thought, her work boots heavy on the stone steps that led to the front doors.

First and foremost, they needed a dead vasmire to put

beside Rylan's bed to keep his regeneration powers working until he woke up. Then, she could figure out what in this ever-loving hellscape of magical madness was going on inside her own body.

Sometime in the last decade, Rooks Hotel had replaced their old wooden entry doors with a glass and chrome revolving unit. It glinted in the night, and a bit of interior light shone through onto the front landing.

As they drew nearer, they found the glass was completely misted over so that everything inside appeared to be nothing but blurry colors.

"I see movement," Callan muttered.

"Yeah, same," Cherry agreed, his shadyr eyes also sparkling like a miniature galaxy.

"Do you think there are people alive in there?" Everly tried to peer through the doors but couldn't see what they'd seen.

The two men exchanged a glance, and Everly didn't like the unspoken words that passed between them.

Callan shrugged. "If there are, you and Harper can work on getting them out while we go hunting."

"Don't try and sideline us." Harper pointed her axe at Everly. "You don't sideline your nuclear option."

Is that what I am? Ultimate destruction, waiting to explode? Everly practiced her calm breathing. *Just focus on one disaster at a time.*

"So is there a vasmire here or what?" she asked.

When Callan looked back to answer, his transformation had begun. Shadows swirled and eddied around his body, dotted by fiery sparks of light. Beneath the magic, his skin turned ash-white, his teeth elongated, his body morphing into a hard, powerful form that hardly looked like his anymore.

"Yep, that would be a vasmire," Everly said. Exactly what they needed.

Denny, Tammy, and Cherry changed as well.

Callan looked them over, striding along like an army sergeant checking his new recruits. Except as vampires.

"Good work. Hold your forms, this place looks rough. Visibility will be poor, and a building like this will have plenty of places for the vasmire to hide out. We can't let it slip past us or we might not get another chance. Taking it down, and fast, is our priority."

Tammy and Cherry nodded, and Denny gave a mocking salute.

"And us?" Everly asked.

Maybe being sidelined isn't a bad idea.

"Stay close. Watch out for the knock-out gas the vasmire can exude—you don't have protection from it, so get out fast if you have to. You two are strictly support, not frontal attack." He directed his final instruction at Harper. "So no Leeroy Jenkinsing."

"Fiiiiine," Harper agreed.

Tammy grunted in disgust.

Callan eyed her sharply. "Come on."

The motor on the revolving doors was broken, so Callan pressed his palms against the glass and shifted the doors manually.

Everly and Harper leapt in behind him, and the rest of the team filed into the next section as it spun around. Everly shuffled carefully over the carpet so as not to tread on Callan's feet, and then they spilled out into the lobby of Rooks Hotel.

The ceiling soared high overhead, lost in a thick, heavy mist that hung over everything.

"What were you saying about avoiding the gas?" Everly tried to breathe shallowly as the fog swirled around her ankles and up to her waist.

Callan sniffed the air. "This is something different. Probably more to do with the beshadowing than coming directly from the vasmire. You feeling faint at all?"

Everly steadied herself, taking a moment to be mindful of how she felt. She was no fainter than usual with her anxiety.

"No, seems okay."

Harper shook her head too.

Callan swung his arm in a sharp gesture, and the three other shadyrs followed him slowly as he continued in.

Harper whispered to Everly. "That means we follow."

"When did you learn military field signals?"

"Last night." Harper grinned.

"Of course you did."

They moved into the vast and misty foyer as a unit. Over to the right, an unattended reception desk was marked by hanging signs for *Check Ins* and *Customer Service*.

To the left, through the churning haze, Everly could trace the hint of an alcove with a bar and shelves of liquor. The space in between reception and the bar held scattered comfy chairs and coffee tables. Everly squinted, unsure if any were occupied. Then behind the hulking, black bar counter, she saw movement.

Callan lifted a fist and everyone froze.

Out of the dark swirls, a man stood at a strange angle, leaning heavily to one side. He moved a metal cocktail shaker slowly up and down as he stared off into space. There was no sound of ice or liquid sloshing within. His bared teeth glinted in the gloom.

"Is he ... okay?" Everly already knew the answer but thought that 'okay' sounded better than asking if he was human, or if he was lost beyond any chance of saving.

"Maybe we should che—Holy shit!" Cherry gasped.

A short, curvy blond woman in a navy-blue skirt suit appeared right in front of them.

Tammy inhaled sharply and seemed to flicker. With a

deep gulp, she stilled again.

"I'm *fine*," she preempted.

The woman swayed in a small circle, the mist following her like a whirlpool. Her eyes were riveted somewhere over Everly's shoulder. A rectangular gold nametag on her jacket read, *Brooke, Assistant Manager*.

Cherry waved his hand in front of her glazed eyes. "Hey, hi there? Are you hearing me?"

"Welcome to—" Her voice crackled.

Her head twitched. She smiled wider than humanly possible.

"Welcome. Welcome to to to to. Welcome ttttttttttttttttt." Her mouth gaped open.

A hushed, unhuman static emerged, like a stifled scream. Then the blond woman sidestepped him and continued a slow journey across the room, seemingly without a destination in mind. She hadn't even reacted to Cherry's very obviously *not human* appearance.

"Wow, that was creepy as all get out," Denny said, cracking open a beer can.

"Did you steal that from the bar? For ghast's sake, dude," Callan hissed.

"What? They aren't going to miss it. Look at them. Too far gone."

He flicked his chin toward the foyer. The haze had cleared just enough to show the silhouettes of half a dozen people, shifting about. Their movements were jerky and repetitive, caught in a nightmarish loop. Soft mutterings came through on croaky voices.

"Non-smoking. Non-smoking. Non-smoking."

"My room issssss ... room isss ..."

"Hell ... hell ... hell ... hello, do you have ... have ..."

Some moved closer. They trudged as if they couldn't lift their feet, eyes glazed over and bodies stiff. Almost zombie-like, but with the most chilling, wide grins plastered on their faces.

"Can we save them?" Everly asked.

"We can save them, and Rylan, by taking out the vasmire." Callan shook his head and pointed across the side, toward a sweeping staircase. "We have to act fast. This is the latest stage of beshadowing I've ever seen."

"How long do you think it's been like this?" Cherry said, as he and Denny moved up to join their team leader.

Callan shrugged. "Don't know. The place is family run—live-in staff. I doubt they've been answering the phones and taking new reservations. Everyone here is non-responsive. Any drop-ins pulling up out front may have assumed the place was closed. It's still weird it got like this without anyone noticing though. It normally takes ages for things to get this bad."

Tammy droned, "All these people, and no one even noticed they were gone. Sounds about right."

Everly shivered. "Can the beshadowing still be reversed?"

"It can, up until when a permanent shroudpool forms," Callan said darkly.

"Let's stop that happening, shall we?" Cherry said.

Callan led them up the wide staircase to the second floor. Everly got the sense he was following something only the shadyrs could feel—whatever magic warned them that an eidolghast was nearby.

Harper whispered, "Are beshadowings always zombie fun-times like this?"

"Oh no, they come in all kinds of nightmare fuel flavors. Anything you could imagine, and all the things you wouldn't want to imagine." Cherry grinned at them in a way that mimicked the zombified hotel guests.

"Quiet," Callan snapped. "It's close."

Harper nodded seriously, lifted the axe off her shoulder, and held it in front of her with both hands.

Everly wished she had a weapon to hold onto, too. Rather than one she had to hold back.

The farther they walked, the more the proximity of the creature strengthened the Howell team's transformations. Their skin hardened and smoothed to resist the vasmire's toothy tentacles. Their breathing slowed to almost nothing to protect them from the noxious gas that oozed from the monster.

Callan had explained that the fangs they grew were venomous and could be used to fight back. But most modern shadyrs found biting their repulsive enemies a bit distasteful. Their vampire form luckily also came with strength that could rend the monsters tentacle-from-tentacle.

Callan stalked down the hallway, his head turning this way and that as he seemed to note the monster's movements. They stepped around an overturned cleaning cart.

The mist was thicker up there, and it undulated around them as the group moved, casting disorienting swirls and shadows. A painting of a lighthouse hung on the wall beside them, dripping black ooze.

A guest emerged from the mist ahead—a man with gray-streaked hair and unfocused eyes. He was in a bathrobe, a business suit underneath, dripping wet as if he'd just showered fully dressed. He dragged a white bedsheet along in one hand.

Something else swirled in the darkness behind him.

"You see it?" Cherry hissed.

Callan nodded.

"Hey, check this out," Denny said loudly from a few feet back.

Rolling his arm like a baseball pitcher, he flung his empty beer can at the catatonic guest. It plinked right off his forehead.

"Score!" Denny cheered.

Callan, Cherry, and Tammy all hissed at him, fangs bared.

The vapor shifted violently, like an ocean parting around a swimming creature.

Everly caught a glimpse of something long and writhing stretching down the hallway, and then before she could scream, it wrapped around the businessman's torso and yanked him away into the pitch-black mist, disappearing again in a split-second.

"You idiot," Cherry growled, pushing Denny against the wall.

Tammy sped off, racing after the escaping vasmire.

Callan yelled, chasing after her, "Not on your own! Damn it!"

From a distance, a soft crunch echoed through the hall, followed by wet, gurgling, slurping noises.

Harper grabbed Everly's arm with a gasp, and Everly's head reeled, nausea rising in her belly. She could feel Harper's long talons biting into her bicep through the heavy fabric of her jacket, but she'd lost the ability to comprehend anything else beyond those sounds of a human body being consumed.

Another wave of nausea hit her. Their target was getting away. They were split up. People were being *eaten*.

Cherry and Denny need to go after the others. They have to get the vasmire. Why isn't Denny saying something dumb?

It wasn't like him not to fling an insult right back again. She looked for them in the mist, and found them frozen in place, Cherry's fists still bunched into Denny's shirt. Both smiling.

Everly choked on panic.

"Harper? We have to get out of here! We have to get—!"

Chapter Three

"We have to get one of those cocktails!" Harper squealed happily.

"Huh?' Everly jerked, startled by the bright light. She blinked away a foggy haze in her eyes to find that she stood at the Rooks Hotel front desk. Harper leaned beside her, wearing an oversized floppy sunhat and eying the bar.

A pretty blond clerk smiled over the counter. *Brooke.* The name floated to the surface in Everly's mind.

"Was that a single or double bed, Miss Boderleth?"

Leaning in like it would help her understand, Everly said, "I'm sorry, what?"

"Do you need a room with a single or double bed?" the clerk repeated pleasantly, as if she had all the time in the world.

Everly's gaze darted as she tried to ground herself. A

nameplate confirmed that the clerk was Brooke. Assistant Manager.

How did I know her name?

Memories of swirling darkness, unresponsive victims, the crunching of bones came back to Everly.

She grabbed Harper's arm. "Something's wrong. This place is beshadowed."

Harper chuckled. "Are you okay? Is this PTSD?"

"No, we were just there … here … but it wasn't like this."

Harper lifted the brim of her hat and squinted down at her. "Babe, that was weeks ago. Really, are you okay?"

Weeks ago? Everly's brow wrinkled.

She turned away to look around the hotel lobby, astonished to find the sun was high and bright, shining in through wide windows.

No more mist hovering over the hotel. The floors and surfaces were all sparkling and new, and a crowd of guests meandered around, laughing and chatting. No zombified snacks-in-waiting to be seen.

The rest of the Howell gang were nearby, too. Tammy and Denny sat across from each other in cushy armchairs, while Cherry and Callan were playing catch with some car keys.

Everly nodded. "Right. Yeah, I'm fine, sorry, just got confused for a minute. Go grab your cocktail while I sort this out, okay?"

Harper gave her a final assessing frown, then pranced over to the bar.

"I'm dreaming. This isn't real," Everly whispered to herself, using the words that had always been able to keep her lucid in her nightmares. "Wake up."

Nothing happened. *Okay, maybe not? But how did I lose weeks?*

A moment ago, she'd been standing in the upstairs hallway hearing a man get eaten by a vasmire. Had the monster come for her next?

Am I dead?

Brooke cleared her throat. "Do you need to check with your party?"

Everly flushed red, realizing the woman no doubt heard her talking to herself.

"Um, yeah. I do." She gave the woman an awkward smile, then crossed the pristine carpeted floor to her group.

Callan came over, intercepting her halfway. "Don't tell me they're out of rooms. I know it's, like, the only hotel in Shroudhaven, but I was really looking forward to a spontaneous vacation."

"A vacation?"

"We deserve one after everything, don't we?"

"I guess. But, don't you think something seems off? What can you remember from the last few weeks?"

Callan frowned, then shrugged and laughed. "Not

much, but that's why we need a break."

"You don't find that weird? I can't remember either. Like we were just investigating the beshadowing moments ago. Remember the guy in the bathrobe? The munching sounds?"

Callan smiled. "That was ages ago. We're safe now. Everything is fine."

Everly nodded vaguely, but his reassurance only creeped her out more. Either she'd somehow fugue-stated her way through the last few weeks, or something else was going on. She looked around for other signs this was a dream. Anything strange or out of the ordinary, even a small detail.

But the proof she got was much bigger.

"Everly?"

She whirled, her heart hammering at the sound of Rylan's voice echoing through the cavernous lobby.

He jogged toward her from the front door. He was still clad in the clothes he'd worn the night of his attack: a tight black t-shirt beneath a gray-green military-style hooded jacket embroidered with the Darkfrey crest. His gaze raked the lobby, taking everything in.

Could he have woken up? Could this be real? Or …

"Dreaming about my brother now?" Rylan smirked.

"So this *is* a dream?"

"You didn't know? I suppose it is the most completely mundane setting I've ever seen your brain conjure up."

Rylan's gaze still swept the space, as though the armchairs would come to life and try to eat them at any moment.

Callan had grown very still beside Everly.

He looked at his brother with an intense expression. "You ... You're here. When did you wake up? I can't remember."

Everly stared at him. "That's a weird reaction for a dream figment."

"What did you call me?"

"Look, just, give us a second, okay?" Everly rubbed her forehead, completely confused about what was or wasn't real.

She grabbed Rylan by the arm and dragged him away from Callan.

They stopped off to the side of the revolving door, near the luggage trolleys. One of them held Harper's set of rose-gold suitcases.

If this is a dream, the details are amazing.

Rylan stared at Everly's hand around his bicep. "You're worrying me. What's going on?"

Everly took her hand back and bit her lip. "You really haven't woken up? This isn't real?"

He gestured to his appearance, which had seemed locked in since his near-death experience. "I don't remember waking up. I remember your last weird dream about the train filled with blood—not one of my favorites by the way—and now we're here."

"Yeah, okay, it was a longshot, but I needed to check. Last thing I remember we were here, at Rooks Hotel, but it was beshadowed. Late stage, Callan said. We were hunting a vasmire because the pieces we've been using to keep you safe are deteriorating and losing their effectiveness."

"They brought *you* to a *beshadowing*?" Rylan barked, tossing a glare at his brother.

Callan remained where they'd left him, still staring back their way with a pinched expression.

"The point is, when we got here everyone was walking around all zombie-like, mist everywhere. Then suddenly I'm here in this dream with you."

Rylan tossed one more glare at Callan, then turned his attention fully to Everly. "You mean, you could still be there, asleep or knocked out? You've got to wake up and get away. Can you wake yourself up? Like I've seen you do before?"

Everly shrugged. "It was the first thing I tried. I can try again, but I think ... Rylan, I think it's an outside force keeping me here. It feels different."

The hard, determined look of a shadyr on a mission faded, and he reached out to take hold of both her arms. "Try."

She drew strength from the dreamy warmth of his hands.

Closing her eyes, she spoke. "Wake up. You're dreaming. Wake up!"

Nothing changed.

A muscle ticked in Rylan's jaw. He turned and studied the Howell team.

"What about them? Can they help? I mean, are those actually my brother and his friends, or are they figments of your imagination?"

"Callan did react weirdly to seeing you." She turned towards the other people in the foyer who were enjoying the warm light and happy atmosphere. "What if this is a dream, but it's not *my* dream."

"Umm, explain?"

"It's not just me here, it's the whole Howell team, Harper, all the hotel staff and guests. Everyone who was in the hotel before."

"And me?" Rylan asked.

"You've piggybacked along with me, but whatever this is, it's not my dream. I think this *is* the beshadowing. Maybe all of us at the hotel are caught in this dreamworld, and our bodies are still out there, bumping around like zombies waiting to be eaten."

Rylan brushed a hand over his face and the look of abject disbelief there. "Could you have gotten into a worse situation?"

"Who knows. I've had to figure most of this out on

my own because you and your brother kept so much from me to begin with," Everly snapped. "Maybe I'd have had a better handle on all this beshadowing stuff if you'd just been up front with me years ago when you packed off to Darkfrey Estate."

To his credit, Rylan looked suitably chastised, but his voice came out stern. "I know. I'm sorry. But the secret was bigger than just you and me. I wanted—"

"Later. We don't have time. We have to find a way out of this mess before the vasmire eats one—or all—of us."

"Then let's go see if the others are themselves enough to help."

They went back to Callan first, who stood with his arms crossed, foot tapping. "You two have some explaining to do. How is Rylan here?"

"You don't remember the last couple of weeks because they didn't happen. We're still in the beshadowing, trapped in this dreamworld. Rylan has somehow hitchhiked along with me, what with him living in my dreams. I don't understand it better than that."

Callan nodded slowly. "If this is a dream though, why would I think he's even real?"

Rylan crossed his arms to match his brother. "Want me to prove I'm real? On a scale of one to wetting yourself in front of Alexis Darkfrey, how embarrassing of an anecdote from your childhood do you want?"

The two brothers stared at one another for a long moment, Rylan with watchful expectation. Several emotions crossed Callan's face—embarrassment, confusion, dawning horror.

"Ghast damn it. We're zombies, aren't we? Like all the others?"

Everly nodded. "That's my best guess."

Callan pointed at Rylan, but looked at Everly. "And he ... You *were* telling the truth. That's actually Rylan. He's *in* your dreams. Like, real in your dreams."

Everly put her hands on her hips. "What, you thought I was psychic when I dragged you to the theater to find the eidolghast he'd killed?"

Callan stared at his brother. "I guess, maybe I thought you'd just gotten lucky. I didn't know what to think."

He gave his head a sharp shake, his eyes glossy.

Stepping forward, he flung his arms around Rylan. "It's so good to see you."

"You too."

Stepping back, Callan couldn't seem to take his eyes off Rylan. "Wow, this is ... How'd you get trapped in Everly's dreams?"

Rylan shrugged. "We don't know."

"Can we discuss theories later?" Everly said. "More escaping now."

Callan nodded. "Let's clue in the others."

They rejoined their group by the armchairs. Movement caught Everly's eye, and she saw her spirit-cougar dash skittishly up the stairs, spooked by the different atmosphere. It had ended up here, too, and clearly didn't like it.

Everly hadn't seen her dragon yet and hoped it wouldn't show up. She had no idea how it would behave in this dream realm, with so many people around. Another reason to get out of there fast.

"Hey, Harper?"

Harper didn't look up from where she lounged in her chair with her legs crossed over the armrest.

She tapped away on her phone with one hand and sipped a peach-pink cocktail from a martini glass with the other. "Hey babe, yours is on the table there. Reception here is amazing."

Denny sat across from her, reading a magazine, and Tammy had wandered away over to the bar, probably when Harper sat down. She seemed to especially have an issue with Bellsy.

Cherry saw Callan and Everly approach first, saw Rylan with them, and his jaw dropped.

Callan lifted his chin. "Yeah man, Mordan Darkfrey's my sugar daddy."

Everly raised an eyebrow. "What?"

Cherry's face changed immediately, as if a veil had been stripped away from his mind. "Whoa. We're beshadowed?"

Rylan looked at Callan, bemused. "Mordan Darkfrey is your sugar daddy?"

Callan shrugged. "We needed a warning phrase for when things really went off the wall, something we'd never normally say. I like to plan for every possibility."

Denny put his magazine down and slapped his thigh. "No way! I didn't think we'd ever need that one."

Callan scowled at him. "We only needed it because you screwed everything up for us with that dumb beer can stunt."

"Oh, come on. It was a perfect bullseye!"

"You know what your problem is?"

"Yeah, my dick's too big."

"Wait, wait, wait, what? Who is who's sugar daddy?" Harper put her phone down and glanced up. Then she caught sight of Rylan. "WHAT?"

Rylan seemed to be key at jarring people to their senses. Whatever constructed reality surrounded them, lulling them into feeling safe, it hadn't accounted for his presence.

Everly reached down for Harper and pulled her to her feet. "Trapped in a dream, wacky dream magics, yadda yadda. Can you wake yourself up?"

Harper's pretty face screwed up. "The vasmire ... the guy in the bathrobe and the ... It *ate* him, didn't it?"

"Yeah, and it's going to eat us if we don't get the hell out of here. Can you wake up?" Everly repeated.

Harper jumped on the spot and pinched the backs of her hands and screamed, drawing the attention of the other guests. "That would seem to be a no."

Rylan patted his brother on the shoulder. "Good idea setting up a phrase like that. I'm impressed."

Callan turned to him with a glowing grin, and they clapped one hand each into a tight grasp, pulling in for another brief embrace.

"This might be the hottest bromance I've ever witnessed," Harper whispered not at all quietly to Everly.

"Who is she?" Rylan asked.

"Harper? I've mentioned her. I'll introduce you two properly once you wake up for real." Everly rushed out. "We need a plan *now*, and we need a plan *fast*. I already tried to wake myself up, but I can't. Whatever the vasmire has done to us, we're in deep."

Cherry's expression twisted. "We're all just sleepwalking the halls, waiting to be picked off and eaten by the monster. The vasmire's own personal buffet. Yeah, not loving this."

Everly chewed her thumbnail, thinking. "If we can get even one of us awake, they could have a chance to save the rest of us."

Rylan's voice came out deadly serious as he said, "I'd bet that as long as your bodies remain in the beshadowing, no one's waking up."

"Tammy," Callan said suddenly.

Rylan frowned. "What about her?"

"She has this ... I don't know, I guess it's an ability, but not something she seems to control. She can teleport to the Dark Corner shroudpool."

Rylan glanced over to where she stood with her back to them at the bar. In her all-black outfit, she looked out of place in the bright and cheery foyer.

"Tammy Kyrstelle? The kid that got kicked out of Darkfrey Estate after she had some part in the Mesman boy's death? She can *teleport*?"

"Only to that one place," Callan went on. "But yeah, like, poof, gone."

"So, what?" Rylan said. "We get Tammy to teleport out of this dream, and she goes right to another dangerous, beshadowed place? That doesn't seem helpful."

"At least she'd be dealing with it while conscious, unlike here. Plus it happens to her every other day, so she's familiar with the area and its effects," Callan clarified. "Once she's out of here, she can bring back up."

"If we can get her to teleport on purpose. I thought it was involuntary," Everly said.

"She just needs a good scare," Denny said, chuckling. "Once I farted loudly and she popped out of existence."

"Your farts would make anyone want to pop out of existence," Cherry scoffed.

"Your general presence would make anyone want to pop

out of existence," Harper added, and Cherry high-fived her.

Callan shot them a look. "Great, so we have a plan. Now we just need to convince Tammy this is a dream and make her zap herself away from here."

"I'm hoping for a two-birds-one-stone situation," Everly said. "Just learning it's a dream might set her off."

Callan nodded, and led the group over to the bar.

The sullen girl leaned heavily on the counter, making a pyramid of empty shot-glasses with her ink-black hands.

Everly cast a concerned look as the bartender poured out another row of five tequilas. "Um, hey. Tammy? Can we talk?"

She side-eyed them, peering at Everly, Callan, and Rylan in turn through narrowed, smokey eyelids. "If you're about to tell me we're in a dream, don't waste your breath."

"You know?"

"I'm just taking the opportunity to get dream-trashed since this dream-bar doesn't card me." She reached over and downed another shot.

Callan pushed the rest out of her reach. "How did you—?"

"Mordan Darkfrey is your sugar daddy. Your voice carries. It's grating."

The signs of a mammoth effort of patience played out over Callan's face. "Did you hear the plan then?"

"Yeah, and it's not going to work. I've never been able

to teleport on purpose. And yes, I've tried." She stretched past Callan, reaching for another drink.

When he wouldn't budge, she leaned over the counter and took a whole bottle.

"Just give up. We can happily dream-drink ourselves into oblivion while our bodies become vasmire-food. There are worse ways to go." She moved to take a swig of the cheap whiskey.

Callan snatched the bottle from her hands and threw it against the wall. The glass shattered in a loud explosion. Everyone in the foyer turned to stare as one. Then as though nothing happened, they returned to their happy selves.

"We're not giving up," Callan growled. "I'm not giving up on you."

Tammy stared up at Callan with a look of pure, teary petulance only a teenager could muster.

Callan scooped both of her hands into his and held them between their chests. "Work with me here, please."

Everly thought she saw a pink tinge rise in the girl's neck and cheeks, but it disappeared almost immediately, as if Tammy had willed it away. "Fine. I guess. Whatever."

"Close your eyes. I want you to picture Dark Corner shroudpool."

The skin at the corner of Tammy's eyes tightened. "Great. My favorite place."

"I know it's hard for you," Callan said gently. "But

you're our only hope right now, okay? You're the only person with the ability to leave."

Tammy took a deep breath, and her perpetual pout and angry glare was smoothed away, replaced by a hint of determination.

"Imagine the place where you typically show up when you teleport," Callan went on. "Picture it in your mind."

Tammy breathed deeply in and out, and her eyelids flickered as if she were seeing exactly what Callan told her to see. "Okay."

"Imagine you're there, standing in that spot. Really visualize it, down to every last detail."

Her shoulders rose and fell slowly with her breathing. She leaned forward, her head dipping as if she were falling asleep. Callan leaned in, too, and placed his forehead on hers.

Tammy gasped, and her eyes fluttered open to zero in on Callan's face so close to hers.

Then she was gone.

"She did it?" Everly gasped.

Callan dropped his hands and leaned on the bar with a long, low sigh. "Well, it either worked or—"

Or Tammy disappeared from the dream for another reason, one no one wanted to say out loud. That she was the first to have been taken by the vasmire.

Callan shook his head. "There's no way to know."

Everly turned to Rylan to find him staring back at her. He frowned and looked away.

"I don't like this." His voice was gravelly.

That they were relying on a surly, nihilistic sixteen-year-old to teleport herself across town to a beshadowed danger zone, make her way alone out of there, get help, and get back to them in time before anyone else got eaten?

Yeah, I don't like it much either.

All faces were grim surrounding Everly. "All we can do now is wait and see."

Chapter Four

I didn't think I'd ever be happy to see this place.

Tammy blinked, clearing the hazy dream world away and taking in the eerie corner of the Wyrdwoods that had ruined her life.

She'd appeared flat on her back, a few yards from the semi-dormant shroudpool that drew her to it like a bath-toy down a pulled plug.

Her heart hammered from the phantom sensation of Callan's forehead pressed against hers. She brushed the tips of her fingers over the place where their skin had touched and shivered. It hadn't taken any visualization or deep thought to send her teleporting out of the hotel and into Dark Corner.

Only the touch of Callan's skin and his face infinitely close to hers.

Ugh. I don't like him. I can't.

Tammy grunted, placed her hands on the cracked, barren ground, and shoved to her feet unsteadily as she tried to come to terms with reality. Getting drawn to the shroudpool always left her dizzy and disoriented, and getting there from the dream left her head spinning.

"And of course, I'm completely sober. Brilliant."

Nothing grew close to this shroudpool. The circle of dead earth reaching twenty feet all around was ringed by dark trees that seemed to move in ways trees weren't meant to.

Tammy rubbed her temples as her gaze was drawn to the shroudpool itself. The rough circular patch of darkness was big enough to drive a car through. A heavy mist seeped from the void-like black mess.

When it was still a fully active portal to the Everdark, it had writhed with a strange depth that could send you mad from looking into it. She remembered thinking it looked like a tunnel filled with shag-pile carpet made from oily black worms. One that would frequently spew out monsters from another dimension.

That doorway was now closed, but not gone, and a haze of evil still oozed out.

Because of what she'd done.

Getting her unsteady feet moving, Tammy stumbled past the one massive tree that stood in the middle of the clearing. Its bark was warped and twisted, its roots encircling the shroudpool. It didn't grow anymore, but sometimes, it screamed.

The interdimensional portal may have been mostly dormant, but this area was still dangerous, so she knew better than to let down her guard. Dark Corner was permanently beshadowed to the point where nothing and no one came in or out—except Tammy.

All because she'd stuck her hands into that shroudpool.

"It's not going to work. We shouldn't be here alone."

Blaise flashes a perfect smile. "Come on, be more positive. Imagine if we can do this, we'll be the heroes of Darkfrey Estate!"

His blond hair flops over one eye. It shouldn't be possible to be that pretty. Tammy smiles, heart in her throat.

Tammy shuddered. The last moment she saw her friend, with his eyes wild and mouth wide and screaming was a memory that tormented her far too vividly.

She'd latched on to his hands. Sunk into the shroudpool up to her elbows. His fingers slipped through hers. She was nearly pulled in after him.

I should have been.

Pain rushed to the surface, and tears swam in her vision. She swiped both blackened hands across her eyes, jaw clenched.

She didn't have time to stand there wishing she'd done

something different. Wishing she'd saved her best friend. The past was the past. She'd screwed up, and this special little punishment of always teleporting to the place of her heartache was her curse to suffer.

But this time, maybe her curse could save some lives.

Fishing about her pockets, Tammy pulled out her phone and tapped to turn it on. The screen remained dark. A crack split across the glass, and when she gave the device a shake, it rattled.

"Ghast damn it. When did that happen?"

Wetness smudged over the phone screen, faintly red against the black. Examining her inky hands, Tammy noted a rip in her jacket, a sting on her forearm, a bite mark the same size as the toothy mouths that covered a vasmire's tentacles.

She shivered.

Was it really that close? I almost got eaten ... Oh well. Better luck next time.

Without a phone, she only had one other option. She rubbed the velvet-short hair on her head and shook the tingles out of her limbs. Then struck out at a sprint for the rusted, locked gate.

There were a couple of permanent shroudpools around Shroudhaven, and each had been fenced off with warning signs stating *Mine Subsidence Area* or *Dangerous Gases* and *Landmine Field, Keep Out.* Anything to strike enough terror into the blivs to keep them out of trouble.

Plus, the Darkfrey gang did their best to patrol the surroundings and get rid of any teenagers who looked a little too daredevilish.

Tammy slithered through the narrow, nearly invisible slash in the chain link fencing while she went over her options. Dark Corner was on the outskirts of Shroudhaven, much too far from Rooks Hotel for her to make it on foot. But close enough to Howell House, and just around the corner from it, the Boderleth home.

Callan had told her to go for help. Lian and Rushelle were there, keeping an eye on Rylan's body. She straightened on the other side of the fence and for a moment, she thought about going straight to the hotel to try to wake up the team on her own. But she knew better than to pretend, even to herself, that she could do anything to help her friends alone.

She hadn't been able to save Blaise.

She was useless. Cursed.

The team needed someone capable.

With the sun gone over the horizon and not a shred of light to shine through the thick, gnarled branches overhead, the woods were pitch black around her. Anything could be lurking out there.

Normally when she disappeared, someone would come and pick her up, but no one conscious knew she was there now.

Running is the worst.

Two deep breaths, then Tammy took off at a sprint down the uneven dirt road toward civilization.

She kept her gaze glued to the horizon, cursing her humanity. She had access to powers that could make her strong and fast, but without an eidolghast nearby, she couldn't transform and *use* said powers.

It was a crappy clause in the shadyr contract. Though in her estimation, the whole package of being a shadyr wasn't worth the hype. They were literal monsters half the time.

She cast out her senses, hoping to catch the scent of an eidolghast close enough for her to transform. In Shroudhaven, monsters were so common you couldn't sneeze without hitting one, and she usually couldn't go anywhere without coming up against their familiar energy.

She didn't have great control over her shadyr side, so even a hint of an eidolghast could trigger her transformation. Just like the dead one keeping Rylan alive had.

Of course, when she *needed* a monster, there wasn't one to be found.

Her lungs burned and sweat clung uncomfortably around her body armor. Soon, the small side lane met with a larger road. In one direction lay the main highway that connected Shroudhaven to Gorhanmere. Relief flooded her at the sight of brake lights in the distance, and a cluster of streetlights that marked the intersection up ahead.

Maybe hitchhiking was a possibility.

A feeling bloomed within Tammy like a ball of fire in her chest.

Nope, hitchhiking wouldn't be a possibility, unless there was a furry convention happening tonight.

There was a weroth nearby—a terrifying creature of void-like blackness with six legs. They were vaguely wolf-like but too boneless and slithery to ever be confused for something earthborn. They had too many joints, most of which bent the wrong way, and Tammy had always thought they looked like slimy, eyeless spiders.

She steered clear of where it lurked in the woods beside the road, but took full advantage of its presence for her transformation.

The burning shadows engulfed her body as she shifted. Her chest and arms widened, tearing her clothes and putting pressure on the custom built, flexible shadyr armor beneath. It was getting too small for her.

She'd grown since she left Darkfrey Estate with it a few years ago, and the Howells didn't have the same resources. It pinched badly but didn't tear. Her legs lengthened and fur sprouted all over her skin.

Tammy ran her tongue over the sharpened teeth in her now snout-like face and flexed her refreshed muscles. On strong, clawed feet, she tore through the dimly lit streets with startling speed.

Up ahead, she spotted the round, swinging sign for Boderleth Antiques.

The closer she got, the more she could sense the pieces of vasmire upstairs, and dark shadows swirled around her werewolf form. She tried to fight it, had to fight it. Her body ached and shifted, trying to be more than one creature at once.

"Liaaaaaan!" Tammy buckled over at the front gate.

The gray-haired woman appeared within seconds. She wore a floor-length knitted cardigan over pajamas, her sword strapped by a belt to her side.

"Tammy? Is that you? What's happened?"

"Trouble," Tammy mumbled.

It was hard to form words around her snout. Though she could feel the weroth's influence finally fading. The vasmire's presence was taking over.

"At Rooks Hotel?"

Tammy nodded.

"They need help?"

She nodded again.

That was all Lian needed to know.

"Rushelle!" she hollered toward the house. "Go get a car, fast!"

Rushelle's face appeared in one of the front windows, her pale golden hair piled atop her head. "Yes, Mam!"

Dark whisps of change surrounded the woman as

she vanished from sight. The back door slammed, and her footsteps echoed away as she leaped across backyards toward Howell House.

Tammy slumped down on the pavement, wheezing, and turned her furry face to the sky. She focused on her breathing, several breaths in and out, counting to five each time. Callan had taught her mindful breathing as a method for controlling her transformation. A way for her to be in charge of when she changed. It never seemed to work for her though.

Lian adjusted her sword hilt and squatted beside her. "Tell me everything. What are we going into?"

Tammy struggled through a quick and dirty explanation of what they'd found and what had happened, words slurred by her mouth full of razor-sharp teeth.

Every second that passed as she waited for Rushelle to return felt like two seconds too long.

I'm already too late. I failed them all. They're probably dead already.

Just the journey from Dark Corner could have been enough time for someone to be hurt. Or eaten. It was another fifteen-minute drive to get from there to Rooks.

Tammy's face scrunched up and she shifted from werewolf to vampire, her body shuddering, exhausted, soaked in sweat.

Lian mumbled and started scrolling through her phone.

"Damn it. This is too big for us. Bloody Darkfreys are always telling us they've got things covered and don't want our help. If that's the case, they shouldn't have let a beshadowing get that bad!"

The phone rang on speaker. Lian held it up in front of her face, the light casting deep shadows over her wrinkled skin.

"Darkfrey Estate," a female voice crackled over the line.

The last word vanished in a snap of static. Shroudhaven's motto might as well have been *Dangerous Creatures, Foggy Nights, and Constantly Bad Reception!*

"Vonny? It's Lian."

The static eased enough to hear Vonny's audible sigh. "What do you want, Howell?"

"Our team is in trouble out at Rooks Hotel. A late stage beshadowing. Need all hands on deck."

"We aren't—" *crackle, crackle.* A line of white noise, and then sudden clarity: "—our problem, Howell."

"My son is in trouble!" Lian insisted.

"Your sons always—" *hiss, crack.* "—in trouble, don't they?"

"Von—"

"Stop interfering," Vonny snapped. "Stay out of it, and we will—"

The static cut off. Vonny had hung up.

Tammy bit her lower lip, thinking of Callan trapped

in that nightmare while a vasmire stalked around his sleep-walking form.

She spoke up into the sudden, charged silence. "We can't stay out of it."

"We aren't," Lian said briskly.

A roar sounded around the corner, and a vintage yellow sportscar, roof down, squealed to a stop in front of them.

Rushelle leaned out from the driver's side, grinning over vampire fangs. "Good to go."

Lian didn't hesitate to swing herself over into the passenger seat, long cardigan flying out like a cape.

Rushelle adjusted her sunshine yellow corset-top as she checked Tammy over with a glance. "You okay, duckling? You look like you went spelunking."

"If by spelunking, you mean I ran all the way here, then yeah."

"From Rooks?"

"From Dark Corner."

Rushelle cringed. "Man, oh man. I hate that you have to go through that."

Tammy's bones still ached from the run, and her heart still ached from the feeling they would be too late. She groaned off the ground and stepped toward the car.

Lian put her hand up, stopping her. "We need someone here. We can't leave Rylan unattended. Don't worry, we've got this."

Heat stung Tammy's face. *Of course. I'm not going. They don't need me.*

She fought the tears back with a roll of her eyes. "Whatever."

CHAPTER FIVE

E verly awoke to chaos.

Somebody tackled her down onto hard concrete. An explosive clattering burst behind them.

She opened her eyes, staring up at the front entrance to Rooks Hotel. The glass of the revolving door flew through the air, landing like hail all around her. She covered her face with her arms.

The body that was on her moved away, leaving bursts of bright yellow in Everly's clearing vision.

"They're waking up!" The voice was familiar. *Rushelle?*

Everly sat up in a cascade of glass shards. She craned her neck to glance up.

The buxom woman in her sunshine yellow halter top grinned down at her, showing off her pointed fangs. "It's okay, duck. It's us, you're out."

Her face was pale, strange, and monstrous, but there was no mistaking Rushelle.

Everly looked around for Rylan as reality settled before her darting eyes.

I'm out of the dream.

A hint of movement to Everly's left drew her attention. Denny and Callan stirred beside her, both still in vampire form. No Cherry. No Harper.

Where are the others?

Denny's eyes opened, staring straight into Everly's. The corner of his mouth turned up. "Look at us, waking up next to each other."

Ignoring him, Everly got her feet under her and stood up with Rushelle's help. "Where's Harper?"

"I don't know, honey. Found you three first, bobbing about like the world's happiest zombies. Herded you out quick smart. I was just about to go back in for the others, but I think Lian's found the vasmire."

Something crashed, and a deep, inhuman howling followed. Everly turned to the gaping, shattered entryway to the foyer. Within, the mist swirled and forms moved inside it.

Callan stumbled to his feet. "We have to go help."

Rushelle grabbed his shoulders to steady him. "Whoa there, sugar. I'm going. Take yourself a moment to recover."

Callan bared his fangs and shook his head, long hair

whipping. He knocked her hands away.

"I'm ready. I'm not losing anyone on this mission." He took off at a run.

Rushelle raised both arms and groaned. "I just dragged your zombie asses out! Run back into that beshadowing before you've recovered and who knows how long you'll last a second time."

"Don't worry about me. I'm good here. Not planning on going anywhere," Denny said, pillowing his hands under his head.

Everly winced an apology to Rushelle. "I have to find Harper."

She dashed back into Rooks Hotel, leaving the woman behind swearing about *these crazy kids*.

Everly was met with a face full of dark mist. It parted, and the vasmire loomed right over her.

Bulbous gray flesh swirled and whipped past her eyes. Toothy circular mouths covered the tentacles, grinding and snapping. Multiple sets of coal-black eyes opened and blinked at her. Three wormy tentacles shot out toward her with an odd crackling sound.

A figure burst into Everly's field of vision with an animalistic snarl, bringing down a jagged black sword on the slithering appendages. The sword clanged against the floor, and the monster screamed as those limbs were separated from its body.

After striking, the newcomer froze in place, statue-like, head tilted as though in concentration. When transformed, the shadyrs sometimes became so different from their usual selves that Everly could never tell their identities unless she knew what they were wearing.

But she knew this was Lian. Her sword. Her salt and pepper hair. Her long, knitted cardigan. Her ... pajamas?

The vasmire withdrew, whipping around the room frighteningly fast. A second shadyr, Callan, lunged at it, digging his hands deep into the creature's flesh.

"Great googly-eyed gods, I've never seen one so big!" Rushelle joined the fray, skidding to a stop to take in the mess, then yelled, "Lian! To your left!"

Like clockwork brought back to life, Lian slashed, her sword flashing in a strong and precise movement. More dismembered tentacles fell. She returned to a holding stance, as zen as a samurai.

Everly couldn't fit the Lian she knew—caring mother, homemaker—with this violently beautiful creature. She tore her astonished gaze from Lian, searching for Harper or Cherry in the misty shadows.

As big as the foyer was, the vasmire almost filled it. Not in solid mass, but in its length, a web of writhing tentacles. Rushelle took a running leap, flying across the space and landing close to Callan.

"Welcome to ... to to to."

Everly jumped out of her skin as Brooke appeared in front of her again. She gave the sleepy-eyed clerk a gentle push toward the open front entrance, hoping momentum would carry her all the way out. Then she ran for the staircase.

Everly dodged the vasmire's whipping limbs, dashing through the foyer, her eyes darting for signs of her best friend. Would she still be upstairs? She could have wandered anywhere while trapped in the dream.

A wet *thunk* was followed by an explosion of pain in Everly's shoulder. One of the vasmire's wildly flailing tentacles struck against her back and sent her toppling forwards.

Sharp pain lanced up her knees and wrists as she hit the floor. She paused long enough to force back the surge of her dragon's light trying to escape in her moment of weakness. As soon as it was reined in, she rose back to her feet, wobbling and gritting her teeth.

She couldn't wait for the pain to ease or the fuzzy black edges around her vision to fade—she needed to find Harper.

Everly raced up the long, shallow steps to the second floor as the thunder of battle in the lobby grew. She glanced back to see how the Howell team were doing. Pale skin and teeth flashed in the mist and gloom. A chorus of muffled shouts as the team communicated were punctuated by the howling creature.

Lian, Rushelle, Callan ... only three shadyrs against the eidolghast. They always said at least four was best to take the monsters down, even ones not as big as this. They were holding their own for now, but for how long?

They need help. But I have to find Harper first.

A sick feeling squirmed in her stomach. She'd brought Harper to Shroudhaven. She'd exposed her best friend to this world. If the vasmire got to her ...

"There's Cherry!" Callan yelled from somewhere below.

"I'll get him out," Rushelle replied.

Everly spun back around, hoping to spot Harper there too.

Lian's sword flashed like a beacon in the low light. Callan danced around the creature's strikes, moving boldly and loudly, clearly attempting to distract the vasmire from Lian so she could land a killing blow.

Then more movement shimmered through the mist near the bar.

Shuffling like a lost marionette, Harper's grinning face emerged from the murky shadows.

She was entirely too close to the vasmire's flailing tentacles. Even with the shadyrs keeping it distracted in battle. And she obviously wasn't in a good frame of mind to get the hell out of the way herself.

Rushelle rejoined the battle, but the time she took to get Cherry clear had put them on the back foot. Lian took a hit to her chest. It flung her clear across the foyer. She landed among potted palms, ceramics and foliage clattering around her.

Everly couldn't distract them again, she had to get to Harper herself.

Harper didn't have a shadyr's tough skin and sharp teeth to fight back. She was a fragile human, and with one chomp, she would be vasmire food just like the guy in the bathrobe.

Everly looked over the railing, but it was way too risky to jump. She broke into a run, arms and legs pumping, skipping down the stairs so fast she nearly fell.

But not fast enough.

Everly skidded to a halt with just a few stairs left, staring in horror.

Something else moved behind Harper. Larger than another possessed human. Larger than anything that had any right to be there. Its form swirled in the shadows, a tangle of snaking flesh.

"There's another one! THERE'S TWO OF THEM!" Everly yelled with every bit of oxygen in her lungs.

The fight seemed to still for just a second, as swear words spilled from every shadyr in the room.

"We've almost got this one, just keep back!" Lian hollered.

That wasn't an option. Not with Harper standing

defenseless right beneath the thing.

It expanded behind her friend, growing ever bigger in a mass of lashing flesh. The way the one Rylan had fought had, right before it landed its killing blow.

Please, no. Please, no.

"Over here, you bastard!" Everly leaped over the railing.

A tentacle shot out and wrapped around Harper's waist.

"No!" Everly screamed, chills racing across her skin.

She set off in a sprint across the floor, desperate to reach Harper before the beast swallowed her whole. How did the vasmire eat? Were the tiny mouths on its tentacles biting Harper even now?

I've got to get her out of there.

The shadyr team attacked their target even more violently, trying to finish it off. The monster was already a mess of bloody stubs, oozing black instead of red, but still it lashed at them, persistent and deadly. All their attention was on it.

Harper dangled five feet off the floor, limp and still grinning disturbingly within the vasmire's grip. In one of her hands she clutched her axe, the sharp edge bumping and scratching bloody marks on her leg.

Everly reached the floor beneath her best friend just as the vasmire pulled Harper out of reach.

"No!" Everly screamed, leaping after her friend's boots. Her fingers fell just short.

Not Harper. This can't be happening.

Several tentacles moved away from the vasmire's central mass, revealing a mouth that was wide enough to eat a small car, icicle-point teeth glinting.

"Callan, help!" Everly screamed, panic surging. "I can't reach her!"

She glanced around for his tall shadyr form but couldn't find him. Nearby, a blond head that could only be Rushelle's was obscured, wrapped within a squeezing tentacle, and just beyond her, Lian continued to slash what seemed to be a never-ending number of limbs.

The vasmire was too strong. Too big.

They can't beat it. They can't beat two of them.

Anxious breaths clogged her throat and her heartbeat raged, deafening her. Her dragon roared within, ramming itself against the cage she held it in.

No. Everly used every skill in her mental toolkit to keep her panic attack at bay. She wouldn't let it incapacitate her. Not now.

She grabbed bottles from the bar, flinging one after another at the beast. It paid them no attention. They shattered against it, raining down alcohol and glass.

If I could light it on fire somehow, if I had Harper's axe, if I had something, anything ... Anything except the dragon.

Whatever those powers were, they weren't powers for good, and she couldn't control them.

A deep breath, a firm stance. Everly blinked.

Can't I?

She held her unruly adrenaline back by sheer force of will. She regulated her anxiety through years of hard work. It was always there, but most of the time, she kept it in check.

Maybe she could control the ravenous being of light inside her. Maybe she had been for most of her life.

If she let the energy flow through her, she could use it to save Harper, but then it might as easily turn around and eat her friend, too.

The adrenaline spiking in her system made Everly woozy. She felt faint and worked harder to shake it off.

No, not just adrenaline. This is like before. I'm being pulled into the dream. I have to act, now.

The vasmire pulled Harper ever closer, its dangerously sharp mouth widening.

Everly would not be lost to the beshadowing again.

Everly would *not* let Harper die.

She did the only thing she could.

Okay, dragon, let's do this.

Chapter Six

Brilliant light blossomed from Everly's chest and streamed down her arms, illuminating the darkest shadows of the hotel lobby, burning away the mist. Sparkling tendrils emerged from within her, slithering quickly to the ground to take control.

It wasn't really a *dragon*.

Not in the actual sense of the word. But that was how Everly had always personified her anxiety. When the thing appeared in her dreams—a magnificent, coruscating, snaking body of fractal light—she'd labelled it the same way. Just a mental embodiment of her panic trying to break free.

The tendrils of light lifted her up into the air, putting her head at the same height as the vasmire's alien face. They propelled her forward with a smooth, even gait that almost felt like floating.

Everly had lived with the dragon her entire life, using a therapist to get control of the "feelings." Breathing exercises, mindfulness meditations, growing her field of tolerance, learning to accept her emotions ... It took all that and more to quiet the dragon.

Then one day, it had come *out* of her.

The day she saved herself, Harper, and Callan from the weroth at the theater. Then she learned it wasn't a metaphorical manifestation of her anxiety at all. It was a *thing*, some monstrous, fierce entity that no one could identify.

One that wanted to consume anything it could reach.

A ravenous desire washed over her hard and fast. It was a gnawing, aching need that seemed to come from her very essence, as if it had been locked up inside her and left to fester until it exploded. As the tendrils maneuvered her toward the vasmire, she was nothing but light and hunger.

Whoa there. I'm the one in control.

She asserted her willpower onto the force, directing it to take down the vasmire. The light had other plans. Several arms wavered out toward Harper, and foreign excitement filled Everly at how good the mortal girl would taste.

Back off!

Everly snapped at the dragon, shoving her consciousness between Harper and the light. It took an immense amount of control to steer the dragon away.

Eat the monster!

The light turned its focus away from Harper. Tendrils that had been reaching for her whipped out to wrap around the vasmire. But with it still holding Harper, entangled in its tentacles, Everly didn't trust letting her light have its way. She forced it to hold, to wait.

It roared with yearning. She pushed back, pain splitting through her head from the effort.

Everly noticed with detachment that the Howell team had backed away. Cherry, and even Denny, were with the others now, and their vasmire lay broken and twitching, its last few tentacles still whipping wildly.

There. You get two meals. But don't touch anything else.

With a rush of delight, light streamed to the second eidolghast as well.

Everly closed her eyes, trying to block out the part where the light ate the vasmire's life force. No matter how much power the light consumed, filling her, making her stronger, it still felt *wrong*. Abhorrent and abnormal. The beaten vasmire was gone within seconds.

The one holding Harper lurched and twisted, trying to break free. The void-black eyes and no obvious facial features in its central area made it hard for her to read its expression, but she could sense waves of fear rolling off the beast.

Like the weroth at the theater that had stumbled over itself in its haste to get away from her.

In its effort to escape, it dropped Harper.

She hit the floor on her feet and then fell forward onto her knees. There was a startled cry, and Harper looked up at Everly with awe, yellow sparkles shining in her green eyes. She was at least alert enough to scramble out of the way.

Everly held the light back until Harper had leapt behind the watching shadyrs, then she set it free. More tendrils emerged from her and wrapped around the vasmire. The creature thrashed and screeched but was no match for her dragon. The light began to consume it.

"No, no! Release me," a new voice said. A voice of screaming bats and gurgling lava. "Curse you! Vile monster! Beast of teeth and stars!"

Caught in her stasis behind the light, Everly blinked at the vasmire.

Had it just called *her* the monster? Most importantly, the thing could talk, though she didn't see its giant mouth moving at all. The voice had almost seemed to come from inside her own head.

Vasmire tentacles pressed against the light, sizzling as if the flesh were touching flame. The light took pleasure in the vasmire's fear, and purred sickeningly as it dragged the monster's essence into it.

Everly imagined the dragon inside her, licking its

salivating lips. It had eaten, but it was not sated. It would never be sated.

Finally, the vasmire was nothing but a blob of quivering flesh on the carpeted floor. Dead.

You're done. Time to go.

Resistance, growling defiance, and then the light faded. Everly drifted down to her feet, as if the sparkling tendrils were setting her down with utmost care. She leaned forward and rested her hands on her knees, gulping in air as if she'd just finished running a race.

Lian stepped in front of Everly, her gaze shrewd. "That was some light show."

Everly flushed. Lian knew about the dragon, but this was the first time she'd seen it in action. Could the others tell, just by watching, that the dragon was consuming its victims' lifeforce?

She hadn't really explained the sensation to the others. The tendrils seemed strong enough to physically defeat its foes, to crush the life from them rather than absorb it. Maybe that was all that was happening.

But Everly couldn't shake the sense that something, somehow, was being *eaten*. And it wasn't the physical bodies, which still lay before them.

Everly straightened and rolled the kinks out of her shoulders. Being possessed by the light left her feeling weak and achy for a couple of hours afterward. She hoped that was what she felt now, not her mind being sucked into the dreamworld again.

She asked, "Is it clear? Is the beshadowing gone?"

Cherry kicked one of the dead vasmire bodies. It oozed a little dark gas, but otherwise the mist that had filled the space had vanished. "Dead, and dead."

"Good work, team," Callan said.

His skin was covered in vasmire-black and human-red blood, but if he was injured anywhere, his vampire form must have already closed the wounds.

Cherry scoffed. "Team? We didn't even finish off this one ourselves. Both kills land on Everly's scorecard."

"I was counting Everly as part of the team," Callan replied.

"And the MVP I'd say." Harper still had the axe gripped in white knuckled fingers. "I can't believe how useless I was. I didn't even get to use my new toy."

Everly shook her head. "You were trapped in a dreamworld, it wasn't your fault."

Harper tsked. "Excuses. Next time I'll do better."

Everly barely had time to brace herself before Harper threw her arms around her neck and squeezed painfully. "Thank you. You saved my life."

"Might have saved us all," Cherry added. "I was starting to fall back into that dream world again. Can't believe we all made it, especially with also dealing with this fool."

He threw a fistful of vasmire at Denny.

"Watch it!" Denny swatted the gore off his shirt and grumbled about not being appreciated.

"We did good, for what this was. That beasty was an especially big fellow." Rushelle chuckled, picking something out of her hair. "And then another one shows up! Like, whaaat?"

Callan squatted down beside the second vasmire to examine it. "No wonder this beshadowing wasn't caught sooner. It probably turned dark much faster than normal."

Lian wiped spattered hands on her pajama shirt. "We were lucky to have Everly with us."

A harsh, sudden clapping interrupted them.

A Darkfrey team stood just inside the busted revolving doors, concealed in the low light. They'd obviously been there a while. Several of them leaned against the wall like spectators, and the one man out front—bigger and more muscular than the rest—was slow clapping with extreme irony.

"Wow, just, wow. I mean, we always joke about how useless and messed up the Howell runts are, but seeing it in person is something else," he said, his voice thick and growly.

Callan muttered under his breath and shifted ever so slightly to put himself in front of Everly and Harper.

Everly peeked around him to see if she recognized

any of them, but in their shadyr forms, silhouetted by the streetlights behind them, they were total strangers. She counted eight of them. That meant two braces, as she'd heard their four-person teams called.

"How nice of your pet human to take care of everything for you. Although, she's not exactly human, is she?"

They saw? Everly almost wanted to ask if they knew what she was, but from the man's tone, she guessed it was a no.

Lian swung her long cardigan so it obscured the sheathed sword at her side, then stepped ahead of her team. "You were there long enough to watch, but you didn't bother stepping in to help?"

The Darkfrey shadyr shrugged. "And miss the show? Figured we'd wait and see. Could always mop up if you ghast-lickers bit it."

His flippant tone brought a flush of hot fury to Everly's face. It reminded her of that day in the Wyrdwoods when they'd been ambushed at Nell's animal sanctuary.

The Darkfreys had come in, treating it like a black op. All those animals, the poor, eccentric old crone ... And when Everly found Rylan's unconscious form lying beneath the house in Nell's laboratory, she'd also found a Darkfrey shadyr there, attempting to kill him.

If she hadn't shown up when she did, she had no doubt that they would have lost Rylan that day.

One of them wanted Rylan dead. And it could be one of them in front of her now.

The bulky cut of the man who mocked them—the sound of his voice was familiar.

Everly stalked straight toward them, anger glittering in her eyes.

She approached so quickly, so surely, that the huge man backed away from her.

It was him, the one with the blond crew cut and body of an action figure soldier, who had led the ambush at Nells. She'd seen him before too. Nilson Darkfrey.

Even in his shadyr form, she could tell it was him. Closer now, she also spotted Vonny, Annabeth, and Jasper to one side of him. The four faces on the other side were unfamiliar.

It could be any one of them.

Everly didn't know what to say to them. Fury had burned away all her words.

Vonny snapped, "Howell, come and leash this freak of yours!"

"Don't call her a freak, you murderers!" Harper yelled back.

"We just do our job and do it well."

"You sure replaced Rylan fast," Callan said, striding up beside Everly. "Nilson is part of your brace now?"

The soldier-man snickered. "I'm leader of this brace

now, and it's one of the best since the Howell taint is all gone."

Vonny's face twisted into even more of a scowl at the word *leader*.

Cherry hollered from behind them, "Yeah, best at letting a beshadowing get this far along and not even noticing. You guys are sooo great at your jobs."

Nilson snarled. "Shut your mouth. We know what we're doing. Shroudhaven is the Darkfreys responsibility. You're the ones showing up with your little team of useless misfits trying to get yourselves killed."

Both teams erupted, voices on each side rising over one another.

The din echoed through the high ceiling and stone lobby. Fangs were bared. Any moment now someone could strike the other team.

They didn't have time for this. They needed to get back to Rylan, not get into a fist fight with the larger and better resourced team of supernatural beings.

"Enough!" Everly cried, and a burst of light flashed through the room.

Silence fell as all eyes turned to her.

Vonny stepped forward to stand next to Nilson. She tossed back her blond bob and narrowed her gaze on Everly.

"Jasper told us that your pet human had some kind of freaky power. We didn't believe it at first. If you aren't shadyr, you're human. If you aren't human, you're a monster. So, girl, what are you?"

Before Everly could even consider answering, Cherry pushed his way past her. His hands balled into fists at his sides, and his face was menacing, still transformed into his vampire-like visage.

"Oh, *Jasper* mentioned it, did he? Good little soldier boy. I should have known where your loyalties lie."

Everly glanced at the man in question, and he swallowed visibly. She and Harper were the only people who officially knew that Cherry and Jasper had been secretly seeing each other.

The Darkfrey shadyr was a good-looking guy of average height and build, with silky black hair he usually wore combed back, and dusky skin. Even when on the hunt for monsters, he wore bland, neutral-colored cardigans and pressed khakis.

But the hint of emotion that touched Jasper's face fled, and he said coolly, "I might have mentioned something you brought up while we were talking the other day."

"Talking." Cherry spat the word. "Yes, of course. *Talking*. As friends do. But you know, I think we're done *talking*."

Everly had never heard him sound so angry.

"Lose my number."

Jasper's eyes flashed, but the reaction was chilled by

an icy expression. "Fine. It's no loss at all."

If Everly hadn't known the truth, she wouldn't have seen the sharp look of pain that crossed Cherry's face before he schooled his expression back into emptiness.

The two of them had heated exchanges about their different approaches to being a shadyr in the past, but this felt different. Had the two of them just broken up?

In the distance, the few hotel guests that remained shuffled around, calling out with confused pleas.

Lian turned to her son. "Callan, I think we've said all that there is to say. Let's gather up what we came for, and the Darkfrey team can deal with the rest of this mess. It's *their* job, after all, isn't it?"

With grunts and muttered curses, the Howell shadyrs each scooped up as much vasmire as they could carry.

Nilson spat at Denny's feet as he passed by. "Told you that you suited being in cleanup crew."

Everly was surprised when Denny didn't bite back. He hoisted a large tentacle over his shoulder and walked out, head hung low.

A cold smile crossed Vonny's face. "So Rylan is still unconscious, is he? I heard you were keeping him alive with monster bits. What a shame. He was a good fighter. Must be the Howell in him that made him weak."

Lian's spine went ramrod straight. She whirled on her heel and stalked toward Vonny, her face like fire.

She jammed a finger against Vonny's bulky jacket. "The Howell in Rylan is what makes him strong. It was the Darkfreys that broke him."

Then she turned back and strolled away before Vonny could reply.

Vonny's face was thunderous as she pointed at Callan.

"Get your shit and get out," she said in a low, deadly voice. "And when you give up trying to keep your brother alive, go ahead and bring him home to us. Then maybe you'll learn to start leaving things to the experts."

CHAPTER SEVEN

*C*urse *you. Vile monster.*

Everly barely paid attention to the low hum of conversation between the rest of the campervan's occupants. The night had grown darker and more imposing as Harper steered them back to Boderleth Antiques.

Beast of teeth and stars. A shudder rippled up Everly's spine.

It's like the monster knew me. Knew the dragon.

She needed to talk it out with the others, see if any of them knew what it meant. Rylan's mom was older, had been around the shadyr block a time or ten, so maybe she'd have an answer, or at least know *something*. Right now, though, Callan was busy chewing Denny out for his role in the mess at the hotel.

Everly clutched the cold metal railing and watched

Shroudhaven pass out the window, wishing she was anywhere else.

Lian and Rushelle had taken their own car from the hotel to return to Howell House, stating the "gore duty" could be handled by the young people.

Callan made some futile attempts at eliciting remorse from Denny, but overall the mood in the van was much lighter than it had been on the way to the hotel.

Despite everything, their mission had been successful. They were all still alive. Callan and Denny continued ribbing each other, but it almost seemed playful now. Harper laughed from the driver's seat as if she hadn't almost died. Cherry was the only one that remained quiet.

Denny went on a mournful tangent about the desk clerk and how he'd only gone back into the fight to impress her. Apparently, the woman had run off screaming before he could show off properly. Everyone in the van threw things at him until he shut up.

Swinging to park in front of the Boderleth home, Harper cut the engine and remarked, "We made it. Now, please get that foul-smelling monster out of my vehicle, stat."

"You mean the vasmire bits, or this guy?" Callan pointed at Denny.

"Yeah, yeah. Laugh it up, chucklehead. You just lost my help hauling your gore." He clapped his hands once in Callan's face, hopped out the side door, and wandered off down the street.

"*How* can we smell it? The crates are sealed!" Harper grunted.

Callan grinned wryly. "I think we're the ones that smell."

They evacuated the van, taking a moment to breathe fresh air.

A small figure hovered midway up the front path, a petite shadow, hugging themselves.

"I ... um ..." Tammy took a small step forward, then backed off again into the shadows. "Took you all long enough. None of you died then?"

"Don't sound so disappointed," Cherry snapped.

"Hey," Callan barked at him. "Cool it. We did all survive and we can thank Tammy for that."

"Do I get a medal or what?" A subtle, bitter tone laced Tammy's words, one Callan seemed to miss.

"Don't get too cocky. I still want to talk to you about breaking rank and running headlong at that vasmire. Later."

Tammy rolled her eyes. "You're not the brace-leader of me."

Kicking at gravel on the sidewalk, Cherry said, "Wow, with that attitude no wonder we're a mess. I swear we spend more time babysitting her and Denny than getting the job done."

"Cherry, that's enough. It's this kind of in-fighting that made us such an embarrassment in front of the Darkfreys." Callan squared up in front of him, then put a hand gently on his shoulder. "I don't know why you're in such a mood."

Everly and Harper's eyes found each other's, and their lips thinned.

Cherry's voice was low and exhausted. "We'll always be an embarrassment. We're just the runts after all, the unwanted losers and misfits."

"We can be a good team. We did good tonight. For one hell of a ghast-blighted situation, we survived, we ended the beshadowing, and we got what we went for. I know, Ev here stepped in and finished things off for us, but I'd bet my teeth that even without her, we could have gotten there the long way."

"Hope you like soup." Cherry picked up one of the crates and headed toward the house.

Callan sighed and scratched both hands across his scalp, ruffling his long hair.

"Come on, let's finish up so we can wash this stink off us. Everyone take a crate straight to Rylan's room," he ordered. "Swap the new crate out for an old one, and I'll have the fire ready in the backyard to burn the rotting bits."

Tammy took her crate, lifting it easily in her vampire form, then Harper took hers.

Everly offered Callan a sympathetic smile as she picked up the last crate from the campervan.

He huffed a sardonic laugh. "Back at the Darkfreys, braces are carefully selected for skill level and temperament, so each member complements the others. A brace becomes a perfect, efficient unit. I'm trying hard with these guys but maybe we're just an incompatible group of shadyrs. I don't know what else to do."

Everly offered gently, "Maybe remember sometimes that they are humans too?"

Callan's dark eyebrows lowered and he chewed his bottom lip. Then he nodded and wandered off to the backyard.

They'd started their mission at sunset and it was only mid evening by the time the new severed tentacles were in place beside Rylan and the old had been tossed onto Callan's roaring bonfire.

Everly was dead on her feet. All she wanted to do was kick out the Howell team and then stand beneath the shower until the water turned cold and her fingers pruned. Even the mystery of the words the vasmire had spoken wasn't enough to overcome her exhaustion. It could wait until the morning.

Then Callan suggested a drink at Crow's bar to celebrate and debrief, on him. Harper so enthusiastically agreed that Everly wasn't even given a chance to bow out. She also figured this was maybe Callan taking her suggestion, so she should be supportive and join in too.

"I guess you'll need someone to babysit the almost-corpse again," Tammy grumbled.

Everly bristled. *Rylan's not a corpse.*

She turned to glare at the goth-girl, but when she did, there was such vulnerability on her doll-like face, barely concealed beneath the lazy contempt, that her anger dropped away.

"Yeah," Callan nodded.

Tammy's lips twitched like she'd been slapped, revealing her fangs.

Then Callan continued. "I'll call Mom, see if she can keep an eye on him. Team drinks means you're coming with us too."

For a split-second, the scornful mask slipped right off Tammy's face and only the vulnerability remained.

Then her lips closed into a pout. "Sure. Whatever."

With gore duty done, the shadyrs headed back to Howell House, and everyone split off to get cleaned up. Not long later, Rushelle showed up at Everly's front door with her glittery laptop.

"Hey sugar," she said, grinning. "I'm on Rylan watch tonight. Lian's heading to the bar with the others. Said she wanted to have a chat with you. I'll be right here. It's a good chance to get some words in."

"Oh, okay." Everly hovered near the door as Rushelle walked in like she was at home.

Seeing the blonde bombshell fight earlier, it seemed to Everly that Rushelle was a natural, a force of nature. It was odd that she wasn't part of the team too. She always appeared by Lian's side, willing to help her with anything, but otherwise seemed more interested in her writing than in any kind of shadyr activity.

I guess we can't choose what powers we're born with, but we can choose what we do with our lives.

And now Lian would be at the bar too. Everly could ask about what the vasmire had said. The thought of doing so left her with shivers.

She was considering how she could back out of the festivities, when a freshly showered Harper bounced down the stairs and dragged her out of the house.

After dark, Shroudhaven turned quiet and cold. They didn't pass a single oncoming car on the journey through town, and the dark peaks of the mountains that cradled the buildings looked remote and lonely. Everly might have attributed the overall feeling of desolation to her own emotions, but this was just typical Shroudhaven.

"Take a left here," Everly said as they neared the downtown block where the bar was located.

"Yeah, got it," Harper replied, already turning.

Everly shot her a sidelong glance. "You're becoming

awfully comfortable with the roads here."

Harper scoffed, tossing a perfectly curled lock of dark hair from her face. "It's not like it's New York City. Shroudhaven's too small to get lost in."

Looking back out the window, Everly murmured, "Yeah, but there are other ways of getting lost."

Harper found an empty spot along the curb half a block down and pulled into it, muttering under her breath as she attempted to wedge the camper between two small hatchbacks.

"Ugh, I can't get anything right lately!" She was normally a great driver, but the spot she'd chosen was precarious. Everly hopped out and helped guide Harper in from the curb.

As Harper straightened the van a final time, Everly glanced down the street.

It was mostly businesses down this block, including a solicitor specializing in wills, a dodgy looking small-claims lawyer, and a print shop advertising discounts for lost pet posters.

At nine in the evening, they were all long closed for the day, and this late, very few pedestrians could be found on the streets thanks to the unofficial curfew of sundown. Since returning to Shroudhaven, Everly had spent more time out after dark than she ever had growing up there.

Across the street from their parking spot, Everly

saw movement in the shadows and jumped, her mind immediately going to eidolghasts.

Harper joined her on the pavement. "What? What is it?"

Everly squinted into the darkness and then breathed a sigh of relief. "It's Cardboard Box Barry. I mean, Barry."

The rail-thin, white-haired man stood outside his large cardboard box, swaying as if to a silent song. His long, braided beard brushed back and forth over his heavy-metal shirt.

Harper stared at him, the streetlight setting her profile into sharp relief. "You know what's weird? I haven't seen a single other homeless person in Shroudhaven. Is it terrible that my first thought is that they don't last very long, what with the you-know-*monster*-whats?"

Harper was right, Everly hadn't seen anyone else either. "Barry's been around as long as I can remember though."

She shivered, watching for a moment longer, wondering. Barry twisted his hips and swung his arms to an unheard song. Then, behind him, another form appeared, crawling from behind the blanket covering his box.

Barry stopped dancing and opened his eyes, holding out a hand to help the man to his feet. The newcomer had pale hair, and wore khaki chinos and a polo shirt. He didn't appear to be another homeless man, given the glint of a gold watch on his wrist.

"Does Barry often have visitors to his, um, box?" Harper asked softly.

Everly watched the stranger glance furtively around, offer Barry a brief embrace, and then take off at a quick walk down the street.

As he vanished around the corner, she said, "I really don't know."

"I'm not even going to start to guess what that was about then," Harper said.

A gust of blustery wind raced past Everly. She pulled her bomber jacket closed against the cold as she fell into step beside Harper, surreptitiously glancing at Barry again. He'd vanished, presumably into his box.

The Crow's Nest had occupied the same space in a plain, flat-fronted building for as long as Everly remembered. Its tall, arched wooden door was decorated with iron studs and elegant, black iron hinges. If it weren't for the glittery golden letters spelling the name, the place would look less like a hole-in-the-wall bar and more like a dungeon.

Harper latched onto Everly's arm. "I hope Crowea makes us that concoction she made last time. That might have been the best cocktail I've *ever* had. I think it was the added witchy magic."

Everly opened the heavy door and motioned Harper to precede her, then followed her best friend into a burst of warm, sage-scented air.

The Crow's Nest might have been boxy and boring on the outside, but the inside was a different story. An array of antique lamps graced end tables between mismatched armchairs, couches, and age-stained dining tables.

Colorful scarfs were draped over the lampshades, spilling a soft, warm glow through the room. Fantasy paintings and brightly colored Celtic tapestries hung from the walls and angled ceilings. Curtains and low bookshelves loaded down with books, trinkets, and witchy memorabilia separated the wash of furniture into some semblance of order.

"There's a Mermaid in My Lighthouse" played low on the sound system.

There's a mermaid in my lighthouse, and her heart belongs to me.

There's a mermaid in my lighthouse, and she's staring out to sea.

Like Cardboard Box Barry, just another backdrop to life in Shroudhaven.

Callan, Cherry, and Tammy already occupied a curtained-off space near the corner of the room, and Lian stood at the long timber bar, chatting with Crowea.

Other than the Howell team, only one other group sat drinking on the other side of the room. Everly didn't recognize their faces as anyone she'd seen since getting involved with the shadyrs, but she definitely recognized the Darkfrey crest on their matching shirts.

Great, Everly thought, wincing. *Hopefully they leave us alone.*

"Hey, girls," Lian said, leaning her hip on the edge of the bar to turn and greet them. "There's already a pitcher of Crow's signature blend at the table. I'll meet you over there."

"Welcome back, babies." Crowea grinned and leaned on her glove-covered arms on the bar.

She was a tall woman with a wild blonde/gray curls and a penchant for long, flowing dresses. Though that wasn't the most striking thing about the old Wiccan.

Harper gave the bar matron a friendly wave and then grabbed Everly's arm and tugged her toward the team.

Under her breath, she whispered, "Okay, she's even more creepy the second time around."

"It's the tooth," Everly whispered back.

"No, really?" Harper sassed.

At some point, Crowea had come up against an eidolghast and lived to tell the tale ... but she'd walked away from the encounter with a sharp fang stuck in her left eye.

Scarring fanned out from the tooth, intermingling with the wrinkles on her wise face, giving her an almost villainesque appearance. But she wasn't a villain. In fact, she'd saged Everly so thoroughly the first time they met, that Everly had walked away thinking she herself was, in fact, the villain.

Luckily, Crowea had already fallen back into conversation with Lian, and Everly wasn't subjected to another full body smudging.

"About time you ladies showed up," Cherry said as they approached. "We were just discussing whether or not to leave you any alcohol."

Tammy squinted at him. "What? We were not."

"Okay, fine, I was internally debating whether or not to leave *any* of you any alcohol," Cherry said, pouring himself another glass.

Harper dropped her giant handbag onto the floor next to one of the two empty armchairs and flopped onto the overstuffed cushion. "Sorry we're late."

Cherry gave Harper an indulgent smile, but it didn't really meet his eyes. "I bet Bellsy getting ready is a long and meticulous process."

Despite his flame red-hair, he seemed colorless and subdued tonight, in basic sweatpants and a black sweater. Nothing like his normal, crisp red-and-white racer jacket look. Everly didn't think it was an accidental pick. He was mourning the end of his relationship with Jasper.

Harper returned his smile. Hers didn't reach her eyes, either.

"I also had some open wounds to bandage up, but sure, lets blame the makeup."

Everly shot Harper a worried glance, then slipped into the other armchair, sinking into the soft depression in the cushions until she felt like her knees were above her head.

"What'd we miss?"

"Just basic debrief stuff." Callan picked up an empty glass, offering it to Harper as he reached for the pitcher.

"By which he means, a very *cheery* pep talk about our team tactics, and our *attitudes*," Tammy droned.

After filling Harper's glass, Callan offered Everly one too, with a side of a long-suffering expression.

Everly shook her head and held up a hand, indicating she didn't want any of Crow's potent mixture. She'd had a taste out of curiosity last time, but she had a volatile relationship with alcohol after seeing how it had destroyed her mother's body, mind, and moral code.

Everly's head was such a swirl of dark thoughts tonight that drinking seemed like the last thing she should do.

Tammy picked up an empty glass and held it out. "I'll have hers."

"No, you won't." Callan pointed at a second pitcher across the table. "You've got your mocktail over there."

Everly raised her eyebrows at Callan. As Rylan's younger brother, he must only just be barely legal drinking age himself. Harper was probably the oldest of them all at twenty-one.

"Joy," Tammy muttered. "I was better off back in the

dream-trap. Could have died happy and dream-drunk, but nooooo, someone had to go and spoil it."

"Thanks for that, by the way," Cherry offered. "Sorry I was being bitchy before. We wouldn't have gotten out of there without you."

Harper lifted her glass. "To the hero of the night!"

Tammy shot daggers at Harper, as though expecting a sarcasm that wasn't there. Then everyone else joined in the toast.

Tammy clutched her refilled mocktail glass to her chest, a red tinge rising up her neck and into her cheeks. She had the hood of her black jacket up over her head, and sank back into it like a turtle.

"It wasn't anything. I didn't even get to come back and finish the fight."

"We had Everly—wondrous one-woman-light-show—there for that." Cherry lifted his glass again.

"Which I couldn't have done if not for Tammy getting out and sending help," Everly deflected, just as uncomfortable with being singled out as Tammy.

Callan extended one long leg and nudged Tammy's black boot with his toes. "Quit beating yourself up. You saved the day."

Tammy flickered slightly, then groaned out a fake-barfing sound in response.

Cherry leaned over the arm of his chair toward Harper.

"Truth though, I am so upset that I didn't get to see you go all lumberjack with that axe."

Harper huffed. "I know, right? Do you think it's really a good look for me, though? I've been wondering about training with weapons more, and my heart keeps getting drawn to dual-wielding sickles. Ooh, or maybe a whip sword!"

While Tammy and Callan argued about the legitimacy of Tammy's actions, Harper and Cherry continued to get louder and louder about best weapon options, both for killing eidolghasts, and for perfecting Bellsy's look.

Everly listened, observing the here and now as she worked on her calm. The tightness at the corner of Cherry's eyes spoke to the hurt he was hiding. Everly had noticed that since she sat down, he hadn't once pulled his phone out of his pocket, when before he was *always* texting Jasper.

As for Tammy, there was something different about her when she talked to Callan. Her sullen glare had softened, and instead of staring at the wall or ground as she often did, she made eye contact with Callan as he piled on the praise.

And, Everly could hardly believe it, there was even a tiny *smile*.

Lian rejoined the group, carrying a mug of something steaming hot. She settled onto the couch next to Callan and crossed her legs before taking a dainty sip. She'd changed out of her pajamas, but still wore a long, chunky-knit cardigan and sheathed sword.

The memory of the older woman slicing so deftly with that weapon still surprised Everly.

This was a lady who changed into her pajamas by sunset. She had probably been curled up half asleep with her yappy little dog Birdie when they called her round to watch Rylan so they could leave urgently on their mission.

And yet she was so formidable, when required. Much like Rushelle, she had her priorities decided. She'd never wanted her sons to give their whole lives to shadyr duty as the Darkfreys did. She wanted for them a life as normal as possible. For some reason, that had fallen apart when their father died, and she had only just gotten them back. One of them broken.

Everly offered a small smile to Lian and took control of her nerves. "You wanted to talk?"

Lian took a sip from her mug and nodded. "Callan told me he saw Rylan, that they all did."

"Oh, yeah. In the dream." Everly let out a sigh of relief. She wasn't being accused of being a monster.

"He's really there," she muttered as though to herself. "How are we going to get him out? We don't even know how he's there, or what you are."

"Actually, about that ..." Everly inhaled deeply and rushed out her next words. "Something happened during the fight that I wanted to talk to you about."

Lian inclined her head. "I'm listening."

"Did you know that vasmires could speak?"

The two conversations taking place around them petered off as Everly's friends clued into hers.

Lian nodded. "Yes, it's been thought they have ways to communicate. But it's some kind of eidolghast language. Only other monsters seem to understand it. We haven't exactly had a chance to study it and learn over the centuries."

Everly swallowed hard. *Only monsters understand it.* As if she didn't worry enough she was one of them.

"*I* understood it. One of them spoke to me."

Lian lowered her mug to her knee, her face impassive. "What did it say to you?"

"It called me the 'beast of teeth and stars.'"

"That's ... something," said Callan.

"Yeah, but what?" Everly asked.

Lian stared, her gaze sharp as though it could dissect Everly. "It called you that, like a name? Was that all it said?"

"Pretty much," Everly murmured with a shrug.

"Is that what Everly is, or has in her, or whatever? The beast of teeth and stars? What even is that?" Harper rambled.

"It was so long ago, but I think ..." Lian lifted the mug to her lips, her eyes going unfocused. "I don't know that phrase, not exactly, but there is an artifact at the Darkfrey Estate with a similar name. The Bane of Teeth and Stars."

"That can't be a coincidence," Cherry said, leaning into the conversation.

"But what is it? What am I?" Everly's voice was breathy, anxiety building within, compressing her lungs.

Lian placed a hand on Everly's knee. "I'm sorry, I don't know. That's the only thing I know of that's similar to what the creature called you. It's an ancient shadyr artifact, stored beneath the estate in the protected archives."

"Where you plundered your sword?" Callan pried.

"Slander." Lian covered a sly grin by sipping her drink again. "I may or may not have *obtained* my sword there."

Callan's grin widened for the briefest moment as he and his mother faced off, then he went on. "Can we assume this artifact has something to do with Everly? With the weird light powers?"

Lian's eyes narrowed, and she chewed at her lower lip. "It's not exactly a common phrase. There is merit in the idea that whatever causes Everly's powers might have something to do with the Bane."

"So, how about we 'obtain' this thing, too," Harper suggested. "See what we can learn about it, or from it?"

Lian gave her an amused smile. "It's worth considering. But it and anything related to it are Darkfrey property and well protected."

She polished off her drink. "Let me think on it, maybe ask around a bit. I still have some connections. But that's enough for tonight. It's late and time for me to leave you youngsters to it."

Wiping her palms on her jeans, she stood up. "Be careful on your way home."

Callan shot up awkwardly, as though he were about to either salute or kiss his mother goodbye but couldn't decide which. The rest of the group bid her goodnight, then she wove through the maze of shelves, chairs, and tables, disappearing out the front door.

"This is awesome. We have a name, and a lead," Harper said with great enthusiasm.

"A name no one knows except that one lead," Everly countered.

"Pretty cool name, though," Tammy mumbled. The slight turn at the corner of her lip seemed almost sincere for once.

That smile dropped quickly when Callan reached over to refill Harper's drink, and she touched him on the wrist as a silent thank you. Tammy clenched her ink-black hands into fists and folded them under her armpits.

"Hey, thanks," Everly said, leaning toward the scowling girl.

"It's just a dumb name."

"I meant for saving my life, all our lives. I know you're not a huge fan of your power. I know it seems weird and hard and wrong. But you got it under control and kicked ass."

Tammy's lips twitched, but she rolled her eyes. "Projecting, much?"

Everly chuckled and lifted a hand for a high-five. "Go us, team freaks."

Tammy narrowed her eyes, assessing Everly.

"Don't leave me hanging, it's seriously awkward."

Tammy huffed, smiled, and released a dark hand to slap Everly's palm.

A flash of light burst between their touch.

A crack of thunder and howl of nightmares. Sparks shot out from where their skin made contact. Everly hissed at the sudden pain and yanked her hand back from Tammy's as the entire bar was plunged into darkness.

Chapter Eight

The bar fell silent. Every eye in the place turned to the source of the explosion. Like slow-motion rain, mist descended over the tables and chairs in the darkness, obscuring everything and everyone except for those closest to Everly. Tammy's face scrunched up, mirroring the socked-in-the-gut sensation Everly was hit with.

From the general direction of the bar, Crowea's thick, raspy voice spoke, "Oh my stars."

"What just happened?" Harper shone her phone around their group like a flashlight.

An icy breeze filtered past Everly, shifting her pale hair. It tickled her skin as if someone had brushed their fingers against her. Crow's collection of wind chimes jangled in a mournful tone, each one somehow keeping time with the others in a hideous symphony.

Everly's palm tingled with a million pins and needles in the aftermath of the high five. Her hand still hovered in the air. She jerked her arm back and tucked her palm against her stomach, horrified.

Was that the dragon's light?

Had it manifested somehow? Without her knowledge or permission? Just the idea filled her with bone-deep horror. It was every nightmare she'd been harboring since the moment she realized a monster lived inside her. She shivered, and she didn't know if it was from the growing chill in the room or her own fears.

Tammy groaned and slouched in her chair, tucking both of her blackened hands back into her armpits. "I'm so sorry. My hands are *cursed*."

Surprised, Everly turned her gaze on Tammy. The shadyr thought *she* was the issue? Everly opened her palms and looked down at her hands, a churning pit opening in her stomach.

"I don't think it was you, Tammy. Or, not *just* you."

"It is me. It's always me. I'm always going to be cursed. I ruin everything I touch."

Callan appeared out of the mist, kneeling in front of Tammy's chair. "Not true. Remember, you're the hero tonight. The world needs you. *We* need you."

Tammy's head shook in small, shuddering movements from side to side.

"All right, party's over," Crowea called.

Feet shuffled nearby on the patchwork of rugs covering the floor, then a high-powered beam of light cut through the misty darkness, aimed at the front door.

"Everyone out. Make your way carefully to the exit."

A chorus of groans filled the bar, but the clink of glasses and the scrape of chairs proved the occupants were obeying their bar matron. Everly stood, her elbow brushing Harper's.

"You okay?" Harper asked in a low voice, taking hold of Everly's jacket sleeve.

Everly shrugged, her mouth too dry to speak.

As one, their group moved in the general direction of the front door. They were intercepted halfway there by Crowea. She formed from the shadowy fog like a demon, the eidolghast fang in her eye socket and the scars around it harsh and unforgiving. She had a fat roll of sage burning in one hand, and a military grade flashlight in the other.

"You children all right?" she asked, her one eye sweeping over Everly.

Tammy's face held no emotion and her voice was flat. "I'm sorry, Crow. This is my fault. My stupid cursed hands. Can I stay and help you clean up?"

"No, baby, I got it." Crowea tucked the flashlight under her arm and put a hand on Tammy's shoulder.

The elbow-length gloves she normally wore were gone.

Tammy's eyes popped wide and she tried to back away. "Don't, I'm cursed, you—"

"Hush baby, it's okay. Your pain, however deep and piercing, is not a curse."

Everly exhaled roughly. What was Crowea doing? Was she somehow reading Tammy right now, with her psychometry? Her power to know things about objects and beings she placed her hands on?

The power she flat out refused to use on me.

A tear spilled down Tammy's cheek and she fled the building.

Crowea's singular gaze swept across the rest of them and landed on Everly. "Keep an eye on that one."

As she waved them toward the front door, it was unclear whether she was instructing Everly to keep an eye on Tammy, or the others to keep an eye on her.

"Don't worry about all this, babies. A bit of smudging, some banishment charms, a new protection ward, we'll be good as new."

As they filed from the bar and into the cold night, Crowea's shrewd gaze remained on Everly. The dungeon-like door slammed shut behind them as they gathered on the sidewalk outside.

Tammy was leaning on the wall in the shadows of Crow's Nest, and Callan sighed when he saw her. "At least she didn't try and run home on her own."

"Sounds like she's done a lot of running tonight already," Cherry added, softly.

Across the street, the uniformed Darkfrey group glared back at them as they left. Everly tried to ignore them, but their looks of judgement were red-hot brands on her skin.

Callan stepped closer to Harper. "You guys want to come back to our house? We could pop some beers and watch bad movies."

Exhaustion washed over Everly, but she didn't miss the twitch of Tammy's lips and wrinkle of her button nose. The goth girl folded her blackened hands and turned away.

"We're going to go home," Everly said, then to Harper, she added, "if that's okay."

Harper linked her arm through Everly's and nodded. "Yep. Maybe another time. This has all been some swell life-threatening fun, but we should really go and relieve Rush from Rylan watch."

The group shared goodbyes, and the two girls headed for the campervan, faces down against the sharp wind rolling in off the mountains. They were silent until they'd gotten in, where Harper locked the doors and asked, "So ... What happened?"

Everly stared at her still tingling fingers. "I'm not sure. Tammy and I high-fived, and it caused some kind of ... reaction."

Harper turned the key in the ignition, her face

thoughtful. "Have you ever come into contact with Tammy before?"

Everly thought back over the past few weeks. "No, I don't think so. She's not much of a toucher."

"Like the opposite of Rush," Harper gasped with enthusiasm. "Maybe when Tammy got cursed, her personality split in two and became like a light and dark version of herself!"

Everly snorted a chuckle through her nose. "That sounds weird, even for Shroudhaven, and also Rush is like thirty years older than Tammy. We can probably chalk Tammy's lack of touchy-feely-ness down to her being a troubled teen."

Harper pulled away from the curb and smirked, clearly proud she'd provoked Everly into a laugh. "Or that she knows weird stuff happens when she touches things. Maybe it was just Tammy. She seemed pretty sure about that."

"Maybe," Everly murmured.

Whatever it was, she was just glad no one got hurt.

Everly rested her forehead against the window and watched the streets pass the rest of the way to her old family home, feeling sorry for herself.

It wasn't a normal emotion for her. She'd learned early on that life was hard, and it was her job to put on her big girl panties and keep moving. But everything had changed so fast these past couple of weeks. Even Everly herself.

She just wanted to go back to the way things were. When things were normal.

But if she'd been expecting any kind of normalcy back at Boderleth Antiques, she was sadly mistaken.

Rushelle sat on the front steps, illuminated by her laptop screen. Once the van was parked, the woman closed her computer and met them on the front garden path.

"Had to come and write outside," she said, grinning happily. "Oh boy are things going wonky bonkers in there!"

Everly and Harper cast side-eyes at each other.

Rushelle fanned a hand limply at them. "Oh, nothing serious, just a bit distracting. Although it did give me some ideas for a new book! *A Ghost Lover for the Far King*."

"Great, another one for my to-be-read pile!" Harper laughed.

"Have a good night, ladies," Rushelle cooed, and wrapped her long arms around them both at once, squeezing them in, then wandered off down the street.

"Well, this is our first night with spanking fresh eidolghast bits in the house. Shall we go and see what Rush was talking about?" Harper said.

"I'm not sleeping out in the rose-bushes again," Everly replied.

Around on the creaky wooden porch, she shoved open the back door. A thin fog rolled down the stairs from the second floor. On their level, it had settled into a hip-high cloud down the hallway, stretching in an ocean of pillowy white from the back door through the rest of the house.

Everly hit the switch to turn on the candle-shaped lights that lined the narrow hallway, but their dull bulbs barely penetrated the gloom. Coupled with the brown floral wallpaper, they almost seemed to make everything even darker than if she hadn't turned them on at all.

Harper blanched and waded into the fog so that it moved like liquid around her legs. "This permanent smoke machine thing is not my favorite part of having dead monster chunks around."

Everly locked the back door. "You have a favorite part of having dead things around?"

"Well, it's not the smell either. But keeping Rylan alive is good and watching the little googly eyes you give him every time you walk by his room is a solid bonus. Five stars."

"I'm glad my remnants of a childhood crush on what is now a non-responsive stranger is entertaining to you," Everly replied.

She reached past Harper and flicked the old-fashioned switch on the wall to illuminate the kitchen.

"He seemed rather responsive to you in the beshadowed dream-world—*what in the fresh hell*?"

All the kitchen cabinets were open and swinging, as if in an invisible breeze.

"Okay, that is pretty wonky bonkers," Everly murmured

as she crept into the kitchen.

"Are we being haunted now? How exciting would that be?"

"Not exciting," Everly said. "Not at all. But I think this is just the minor beshadowing effect. Like that's what beshadowings are—haunted weirdness caused by eidolghasts."

She grabbed for the first cabinet door and gently closed it, then waited several seconds to see if it would stay that way.

When it did, she started closing the rest. "I don't know, Harper, maybe you should go stay at Howell House. These fresh eidolghast pieces are doing way more than the old ones."

"Not gonna happen. And quit acting like you aren't just as human as me." Harper opened the fridge and pulled out a yogurt. "You want one?"

Everly nodded, closed the last cabinet, and accepted a tub and spoon from her friend. "That big vasmire is probably extra potent too. It was strong enough in life to beshadow an entire hotel full of people super quick, along with its friend. Even its dead bits are going to be a problem. I don't want to see you get hurt."

"I'm not going to be. Not by this try-hard poltergeist, anyway. A little bit of beshadowing doesn't scare me." Harper peeled the top off her yogurt and spooned herself a large mouthful.

Everly sighed. *That's what scares me.*

Harper had adapted to the weirdness in Shroudhaven *way* too easily and had been approaching it all with her usual high-achiever attitude. But the longer they stayed, the stronger Everly's sense of foreboding became. For the first time, she could understand Rylan's need to distance himself from the people around him, to protect the humans in his life. To protect *her*.

"The only thing that worries me is if the cops show up here for any reason," Harper quipped as she headed for the door. "Imagine trying to explain why we have a body in the upstairs bedroom surrounded by chucks of giant monster-calamari? Or cabinets with minds of their own?"

She motioned behind Everly with a grin.

Everly glanced back and groaned. The cabinets were all open again, swaying in that invisible breeze.

She turned away from the dancing doors, too tired to deal with it again. "I hope he wakes up soon. This life has become a little too weird for me."

In the hallway, Harper paused by the antiques shop door. "Did you have any luck with the carousel music box?"

Taken aback, Everly frowned. "Oh, um, yeah. Early this morning, while you were still asleep. It just had a gear knocked loose. Didn't take much to open it up and put things right."

Since they'd been in Shroudhaven, the two of them had cleaned every living area of her old home—though Everly had steered them away from tackling the basement or the attic just yet. Her childhood phobias ran deep.

Once the house was mostly done, they'd turned their attention to the antiques store.

The place had been boarded up for nearly sixteen years with everything exactly as her father had left it the day he died.

They were tag teaming the project, with Everly repairing and cleaning the better looking antiques while Harper used her skills at sales and marketing to sell them online. As far as Everly was concerned, it was a temporary arrangement, but one that they could be equal partners in.

"Perfect. I think it might be a real collector's item," Harper said excitedly. "I did some research with the pics I took last night. I have a ticket in with this big antiques website to help with verifying it. The thing's over a hundred years old, and the last one in the public eye sold for over twenty thou."

Everly blinked. "What? No way."

"Your dad left you a treasure trove, Ev." She took a few steps toward the door that separated the living area from the store. "I'm going to go do a few mock-ups for the carousel, see if I can't get a stunning portrait to woo potential buyers. You coming?"

"Not tonight." Everly loved working alongside Harper, but she didn't have any energy left. "I'm going to call it a night."

"Suit yourself. Pancakes in the morning, my treat."

"Like you'll get out of bed before me," Everly teased, then watched as her best friend disappeared into the antiques store. She still found it weird to be coming and going through that door. Her entire life had been spent pretending that door, and what lay beyond it, didn't exist.

After her father's death inside the shop, Everly's mother had locked it up and left it to rot. Day after day, Everly had passed that door as if it weren't even there—dark mahogany wood, a frosted glass window covered in dust and grime, and an old skeleton keyhole that kept it closed forever.

Not forever, Everly thought, standing for a moment to listen to Harper puttering around on the other side.

All the tragedies this house had seen, all the neglect Everly had experienced, all the secrets hidden—one day, they'd be nothing but history. Everly would sell the house to someone who could breathe new life into the place and bring a family to fill it with light and laughter.

Everly finished off her yogurt and it sat heavily in her stomach. She felt a pang of regret for the childhood she wished she could have had, then headed upstairs, fighting against the flow of fog, and the chilling fear that there were only more tragedies still to come.

Chapter Nine

Everly didn't really need a second shower that night, but *wanted* one in order to chase away the icy butterflies that had made a home in her chest.

Tonight, she'd controlled her dragon. They'd beaten a beshadowing and provided Rylan with what he needed to stay alive. Monster parts for days.

But how many more times would they have to repeat this? How many more times *could* they?

They'd barely survived, even with calling in backup, even with using the ravenous power within Everly. What if Rylan didn't wake up this week, this month, this year? How long would it take before everyone had enough of hunting Vasmire for his life support?

I won't ever give up on him. I'll keep him alive, no matter what.

Everly towel-dried her hair and checked the bedroom. Harper still hadn't come upstairs from the shop, though with the way she nitpicked every last thing about her photography setups, Everly assumed she'd be there half the night. Inching the lighting to the left. Trying different colored gels. Finding the perfect angle to show off the carousel's bright colors.

Harper hadn't earned her status as an influencer without the eye, talent, and hours worked late into the night to back it up.

Dressed in clean leggings and an oversize, threadbare t-shirt, Everly snuck downstairs with a gurgling hunger in her belly. Her own hunger, this time, and not the all-consuming hunger of the light. They had missed dinner, and one yogurt wasn't enough of a replacement.

She tiptoed past the antiques shop so she wouldn't disturb the artist at work, then pushed through the door into the kitchen, not bothering with the light switch.

The cabinets all hung open, though they were no longer swaying with their synchronized, haunted dance. Everly took a moment to close them all, again, and glared at them in a silent dare to pop open one more time. She'd take the damn things off their hinges if she had to.

Everly pilfered a granola bar from the box on the kitchen counter and stood over the sink, munching on the chewy chocolate and oats mixture. She hoped it would be enough to quell her stomach so she could sleep, although the churning inside her wasn't only from hunger.

She had almost lost Harper tonight. An eidolghast spoke to her, calling *her* a monster. And whatever that thing was between her and Tammy.

How has life gotten so crazy?

The lacy white curtains hung open over the window, revealing the quiet street outside and the dull glow of streetlights. All the neighbors were tucked inside their dark houses, seemingly sound asleep by the lack of glowing windows.

Trees shifted and bent beneath the breeze, and even through the old, wavy glass, Everly could hear the clack of their branches beating against one another.

Movement broke the stillness.

Everly stopped chewing and leaned forward, her gaze raking the street. The night Rylan had been attacked, she'd watched him get struck down through this very window.

At first, she'd thought he'd been fighting a tall man in a gray cloak, but things had been ... off. She knew now, of course, what a vasmire was, and how they lurked around Shroudhaven.

But instead of a vasmire slinking through the shadows on her street, she saw a familiar long, sleek tail and a flash of predatory eyes pass through the streetlight, then vanish down the sidewalk next to her house.

The cougar.

He was one part of all this craziness Everly actually liked.

Everly smiled and hurried to the fridge, pulling a slim packet of ground beef from the bottom drawer. She'd picked up several slabs of meat a few days before just for such an occasion. She ripped the plastic off and carried it to the back door on silent feet.

The smoke of the gore-burning bonfire, still smoldering in the bare far end corner of the yard wafted to Everly as she stepped outside.

The cougar lurked near the old, overgrown swing set, peering out through the weeds and ivy. His tail flicked and he marked Everly's every movement as she stepped down off the porch and walked up to him cautiously.

He'd clearly been young when he'd died, because he was still much smaller than a normal cougar. His coat still showed some of the spots juveniles have which are lost as they matured. He was still big enough to be a threat, but considering he had been brought back to some kind of undead life by Nell, Everly wasn't sure he'd ever grow another inch.

Everly crouched and set the plate of meat in front of him. "Heya, Zozo."

He leaned down and sniffed at the meat, then moved up to snuffle at her fingers. He'd been getting tamer by the day. The first few times she'd brought him food, he'd run off when she got too close, and she'd left his plate in the weeds for him.

But still he kept coming back, always nearby, as though drawn to Everly. And still his hazy visage haunted her dreams. Connected, somehow.

Zozo snuffled her fingers, then dug into his meal, snapping at the bloody meat with sharp teeth.

"You'll never believe the day I've had," Everly told him, settling down on her knees.

Though he didn't look up at her, he huffed as if to let her know he was listening.

"You wouldn't judge me, would you, if it turned out that I was a monster?"

A low, satisfied growl rumbled from Zozo as he ate.

A lump formed in Everly's throat. If she could tell her zombie cougar friend all her worries and fears, could she tell the others?

But before she could open her mouth to speak again, the back door creaked open and the porch light flashed on.

Harper's voice called, "Ev? Is that you out there?"

With the barest rustle of grass and leaves, Zozo was gone.

Everly frowned after him, sad to see him go, then got to her feet and waved. "Yeah, it's me. I'm here."

Harper stood on the porch, haloed by the dim glow of

the candle lamps in the hallway behind her. She'd pulled her long dark hair into a messy bun that looked effortlessly classy. One suspicious eyebrow lifted toward her hairline.

"Whatcha doing?" she sing-songed, in a tone that also held an unsaid *"Should I be worried?"*

Everly walked back up the cracked concrete path, dodging weeds higher than her ankles. One of these days, she'd need to tackle this jungle. For now, though, it gave Zozo plenty of places to hide.

But how would she explain to Harper that she was feeding an undead cougar?

She could already imagine Harper wanting in on a pet kitty, no matter how Frankensteined. But just because Everly felt some strange connection to the beast, didn't mean it was safe.

She hopped up the three shallow stairs leading to the porch. "There's a stray cat I've seen around. I've been leaving it food."

Lying to her best friend left a gritty feeling in her mouth. But Everly didn't like the way Harper had adjusted to the dangers of life here, or the way she dove headfirst into the paranormal as if it were her goal to experience it all, as if it were just another thing to master. The more Everly could keep her separated from that world, the better.

The last thing she wanted was for Harper to get attached to Zozo.

Like I have? I shouldn't have named him.

Neither of them should be forming attachments there. Because as soon as they were able, as soon as Rylan was awake and well, they would leave Shroudhaven and all this danger behind forever.

Unless I'm one of the dangerous things.

Harper's eyebrows lifted a little higher. "I'm not sure if leaving meat out for random wildlife is a smart thing to do in this area, babe. But I love the sentiment."

"How'd your shoot go?" Everly grabbed her elbow and tugged her back into the misty house.

"I got some beautiful shots of the carousel. I'll list it and start marketing tomorrow. This one is going to be such a winner."

"Great." Everly clicked the deadbolt into place behind them. "I'm going to check on Rylan one more time before I go crash."

"Mm hm." Harper's full lips flattened into a smirk. "I bet he can't wait to see you again too."

"What do you mean?"

"I mean he's clearly into you."

Everly huffed. "He's in a coma. I don't think you can tell anything he's into right now."

Harper stuck her tongue out. "Stop being obtuse. I mean when we were in the beshadowed dream, duh. He looked at you like you were the only person in the room."

"He's probably just gotten used to ignoring other people since being in my dreams, because normally any other people aren't real," Everly pointed out.

She led the way up the stairs, fog parting around her ankles, weirdly warm in places in a way that felt even creepier than the cold spots.

Harper slid her hand up the banister with a dancer's flourish. "The way he looked at you was real. Like every muscle in his body—which is a whole gorgeous bunch by the way—seemed to tense up when you were near."

"In irritation, maybe?" Everly rebutted.

"Did you not hear me telling you to stop being obtuse? Should I say it louder?" Harper cupped hands around her mouth as though about to yell.

Everly lifted a hand in front of her. "Rylan just wants me out of this town and out of his life, and he's made that perfectly clear. He's changed so much from the boy I used to lo—know."

Everly coughed, a futile attempt at covering up her slip.

Harper tilted her head innocently and fluttered her long-lashed eyelids. "Well, if I were you, I'd be taking this remarkable opportunity you've been presented to get to know him again. Like, I'm surprised you haven't gone to sleep already. Honestly, now I've seen what you see in your dreams, I'm surprised you're awake as often as you are."

Everly blushed. She had to admit, she spent many of

her waking hours counting down to when she could fall into her dreams with Rylan again. But she didn't have to admit it out loud.

Having Rylan all to herself in her dreams was a bad, guilty sort of pleasure Everly refused to indulge in.

"It would be much better to see him up and around again in the real world," Everly said.

Whether he likes me or not.

"Obviously that is the ideal outcome, but don't dental-check your gift horse, you know?" At the top of the stairs, Harper air-kissed Everly's cheek. "Sweet dreams!"

Everly stuck her tongue out in reply.

Harper wriggled her fingers in a wave and took over the bathroom for her nighttime facial cleansing ritual.

Everly stopped by her old bedroom to peek in at Rylan.

He lay as still as stone in the fall of golden light from the hallway, his skin pale, and his breaths apparently nonexistent. The fog was even denser in his room, billowing from the crates of dead vasmire bits and turning every corner dark. Shadows crept in nightmarish patterns along the walls, shuddering and slithering like snakes.

Everly steeled herself and ignored the weirdness as she ventured into the room. At Rylan's side, she placed the tips of her fingers beneath his nose. His soft breath fanned over her skin, sending goosebumps up along her arms, and her heart into a gallop.

She pulled her hand away again before the urge to stroke his cheek became too strong.

He was still breathing. That was all she needed to know.

That was all she could hope for right now, but didn't know how long it would last.

Chapter Ten

The boxy old TV showed Rylan hurrying down a sidewalk, his hands shoved in his pockets and his eyes trained on Everly through the screen. As he moved closer, the streetlamps behind him went out, chasing him with a sticky, malevolent darkness.

"I'm asleep. This is a dream," Everly said out loud.

The dreamlike haze resting over her senses vanished. Without significant effort, the setting of the dream would do whatever her subconscious felt like doing, but at least she would have control of herself.

Everly found herself in the living room, on the couch where she'd fallen asleep. She sat up and shoved the sleeping bag away, putting her feet down on wet floors.

Water poured through the open doorway behind the couch, and lily pads floated past her on the currents.

Hundreds of frogs swam and hopped around, jiggly and shiny, filling the wet space.

Zozo splashed after the largest of the vivid green plants, batting at it with one of his oversized paws. He was still ghostly in the dream world. Everly wished the cougar could speak, so she had some idea of whether it was really its conscious self, like Rylan was, or just an ever-present dream figment, like Rylan used to be in her dreams before his near-death experience.

She guessed it wasn't the cougar's complete life essence trapped in here like Rylan, since it was still able to move around normally out in the real world.

Looking up at the ceiling, she could see her dragon turning lazy circles in the sky above, even though the roof wasn't transparent. She simply *knew* it was up there, so entwined with herself she could sense its motion, its feelings. It almost seemed to be sulking at the control she'd exerted over it.

That's right. Just keep your distance.

On the television screen, the darkness chasing Rylan had solidified into black water, filling the world behind him as he increased his pace to a sprint. He grew larger, his face taking up the entire television as the inky liquid filled in around him. He reached out, his hands coming through the glass.

Everly lunged forward and grabbed a hand in both of

hers, pulling back with all her strength. Frogs squirmed around her knees and despite knowing it was a dream, Everly hoped she wasn't crushing any.

Rylan's head and shoulders pulled free of the saturated TV world, and he gasped a deep breath. His hands were slick and Everly's grip slipped. She fell back onto the lounge.

With a slurp and splash, Rylan hauled the rest of his body out of the television. He rolled face first, doing a graceful somersault across the lily-pad floor that thumped him right up against Everly's legs. A few frogs that had been in his path shook themselves off and hopped away.

Dripping wet, Rylan glanced up at her and remarked, "Your mind is a terrifying place, Boderleth."

"Tell me yours is much better," Everly shot back with a grin.

"Touché." He wore the same hooded jacket and jeans he'd worn the night the vasmire nearly killed him.

He hopped to his feet in one smooth movement, his body all hard angles and grace, and then turned to dump himself onto the couch beside her. Dark liquid clung to his eyelashes and made his clothing cling in messy wrinkles to his skin. Droplets sparkled as he rubbed his head and face, then he leaned back with a tired groan.

Everly readjusted to make room for him, and as he hit the cushions, she was struck with the acute sense that she felt naked.

Oh my ghost, don't be naked, don't be naked.

She glanced down at herself and sighed in relief to see she wore a close approximation of what she'd gone to sleep in. Only the threadbare t-shirt felt entirely too thin.

Better than nothing, she thought, glad she'd yet again been spared the humiliation of *that* kind of dream while Rylan was around to watch.

Rylan's eyes were on that shirt as she turned back to him.

He threw his arm over the back of the couch and cleared his throat. "Glad to see you made it out of the beshadowing situation in one piece. Everybody okay?"

"Yeah, everybody's good." She gave him a basic run down of all the waking moments since she'd last seen him, as she'd become accustomed to doing since he was separated from the real world. The TV had emptied of its black liquid, and played through a strange, birds-eye view of time-ramped scenes from Rooks Hotel.

Once the basics were out of the way, Everly looped back around to the hard part. "When I used my light powers on the vasmire ... it spoke to me. And ... I understood it."

Rylan remained silent, his brows lowering over olive green eyes.

Everly sighed out the words. "It called me the beast of teeth and stars."

"Did it call you that, or the *dragon*?" Rylan glanced

around as though checking for it, but it had remained at a distance.

"I don't know. Are we separate? Am I the dragon or is it something else inside me? Either way, I don't know how I got like this. My parents aren't around anymore to ask them whether they were something other than human."

"They weren't shadyrs," Rylan said.

Doesn't mean they weren't something else.

Everly shrugged. "Even with this name, we've only got one lead. Your mother thinks we might find answers with some kind of relic that's being kept at Darkfrey Estate that has a similar name. Unless you learned anything while with the Darkfreys that might give us some insight?"

"No. I haven't heard that name before. But I was never very good at shadyr history, that was more Annabeth's thing. Put most of my effort into learning how to kill eidolghasts, honestly."

Everly shivered as the water around her feet slowly soaked up the fabric of her pants. But the chill that left her shaking was more due to the fact the boy she used to know had spent his life training to be a killer.

When he'd left home at thirteen years old for Darkfrey Estate—when they'd stopped being friends—she would never have guessed that was the reason why.

Rylan rubbed a thumb over his chin as he watched her. "I think it's clear you aren't a shadyr, but you're definitely not entirely human."

"What other options are there? Eidolghast?" Everly asked quietly.

Like the things you kill.

He reached out and placed his hand on her knee, squeezing gently. "You're not an eidolghast."

"But I am a monster." Everly let the words fall between them with all the weight of her worries.

All the things she hadn't been able to tell anyone. The way she seemed to consume things that left her feeling sick right down to her marrow.

Before he could argue with her and make her feel worse, she went on, "At least I could help get the vasmire for you."

Rylan turned away from her, his jaw and arm tensing. "I hate that you had to do all that just to keep me alive."

"Nobody who went today had any qualms about what we needed to do," Everly pointed out. "Your mom loves you. Your brother adores you. The rest of the Howell team cares about you. I ... care about you."

His eyes flashed up at hers. "I care about you too. Which is why I hate you putting yourself in danger to keep me safe. I need to find a way back into my body."

Everly rubbed at the goosebumps that sprang up all over her arms. "Any ideas?"

"None." He leaned forward and placed both hands over his face as he slouched down.

The motion made the cushions sink so that Everly angled in toward him, and their sides pressed together.

He didn't make any move to pull away.

Everly's breath shuddered. Even in the dream, she could feel his warmth, smell the familiar soap scent of his skin, hear the breaths in his body. He was long and lean, his muscles hard against her full curves. She was certain he could feel the way her heart pounded being so near to him.

As if in response to how she felt, the lily pads still floating by on the watery floor began to look suspiciously heart-shaped. With a bit of will, Everly managed to change their surroundings until water became sand and a purple sun beamed down from overhead, casting everything in a hellish glare.

Though they were still on the damn couch. Touching.

"What have you tried so far?" Rylan asked, his gaze sweeping the glaring horizon.

Giant, lumbering shadows walked just out of sight, nothing more than dark shapes despite the sun. They reminded Everly of Nell's undead animals darting through the trees of the Wyrdwoods.

Everly blew out a breath. "Well, we stuck needles between your toes."

Rylan looked over at her, horrified. "Ow."

"That was Callan's effort," Everly added, and thought, *his lips are so close.*

Everly shifted away from him in the guise of pulling her legs into a crisscross beneath her. She needed space from him. Room to breathe. Room to wash all the desire from her mind before it drove her crazy.

I don't even know who he really is anymore. These feelings are just a hangover from my childhood. Calm yourself the heck down, woman.

"We've also tried smelling salts, adrenaline injections, and throwing water on you—scalding and iced," Everly said, ticking each of the options off on her fingers.

An amused grin quirked up the sides of his lips. "What I'm hearing is that my supposed friends and family have been torturing my unconscious body."

Everly grimaced. "It does sound a little like that, doesn't it?"

They shared a laugh, and as Everly watched his face, her heart skipped a beat. She hadn't heard that laugh in what felt like a lifetime.

A true laugh that trickled up from deep within him and illuminated his face. It transformed him from the buzz cut, military Darkfrey shadyr into someone more familiar. A shadow of the boy he'd been years ago, when he was her best friend, first crush, loyal protector.

She wanted him whole again back in the real world.

But a deep, secret, selfish part of her wanted to keep him here in her dreams, where he belonged only to her, where his time could only be passed in her company. A yearning hunger that wanted to hold onto him forever.

We won't let him go.

Everly's eyes widened.

We? This wrong, selfish desire to hold onto Rylan ... was it coming from her, or the dragon?

She glanced up at the sky. She'd sensed the dragon there above them, but had studiously ignored it. Instead of a ceiling, there was a canopy of leaves overhead now, and the dragon stared down at them both through the shivering foliage.

Somehow, she, or her dragon, was holding Rylan's spirit within her. In a way, she'd felt like she and Rylan were connected on some metaphysical level ever since that day in the woods when they met as children, both of them lost until they found each other. Connected the same way she and Zozo were now.

But something changed when Rylan almost died. That connection became a full-blown soul-kidnapping.

Is that related to the feeling of consuming things I get when using my powers?

But the other beings whose lifeforces she'd consumed—Nell's husband, the vasmires—they hadn't ended up in her dreams. They were just gone. Or maybe never eaten at all.

I should tell him.

The self-rebuttal came fast. *And have him think I'm a*

soul-sucking monster?

"Okay. What other options are there for getting me conscious again?" Rylan said, interrupting her reverie. "Let's talk pop culture and literature. Rip Van Winkle. What woke him up?"

"Um, nothing. I think he just woke up on his own."

"Might still be a possibility," Rylan said, "but not one I'm willing to wait for."

"Odin from Norse mythology had a sleeping thing happening, but again I think he woke up himself."

Rylan huffed. "Who didn't wake themselves up? Sleeping Beauty?"

She woke with a kiss.

Everly flushed from the roots of her white hair to her toes. "Yeah, I guess, but these are just fairytales."

Rylan looked her right in the eyes. "Just hang on a moment. I mean, have you, uh, touched me, much, since you found me?"

Everly straightened in her seat and stammered. "What? No! I mean, no, your brother and Cherry carried you. Your mom, she makes sure you're clean—"

Rylan winced. "I guess that's the least mortifying option of many?"

Everly continued rambling. "I haven't ... I just, I check your pulse, signs of life, but that's all."

Rylan ran a hand over his short hair. "Okay, but it

could almost make sense, right? If my consciousness is here, in you, and my body is out there ... what if more direct contact between your body and my body is needed, to put me back?"

Everly's skin turned molten. She suddenly found herself super glad she'd moved away from him, because if she hadn't, right now he'd be feeling her go up in flames. She burned in a way that could turn the sand around her ankles into glass.

"You want ... me to kiss you ... like you're Sleeping Beauty?" she clarified.

He shrugged, looking embarrassed himself. "I guess. I don't know. But it's worth a try, right? We're in new territory here."

A kiss just to save his life, Everly thought, crestfallen.

She wanted to kiss him for real, and for him to kiss her back like he meant it. Not stand over him like some savior princess and hope her lips on his cold, hard mouth would bring him back from the dead.

The sand around them shifted, rolling like waves coming to shore at the foot of the couch. They started growing, pulsating in time to her heartbeat, and Everly hoped this wouldn't evolve into a twisted version of her tsunami dream. She closed her eyes, trying to control the world in her mind, and calm the emotions shivering through her.

"I'll try it," she promised, carefully keeping her emotions from her tone. "But there's got to be another option. Isn't there some local legend about a place you can make wishes?"

Rylan's face darkened. "Absolutely not."

The wishing stone was a story Shroudhaven kids told each other, but as with Santa, generally grew out of quickly. It was a large stone, jutting out from the small island in the middle of Myrkur Lake, rumored to grant wishes—if you could get to it.

But since she'd learned that nothing in Shroudhaven was *actually* just rumor, and most of the weird stuff had a basis in shadyr fact, she was assuming the wishing stone might be real too. Rylan's response seemed to verify that.

"But maybe it could help us," Everly argued. "Maybe one wish could bring you back."

"It's not what you think it is." Rylan grabbed both of her shoulders and turned her to face him, his gaze serious. "The whole lake is beshadowed. A shroudpool formed out there, and in a effort to block it off, shadyrs had the area dammed and flooded. But that water and island are still ghost-twisted and deadly. Promise me you won't go out there."

"But what about the stone? Could it be something, something real?"

Rylan grunted. "Put it this way. Have you ever heard

anyone say they went out there and had their wish granted?"

"No, but—"

"And how many tragic, accidental deaths by drowning have you heard about from that lake?"

"Some. A lot. Okay, I get it, bad place."

"Bad place," Rylan echoed. "Like most of Shroudhaven."

His hands slipped away from her shoulders as though exhausted, and he stared out over the rolling dune-waves. "A place I wish you'd just leave."

Everly's nose wrinkled with the effort to hold back tears. She'd considered it. Giving up, leaving Shroudhaven to return to where she and Harper weren't at threat of death-by-monster every day. If she gave up, Rylan could remain like this, hers and only hers in her dreams.

No. She couldn't do that to him. She refused to stop until he was back in his body.

But scarily, part of Everly wanted to keep him trapped. Part of her wanted to never, ever, let him go.

CHAPTER ELEVEN

Jasper and his brace stayed at Rooks Hotel only until the cleaning crew arrived, but Jasper struggled to stay focused.

Don't let anyone see. No one can see that you're hurt.

As part of a hunting brace, they were at the top of the Darkfrey pecking order. That was where Jasper liked being, where he'd worked hard to be—a place of power no one else in his family tree had ever achieved.

Braces didn't have to do the dirty work. The cleaners would deal with removing any trace of monster remains, help any lingering civvies out of the building, and make some excuses about a gas leak or explosion.

The hotel staff and guests would still have some strange stories to tell about their experience, but who in Shroudhaven didn't?

Their sleek black van trundled up the steep drive of Darkfrey estate. In the back seat, Jasper clenched his hands together to keep them from shaking.

It's over. Really over.

None of his team gave him a second glance. They couldn't see through his calm exterior to his malfunctioning heart inside. It jittered and thumped and cracked against his rib cage, frantic to beat itself into oblivion in its pain. Jasper grimaced.

Get it together. It's better this way.

Vonny pulled the van up to the gates and rolled down her window to key in the security code. A burst of chilled night air rushed in, and Jasper inhaled it deeply as though he hadn't breathed since his final words to Cherry. The gates opened, and Vonny closed her window as the van rolled into motion up the long drive.

Dark forest thinned the higher they rose, and then the trees opened around them on a wide, angled plain covered in the estate's training areas. The hulking shadow of Darkfrey Estate sat atop the hill, windows blazing with light like something out of a gothic horror movie.

A hint of movement atop the crenellated ramparts proved that the night's guard had already set to work. Ghasts didn't typically try to barrel onto Darkfrey's gated property, but it wasn't unheard of, either.

A group of shadyrs in maroon sweats played basketball

beneath glaring white lights on one of the courts, but they were the only visible occupants at this time of night.

The other illuminated training areas were empty, fog wisping over concrete and turf to give the grounds a desolate look. Most of the estate had already retired to their rooms. After his brace debriefed with Mordan, Jasper had every intention of shutting up in his own room.

And not crying. *There will be no crying.*

His throat tightened. He couldn't lose it in front of the others. He dug one thumbnail into the other.

Red welled up in the crease of his nail, shiny in the passing lights. The pain helped him chase away thoughts of his boyfriend. *Ex*-boyfriend. Jasper was a Darkfrey, and that meant he was strong, in control.

Only the mission mattered. Only the fight. Nothing else.

Vonny pulled the van up the circular drive before the front door and threw the vehicle into park with more force than necessary.

She'd been in a mood ever since her run-in with the Howells, and most of the brace had given her a wide berth so they didn't get caught up in her ire. She may have been barely over five feet, but Jasper knew intimately that she could kick his ass.

He had learned early. The hard way, with the scars to prove it.

The tiny overhead light bloomed to life, chasing away some of the darkness pressing in from outside. Vonny opened her mouth, her face clearly ready to bark orders, but Nilson stepped in front of her.

"Straight to Master Darkfrey's office," he commanded. "He's expecting us."

The big, blond brute had replaced Rylan in their brace, and he'd come in with a bang, vying with Vonny for control—something Vonny thought she'd finally claimed. Even for someone as imposing as him, Jasper didn't think Vonny would have ceded command. But being Mordan Darkfrey's son counted for something.

Jasper avoided Nilson's shrewd gaze and stayed close to Annabeth's heels, the two of them following Vonny into the building. Something about the older man set Jasper's nerves on edge—like he could see through Jasper, straight to his secrets.

Secrets that could get him kicked out of Darkfrey. Being gay wasn't overtly against the rules, but being different in any way often ended in expulsion. Mordan Darkfrey liked traditional people and traditional methods, and his values seemed to trickle down to most of the shadyrs in residence. Jasper wasn't willing to play the odds.

He kept his gaze firmly on Annabeth's auburn hair as they navigated the maze of halls toward Mordan's office. The oppressive walls of Darkfrey's lengthy corridors pressed in on him more than usual.

It wasn't the suits of armor that disturbed him, or the oil portraits of white-faced old shadyr families, or the dull, flickering glow of the lights, all of which could be somewhat spooky on a night like tonight.

It was the way Jasper didn't quite belong.

Jasper's brace piled into the Victorian cage elevator. The rickety shaft was barely big enough for the four of them, which made it claustrophobic with Nilson's oversized bulk.

Vonny yanked the metal folding door closed and smacked the button. Nilson glared down at them from above, breathing like a bull. Rumor was he hadn't been pleased with his last brace, and the way he looked at them, Jasper wondered if anyone would hold up to his standards.

They exited the elevator in the long, shadowed hallway outside Mordan's office. The lights never seemed to be on at any point except right in front of the elevator, giving the entire floor a kind of "hands off" vibe.

The double doors to the office soared high overhead, made of black wood and both decorated in intricately carved knots. Formed in the center, where the two doors met, was the Darkfrey coat of arms, made of a crescent moon, twin, fang-like blades, and skulls.

Vonny tapped the button on the intercom. A moment later, the lock on the door clicked, and the doors opened outward to admit them.

Mordan sat behind his huge mahogany desk with his back ramrod straight while he perused an open file. He wore his typical garb of a well-tailored smoking jacket in deep shades of purple and gold, and his silver hair was tied back in a low ponytail.

The walls framed him, covered in built-in shelves loaded down with books, statues, trophies, and other artifacts, while the massive wall behind Jasper held an array of animal heads forever frozen in death. Any time Jasper stood before Mordan in this room, he could swear he felt their eyes on him.

Between the lush maroon carpet and the thick drapes over the windows behind the desk shining like gold, Mordan looked like a king lording over his kingdom.

Jasper often felt like that was the truth, too.

Mordan didn't look up right away, continuing to read whatever paper was on his desk that merited his full attention.

Their brace stood like soldiers, hands clasped at their back, feet spread shoulder width apart, waiting patiently for him to acknowledge them. In the time he took, the other brace who attended Rooks trickled in and posted up behind them, ready for the debriefing.

After a few long, silent moments, while the richly appointed grandfather clock behind him ticked away the seconds, Mordan flipped the manila folder closed.

He raised a gaze as nebulous and silvery as his hair, and remarked, "Proceed."

"Rooks Hotel has been secured, sir," Nilson exclaimed.

"Good work," Mordan said, giving a single nod. "Any trouble with the Howells?"

Nilson took a second to snarl, and Vonny stepped in before he could reply. "Yes, sir. There was a notable event involving the Boderleth woman."

Her voice always went lower, more raspy, around Mordan, as if she felt like she needed to exude a more masculine vibe to be taken seriously.

She probably does, Jasper thought.

Mordan's old-fashioned values made him favor the men under his employ.

Mordan leaned back in his chair, his weight resting on one arm. "Oh?"

"The rumors appear to be true," Vonny said shortly. "She's not human."

Jasper kept his expression neutral as Vonny described in detail what they'd seen. Guilt made his skin crawl, and he fought the urge to dig at his nails again.

He knew that what they'd seen had to be reported. It was too big and too *weird*, even by Shroudhaven standards, not to report it. But it still felt somehow like a betrayal. If only they'd gotten there too late to see, it wouldn't be any of their business.

It could remain a secret, like some things should. But he'd hurried them to the site, secretly worried about Cherry's safety. And they all saw what Everly could do, the light, the sheer power. And Jasper lost Cherry anyway.

When Vonny finished her explanation, Mordan leaned back in his chair as though bored of the proceedings. "Interesting. Well, if that's all, Vonny, I'd like—"

Jasper startled, his gaze moving between Vonny and Mordan. That was it? She wasn't going to bring up Rylan and why the Howell team ended up in that situation?

"Um, sir?" Jasper's heart beat faster as he stepped forward.

Mordan's silvery gaze turned on him, surprise visible in his eyes. It wasn't done for one of the subordinate brace members to be so bold, and Jasper knew he was risking undue attention by stepping out. Nilson and Vonny shot him narrowed stares.

But Rylan had been part of his brace. A good fighter, good shadyr, and good friend. The Howell team were risking their lives to keep him alive with a resource the Darkfrey cleaners were incinerating daily.

Jasper cleared his throat. "Sir, if I may speak?"

Mordan raised an eyebrow, but made a flippant hand gesture indicating for him to continue.

"The Howell team have submitted multiple requests for vasmire remains to assist keeping Rylan Howell stable in his strange coma. I can't see the logic in denying them. Approving those requests would at least keep them out of our way in situations like this, and I also feel as though helping to keep Rylan alive is a worthy cause."

And that maybe the only reason not to, is that someone doesn't want him to remain alive. That was something else Cherry had once whispered to him, something so crazy and scandalous Jasper didn't even consider passing it along.

"It isn't your job to 'feel,'" Mordan said sharply. "Your job is to fight back the forces of darkness and do as you're told."

Jasper inhaled sharply. "Yes, sir!"

"I don't appreciate my logic being questioned. Remember your place, shadyr." He paused and looked around the room. "Vonny, please remain so you and I may talk privately. The rest of you are dismissed."

She nodded, then turned to glare at Jasper, her lips curling in a snarl that promised retribution.

Jasper looked down at his boots, shame racing through him. He fell into line with his brace and headed for the elevator, berating himself for speaking up. He shouldn't have said anything. He knew better than to step out of line.

But Cherry had that effect on him. As the elevator trundled down to the first floor in silence, he thought of the way being with Cherry had made him feel.

Cherry made him want to be different. Better. Braver.

That had been the most intoxicating part of building their relationship, when he'd discovered there were qualities hidden deep inside himself, if he only had the courage to bring them out.

But he didn't. He couldn't. As upset as he was to lose the person who made him want to be more, Jasper knew his place was with the Darkfreys. He was on the right side, the side of power, the side fighting for the very existence of their world. He was going to be fine.

As long as Cherry didn't out him in revenge.

The thought sent a tremor down his spine. He said good night to his brace, avoiding Nilson's gaze, and then took the staircase that led to his tower dormitory.

Darkfrey Estate was his home.

If he wasn't a Darkfrey, he was nobody.

Chapter Twelve

Rylan and his family are shapeshifting monster hunters. Someone from Darkfrey estate tried to get him killed. Someone who is doing creepy things with black bones. Rylan needs to get back in his body. Plus, I need to find out what's going on with the light inside me. What is the beast of teeth and stars?

And did Rylan really ask me to kiss him?

After waking up from her conversation with Rylan, Everly's mind raced with everything she knew, everything she'd learned since coming back to Shroudhaven. She couldn't shut down the endless swirl of information.

Everly finally gave up on rest as the sky outside the window was beginning to tinge with morning pinks and reds.

She rubbed sleep from her bleary eyes and shuffled

downstairs to brew a coffee, adding an extra shot for a little more *oomph*.

She sipped from the warm mug, standing over the kitchen sink as she watched the neighborhood awaken.

Across the street, a bent-over old woman emerged from her house to water the flowers in her front garden. A few houses down, the dentist who worked out of his three-story Victorian hung his *Open* sign, his sapphire blue scrubs a startling splash of color on the gray, misty morning.

Farther down on the corner where the street ended, school kids trickled to the stop sign in twos and threes—never alone—to wait for the bus.

Normal, everyday life in Shroudhaven, Everly thought. *And it's a total lie.*

These people had no idea that monsters roamed their town after dark. They had no idea that a mad witch in the woods had been bringing dead animals back to life, or that there were portals throughout the area connecting Shroudhaven to another dimension full of horrifying beings.

There were stories, rumors, but overall they were blissfully unaware. Oblivious. Especially in the light of day when intuition whispered it was safe because the things that went bump in the night were sleeping.

Everly herself would have been in the dark still if her mother hadn't died. She wished she were back in her city apartment, ignorant of all of the shadows in Shroudhaven. Back when her only worry was keeping her anxiety at bay and making sure Harper was safe from her ex.

Back when people like him were the only real monsters.

"You're up early."

Harper's voice broke through the silence of the kitchen so abruptly that Everly jumped. Coffee sloshed over her fingers into the sink, and she hissed, quickly putting her mug down and reaching for a towel.

Harper raised her eyebrows as she reached for the cabinet door to extract a mug. She still wore her cream-colored silk matching night set under her open robe, but her feet were bare, toenails colored in a glittery pink.

"Sorry. Jumpy this morning, huh?"

"Thinking about monsters," Everly replied, drying away the spilled coffee on her fingers.

Harper carried her mug to the coffee pot. "Literal or metaphorical?"

"Yes."

"I suppose both is an option. We're spoiled for choice, aren't we?" Harper filled her mug, adding a heaped spoonful of her flavored creamer. "Do we have plans today? Monster related or otherwise?"

Does kissing Rylan count?

Everly cleared her increasingly dry throat. "Not that I know of."

"Good. I'm going to get an early start in the shop. I didn't like the way the Waterford crystal pics came out. Too many rainbows."

Everly laughed. "Since when do you put a limit on rainbows?"

Harper made a face and picked up her mug. "When you can't even see the vase for the sparkles. Meet you there?"

"Yeah. I'll join you in a few."

Everly listened to her best friend's light footsteps pad down the hall, then the creaky back door to the antiques shop opened and clicked shut. In the ensuing silence, the school bus arrived at the end of the block, lights flashing while kids piled on.

She envied them for still being kids. Her most treasured memories were still from the time before Rylan's father died, when it was him and her, best friends against the world.

A time when they could spend their days trying to teach Birdie tricks, or building a fort down by the creek, or sitting in a mulberry tree, staining their mouths and hands blood-red and pretending to be vampires.

Did he know then? Did he always know what he was?

Rylan's questioning of her memory of when they first met now had a deeper meaning.

At five years old, she had run away from home to escape her mom and her male companion, and gotten lost in the

Wyrdwoods. A place many people didn't come back alive from. Rylan had run away too, although she was never truly clear on the reason why until learning about shadyrs filled in the blanks.

He was worried he was a monster.

She remembered telling him that he wasn't. She'd felt so sure about that, because it was the grown ups in her life who were the monsters.

In her dream when they'd talked about it, he'd asked if she remembered him looking *different*. Everly tried to bring a clear vision of him at the time forward.

But it was so long ago, and she had been weak and delirious by that point. But maybe he had been in a shifted form then. Only five himself, he'd carried her all the way out, back to his mom for help. That wasn't normal.

He'd known at least that long, what he was.

He'd done everything he could to protect her since that day, too.

She knew what Rylan expected of her. He'd been clear that he wanted her to kiss him in the hope it would wake him up. The idea thrilled her and frightened her all at once, and she knew she needed to get on with it.

But she dawdled over the sink, taking her time with her coffee, procrastinating by washing the few dishes left from the night before. When her cup was empty, and there was nothing else to distract her, Everly took a deep breath, let it out slowly, and then headed back upstairs.

The door to her old room hung open, but the sunshine beaming in from the rest of the house couldn't penetrate the darkness that lay beyond. The beshadowed weirdness had eased already, but the worst of it remained in there, oozing across the bedroom walls.

Everly's skin crawled from the cold rolling out, and as she stepped up to the threshold, she waded into a knee-high wall of mist.

On the bookshelves along the wall, the vasmire pieces seemed to hum with unrestrained tension. The tentacles pulsed like they were alive and breathing, though Everly knew it was just a symptom of the minor beshadowing caused by their presence.

She stared at Rylan in the dim room, her heart pinging against her rib cage. Was she really going to do this? Kiss him while he was in a coma?

Sucking in a steadying breath, she took a step into the room and tried to turn the overhead light on, but the switch flicked uselessly. She considered getting a flashlight. So she didn't have to be alone in a dark room with strange things happening all around her, and it would be handy to check for signs of life and—

Stop it. Stop putting it off.

Everly walked up to the edge of the bed quietly. He lay atop the covers, eerily still, his pale skin nearly glowing in the dark.

Should she just … lean over him? Sit beside him?

She waffled between her options, unsure whether she was doing the right thing. The idea was silly—she couldn't fix him with a kiss. She needed to find a way to get Rylan's spirit out of her head and back into his body, but there was no way a kiss was enough.

Whatever metaphysical thing had happened to put him inside her dreams, she needed a reversal of that.

Plus … what if this was the only kiss they ever shared? And he wasn't even awake to kiss her back.

Just do it, she chastised herself.

A person couldn't win the lottery if they didn't buy a ticket. She'd never know if this crazy plan would work unless she just went for it. Rylan must have thought it had at least a small chance, or why else would he have suggested it?

She took a few more deep breaths to calm her racing heart, and gave her hands and arms a good shake to brush off the jitters. Then she sat down on the edge of the bed, put her hands on either side of his head, leaned over, and kissed him.

Though his shadyr skin was hard like stone, his lips were soft, and cool. They parted ever so slightly under the pressure of her mouth, and for just a moment, she imagined he was kissing her back.

She'd imagined her lips on his countless times, imagined

how fireworks would explode around her, how she'd melt into him, turn to liquid heat, fall to utter pieces beneath his touch.

None of that happened.

He didn't move. He didn't wake up. He remained as cold and immoveable as a statue.

Everly ended the kiss and pulled away, though she didn't sit up. She stared at his closed eyelids for any hint of movement, but they remained still, as her own eyes filled with tears.

"Dammit." She shoved away from the bed, turning her back on him as the hot tears spilled.

Harper stood in the doorway.

Everly froze in mid-stride, halfway between the bed and the door.

Embarrassment flooded her neck and cheeks with heat. "It's not what you think."

Harper leaned her hip against the frame. "You were trying Sleeping Beauty's kiss."

"Oh. Then it is what you think. It was Rylan's idea. He asked me to try."

"Didn't mean to interrupt, just came for my slippers."

"Didn't work, anyway." Everly wiped her wet cheeks, only spreading the salt-water as more and more tears fell. "I just want to fix him. I *need* to fix him."

"I know," Harper said gently. "And you're going to."

"What if I can't?" Everly's voice cracked on the last word, and pain blossomed in her chest, shooting numbing chills down her arms. "What if this is it? What if he's just broken for good? What if he's trapped in my mind forever and we can't continue keeping his body alive?"

With every word, her tone got higher pitched, the words came faster, her heart beat painfully loud in her ears. Tremors rattled her hands.

"What if he *dies*, Harper? For real this time? It'll be all my fault because I couldn't find a way to let him go. What if I never—"

She cut off. Her throat closed and all the breath in her body had vanished. The tension in her chest extended upward, shooting pain through her neck and scalp.

The dragon shifted restlessly, and she could see its light just out of sight inside her. Feel it scraping at her walls, waiting for this weakness to set it free.

"N-no, *no*," Everly stammered, backing away from Harper.

She backpedaled furiously, all the way into the corner of the room, where her back slammed against the bookshelves that held the vasmire tentacles.

The force of the hit kicked her legs out from beneath her and she slid to the floor, reaching desperately to catch herself on the shelves. Instead, she grabbed a crate of putrid monster flesh and dumped it on the floor beside her. Foul-smelling fluids spattered her leggings, and she cringed away from the pile with a short, sharp cry.

The light was everywhere. Inside her, all around her, brightening this dark, beshadowed corner of the room. Her heart pounded, and the grip around it tightened even more. Despite the cold, misty air, sweat broke out on her forehead, even as her skin felt frozen solid. She heard a frightened voice and some part of her recognized that it was *her own*, but it didn't sound right.

"No, no, I won't let you. Stay inside. No, no, no."

There was nothing, nobody, there that she could let the dragon consume.

Her vision tunneled until all she could see was Rylan's corpse-like form on the bed.

Harper's fingers dug into her shoulders, drawing Everly's attention. "Ev, hey, Everly, look at me. Breathe. You're okay. You can control this."

"I ... I can't!" Everly gasped the words out, her breaths like knives in her throat.

"Yes, you can," Harper said firmly. "You will. You do it every day. Look at me. Breathe with me."

Everly forced herself to look into Harper's bright green eyes. The two women stared at one another for a long moment as Everly anchored herself in Harper's gaze, and then Harper took a deep breath and let it out.

"Nice and slow. Press your feet down, ground yourself,"

she said, then pulled in another deep breath. "Come on, you know what to do. You've got this."

I've got this.

It was hard, in the moment, to feel as though she wasn't dying, to feel as though anything could help, that everything wasn't pointless. Everly struggled to maintain her hold on reality, as the dragon wailed to be released.

But she'd survived this before. She'd lived through every panic attack that had ever struck her down. She would survive this too. She knew how. She set her trembling legs as firmly as she could onto the ground. She pulled back her shoulders, expanding her chest.

She focused on Harper's breaths, on mimicking her, one breath at a time until her heartbeat slowed, and the sparkling lights and dark edges of her vision widened.

"There," Harper said, like she'd put the finishing touches on her grandest photographic masterpiece. "Are you all back together again?"

Everly nodded. Her hands still shook, but she no longer felt on the verge of her heart giving out. The exhaustion that hit on the other side of a panic attack felt like slurry filling her veins. She wanted to crawl into her sleeping bag and snooze for the next week.

"Thanks. I'm sorry for freaking out."

"Psssh. What you should be apologizing for is making me crouch down in these nasty vasmire parts. Look at my slippers, Everly. Just look at them." She wiggled her toes with an audible squelching sound.

"I'll buy you new ones."

"Babe, I have five pairs and I didn't like these ones anyway." Harper grimaced and held out a hand. "Come on. Let's get away from the dead monster for a while. I'm sure it's not the best for a happy state of mind."

Harper pulled Everly to her feet then tossed an arm around her shoulders. "You're going to be okay. And so is Rylan. You'll figure out how to free him. I know it."

Everly nodded, giving Rylan's sleeping body one last glance before Harper steered her out the door.

Will I?

It was going to be hard to free him when an essence deep in her being screamed that it would never let him go.

Chapter Thirteen

After pulling herself together—plus a shower and a little more coffee—Everly joined her friend in the antiques shop. Maybe if she focused on working with her hands, she could get a break from the overwhelming worries beating at her mind, and the echoes of the eidolghast's voice screaming *monster, beast.*

And the building evidence that the vasmire was right about what she is.

She and Harper had set up a temporary workshop-slash-photo studio in the front room, since it had the most natural light and available surface area.

Harper had made use of an antique table in the corner for her photography and tech needs, while Everly had turned the old L-shaped checkout counter into her repair station. The monstrous wooden bench was covered in paint splattered drop cloths she'd found in the storage room, and the entire contents of her toolbox were scattered across the surface.

It had taken more than a few rounds of dusting, sweeping, and vacuuming to remove the gray tint of neglect from the antique store. Of the items that could be salvaged, most still needed individual cleaning as well, but the cobwebs no longer dangled like ribbons across the rooms and the air was more breathable. The rats, also, had been banished.

Every time Everly sat on the old barstool behind the counter, she flashed back to her dusty memories of her father.

Being in that forbidden space had been painful in those first few days of cataloguing the store. As though her father's specter hung in the air, accusing her of his death, of dismantling the store that had been everything he'd cared about.

His presence was everywhere: in the selection of antiques he'd curated, in the 'Do Not Touch' signs, in the corners and shadows and slants of light. Her father's heart and soul existed there, even though his body didn't.

She'd been only three years old when he suffered a heart attack right in front of her, just next door in the books and collectables room.

Everly still blamed herself. She'd broken one of his

favorite pieces, and his fury had sent him into cardiac arrest. Her mother had done a great job of piling on the guilt, too, so it had been a pain she'd lived with all her life.

Though her memories of that day were fuzzy, like she was looking through a translucent veil, she remembered light. A flash of brilliant light.

A flash she'd discounted as faulty memory for most of her life. But in the new awareness of all she'd learned and experienced in Shroudhaven, all her old memories were being scrutinized.

There had been a light.

Like the dragon had been there then, too.

Maybe it had always been part of her. The thought made her shudder and she put those dark musings out of her head.

For several hours, Everly threw herself into repairing the old German cuckoo clock Harper had tasked her to fix. She was no clock expert, but she had the internet—spotty as the connection could be—and an eager ability to teach herself how to fix anything.

It had served her well when she'd been kicked out by her mom at fifteen and bluffed her way into adulthood early, scoring maintenance jobs with a couple of forged documents and online tutorials.

Focusing on something she *could* easily fix helped ease the knot of tension in her chest.

Around noon, a shadow appeared on the other side of the lace-curtained front windows. The silhouette passed the window like a wraith, then appeared on the other side of the frosted glass window at the front door.

Everly froze, miniature screwdriver hanging in the air over the open door on the clock.

Three sharp knocks echoed through the high-ceilinged room.

Harper straightened and lowered her camera, brow furrowed as she glanced at Everly. "Are we expecting company?"

"No. And any company we *know* would use the back door." Everly slipped off the stool and went to answer the knock.

"Um ... Hello?" Everly squinted into the daylight at the red-headed shadyr on the front porch.

Annabeth was in her usual uniform of black pants and a Darkfrey jacket, the hood up over her auburn hair. She was taller than Everly by a couple of inches and had a cute button nose and a galaxy of ginger freckles on her cheeks.

She offered a wobbly smile. "Everly, right?"

"Yeah, we've met before."

"Oh, I know, but not really, well, only ..."

"Only when it was our-team-versus-your-team fun times?" Everly offered the stuttering girl.

Annabeth gaped but recovered quickly, her lips firming

into a straight line. She extracted a small maroon envelope from her pocket and held it out. "From Master Darkfrey."

Harper peered over Everly's shoulder. "You sure it's not poisoned?"

Annabeth's brow furrowed. "Um. No?"

Harper flashed her teeth in a mockery of a smile. "No, it's not poisoned, or no, you aren't sure?"

"Harper," Everly admonished.

"What? It's an important distinction," Harper said, laying on the mock innocence.

The envelope felt heavier than its size allowed, and the front bore Everly's full name in spidery gold script. She turned the envelope over to find it sealed with wax in the shape of the Darkfrey crest. The tiny skulls with their hollow eyes stared up at her, threatening.

Slipping a finger beneath the lip, she opened it and withdrew a note made of thick, textured cardstock. It was as dark maroon as the envelope and held the same spidery gold handwriting.

"Dear Miss Boderleth, please accept my regards and welcome to Shroudhaven," Everly murmured. She read onward, each word furrowing her brow further. "He wants me to come for tea."

"Why?" Harper asked, drawing out the word suspiciously.

"Since my first visit to Darkfrey Estate wasn't 'under

the best circumstances' he wants to 'welcome me properly,'" Everly quoted.

She exchanged glances with Harper and wondered if her best friend had the same thought she had: Mordan Darkfrey wasn't interested in a social call.

"Right. Nothing to do with you glowing up Rooks Hotel then?" Harper murmured.

It seemed she and Everly were on the same wavelength.

Everly nodded, then took hold of the door. "Well, thanks for bringing this by. I'll give it some thought and call the number he left if I decide to go."

But the shadyr stepped forward, putting the toe of her boot against the wood before Everly could close it. "Wait. I … can I see Rylan? Please?"

"He's still not awake."

"I know," Annabeth said, subdued. "I just … wanna see him, you know? He is—was—my brace partner."

A sudden flash of jealousy and protective fury coursed through Everly's veins, and the feeling was so foreign, she felt like she'd stepped outside her own body.

"If you cared about him, you'd help us keep him alive," she snapped.

Annabeth's eyes widened and her mouth pursed. "I know. I would if it were up to me. If you just gave him back to us, I'm sure—"

"That's not happening."

Annabeth's face twisted as though something had broken inside her, and she put a hand over her eyes for a few seconds.

When she withdrew it, her expression was calm and neutral. "I just want to see him, just for a moment."

Everly turned to Harper, unsure. Despite the firm line of the shadyr girl's mouth, there had been a hint of pleading in her tone. Harper shrugged.

Annabeth had never been outright antagonistic to her and her friends like other members of her team. She seemed innocent enough, for a Darkfrey. Why should Everly be so rude as to deny her simple request?

Except ... Annabeth could be the shadyr who tried to kill Rylan the night of the raid at Nell's animal sanctuary. She couldn't let her guard down around *any* of the Darkfrey residents. But she could let the girl see Rylan. Accompanied. It could be a chance to try to trap the shadyr into revealing herself, if she was the one.

If she did want to kill Rylan, would I have a chance to stop her? She could use the monster bits to shift into vampire form and then I'd be no match for her.

But I do have my dragon.

And if Annabeth tried something on Rylan, Everly knew she wouldn't hesitate to let out her light.

Everly shrugged as casually as she could, and stepped aside to let her in.

Harper stayed behind to keep working, saying she'd had enough of the vasmire tentacles for one day, so Everly led Annabeth through the house alone. They didn't speak, though Everly could sense Annabeth's curiosity about the house, and the quiet, contemplative way she studied her surroundings.

At the door to her old bedroom, Everly motioned to the darkness beyond, then let Annabeth go inside first while she waited at the threshold. She held her breath, watching for any sign of change, or attack.

Annabeth's steps faltered halfway into the dark room. Ambient sunlight from the living room down the hall illuminated the back of her military jacket, casting her shadow over Rylan's face.

"He looks dead," Annabeth said quietly.

Everly wanted to question whether that was what Annabeth wanted, but the dull tone hadn't hidden the fear in her words.

She sighed and said softly, "He's not. The pale skin is because he's partly in vampire form, regenerating."

Annabeth nodded slowly, turning to the crates, nose wrinkled. Some had popped their lids, the gore inside expanding as it decayed.

Everly watched the woman carefully, but there was no sign she was going to shift. She seemed younger than her, more like Tammy's age, but clearly had complete control over her abilities. Everly guessed she wouldn't be part of an active brace if she hadn't.

Annabeth looked around the room at the strange black shapes pulsing along the walls and the mist pouring from the crates. "This is dangerous for you and your friend."

"We're managing just fine." The words were snappier than she'd intended, but the Darkfrey shadyr had no right to lecture her about the vasmire pieces keeping Rylan alive, and wasn't about to scare her into letting them take Rylan away.

Annabeth walked up to the edge of the bed, and Everly jolted a step forward after her, breath hitching. The shadyr reached out and pressed her fingertips to Rylan's neck. Checking for a pulse, but also something more, something lingering. Everly shifted uncomfortably at the sight, jealousy surging. She wanted to scream at her to stop touching him.

What is going on with me? He doesn't belong to me, in any way.

Rylan's presence in her head must be doing this, making her possessive, thinking of him as hers and hers alone. But it wasn't true. It never would be.

"The two of us, we ended up at Darkfrey estate in the same circumstances," Annabeth said without looking back at Everly.

Her voice was soft, as though it were more for Rylan

than anyone else. "An eidolghast attacked my home, too. Killed my mom. Years after it happened to Rylan, but I think the pain was still fresh for him. It connected us."

A deep chill ran up Everly's spine.

Rylan's dad was killed by an eidolghast?

That wasn't the story she'd been told. But now she found it hard to be surprised that it wasn't just an animal attack. She'd wanted to be there for Rylan when he was grieving, but he'd shut her off, pushed her out of his life entirely. But he didn't shut out Annabeth.

"I'd only been in his brace since Callan left, but we were so good together." Annabeth's fingers slid up to his cheek and then down his jawbone, hovering just below his lips.

Oh.

Everly drew a sharp breath. "You're in love with him."

Annabeth turned toward her, vulnerable, watery eyes hardening fast. "What does that matter to you?"

Why didn't I see it, why didn't I think?

Of course there would have been someone in Rylan's life who loved him.

Why wouldn't it be this stunning, capable, hard-edged young woman? Why wouldn't he love her back?

I have to know. But I don't want to.

Everly's lips opened and closed a few times before the words got out. "Is ... is he in love with you?"

Annabeth laughed bitterly. "No. I worked out pretty

quick that his heart's buried under a brick wall. It belongs to someone else."

Everly's heart skipped a beat. "Who?"

Annabeth's wry grin spread as she took Everly in, as though seeing her for the first time. "Huh. I'd almost guess you had a thing for him, too."

"We were friends." The denial came too fast, too off pitch.

Annabeth strolled up in front of Everly, eyes soft with sympathetic solidarity. "Right. Sure. Good luck with that. But I'm telling you, his heart is already taken."

Everly folded her arms, as though that could hold in the churn of acid burning her insides.

Annabeth straightened up, almost at attention. All the softness had gone from her face again.

"Thank you for letting me see him. Look after him. He's a good man."

As the shadyr passed by her into the hallway, Everly glanced at Rylan's sleeping form. Was Annabeth right? Did he love someone else?

Of course he could. In all the years they'd been apart, of course he would have had relationships, could have been in one right now. She knew there was at least one reason why Darkfrey shadyrs kept their romances secret.

After all the other massive secrets he'd kept from her, one more wouldn't be a surprise.

Everly didn't hesitate to get in touch with Lian to let her know about her invitation. It was decided she should come over for dinner that evening to discuss options.

Callan showed up at dusk, tag-teaming them for Rylan watch duty. Everly and Harper left in the campervan to drive to Howell House.

Up until recently, she would have just walked the couple of short blocks, but now that she knew what came out after dark, she wasn't interested in tempting fate. The campervan drove like a tank, and if they came up against a wandering vasmire or weroth, Everly intended to use it as a weapon.

She was much too aware of Mordan Darkfrey's fancy invitation in the inside pocket of her red bomber jacket. She didn't like that he knew her name or that he knew what his shadyrs had seen at the hotel. She needed Lian's advice.

Howell House sat alone in a large field at the end of a birch-lined drive. When Mr. Howell had been alive, the place had looked like a palace—white gingerbread trim always freshly painted, ivory siding as bright as the sun, the flower and herb gardens like something out of a fairy tale.

While Lian had maintained her gardens with the same colorful eye for detail as all those years ago, the rest of the house had faded and cracked. As if her husband had taken the vibrancy with him when he died.

They hadn't even knocked on the door when they heard Rushelle's voice. "Come in!"

Everly shoved open the creaky screen door to find the house filled with the smell of cooking. Lian's bolognese. She knew it immediately and the scent was so familiar it sent an ache of nostalgia into her chest.

She and Harper headed to the kitchen, where Rushelle set the huge, farmhouse table, and Tammy sat slumped in her seat, hood up, ear buds in, a patch of darkness in the warm space. Across the room, Cherry and Denny argued.

"Bellsy is, like, my new best friend," Cherry said, waving his hands around. "And no offense, but I'm pretty sure she hates your guts, so ... I'm sitting next to her, and that's that."

"Nope. No, siree," Denny said, rocking back on his heels with a little smirk on his bearded face. "I got dibs."

"You can't dibs a person!"

"But I did, so suck it up. Hope she wears something low-cut. Girl's got nice—"

"Girl's here!" Harper interrupted loudly.

"Tits," Denny drawled, unperturbed.

Tammy made a far too realistic gagging sound.

Harper tossed her perfectly curled hair back. "I've got a nice AVO lawyer too, happy to show that off."

Denny opened his mouth, but Rushelle straightened, looking like a vengeful Norse goddess as she slammed her fists on her hips and glared. "Do I need to serve your dinner to go, mister?"

"Was just a compliment," Denny grumbled under his breath.

Under the continued pressure of Rushelle's stare, he gestured zipping up his mouth and dropped into a chair, slouched and sulking.

Cherry put his arms out and welcomed an embrace from Harper. Over her shoulder, he stuck his tongue out at Denny, before taking a seat as far from him as possible. The hushed conversation between him and Harper started up immediately.

Across the kitchen, Lian hefted a huge cooking pot to the sink, momentarily disappearing into a cloud of steam as she drained off the pasta.

Everly sidled up to the counter across from her and pulled the envelope from her pocket, tossing it next to a cutting board. "Here it is."

"Fancy." Lian set the pot down and opened the envelope, raking her gaze over the short message. "What a polite way to invite you to an interrogation."

"My thoughts exactly."

Lian tossed the envelope and card back on the counter. Grabbing a ladle, she spooned a thick, red sauce into the pasta.

"Even if we did know what caused your powers, that's information we don't want the Darkfreys to have. And we certainly don't want them working it out first."

"Do you think they'd hurt me?"

Lian stared into the pasta as she stirred the sauce through. The silence grew heavy before she looked back up and tossed Everly a small, encouraging smile.

"We wouldn't let them. But still, you're different. Mordan and his army don't treat 'different' well."

Everly glanced over at Cherry. He and Harper had stopped their conversation. Despite a casual smirk, there was a darkness of pain in Cherry's gaze.

"Then I should decline the invitation?"

Lian's smile widened. "Oh no. We're going to accept."

"We?"

"Yes, you and me. You're not entering that place on your own. We'll approach the meeting with caution, keep up appearances for Mordan," Lian said. "Because this could be our one and only opportunity to get inside Darkfrey Estate."

She put the ladle down in the sink and chuckled almost mischievously. "Mordan thinks he's going to get info from us, but this is our chance to get something from them."

"The Bane of Teeth and Stars?" Everly said.

For some reason, the phrase turned her stomach sour,

but a hint of excitement followed. This could be her chance to find out what she was, what the dragon was.

From over at the table, Harper squealed. "We're going to do a heist?"

Lian grinned as she took the cordless phone off the wall and held it out to Everly. "Let's go to tea."

Tea, with Mordan Darkfrey. Everly may as well be walking into the lair of a monster.

Chapter Fourteen

In the light of day, Everly expected the gates to Darkfrey Estate to be less foreboding.

Of course, the "light of day" in Shroudhaven was often dim, gray, and misty, so instead of bright sunshine glinting off the black wrought iron gates, the atmosphere was more that of a gothic movie.

Low-hanging, gunpowder gray clouds threatened rain and cast the forest in a haze that made it look darker than it should be. Everly shivered in her seat at the presence of those gates, and what lay beyond.

Lian rolled down her window and pushed a button on the intercom.

A beat of silence passed, and then a crisp, authoritative voice said, "Yes?"

Lian leaned out her window. "Lian Howell and Everly

Boderleth to see Mordan."

"Do you have—"

"Yes," Lian cut in. "He's expecting us."

After a drawn-out pause, the voice at the other end said, "Pull around to the front door and an escort will be waiting for you."

The gates began to creak open, and Lian hit the toggle to roll her window up.

"An escort," she scoffed, carefully pulling through the gates before they'd finished opening. "Sounds like someone is feeling a bit threatened."

By me?

Everly didn't like that idea. "Is that going to be a problem?"

"No, we'll work it out. This isn't my first rodeo."

"Your sword?" Everly fished.

Lian flashed a mischievous grin.

They fell into silence as Lian navigated the twisting driveway through thick, dark woods.

Everly lay her head back against the headrest and thought about how strange it was to see this side of Lian. When she'd been a kid, Lian had just been Rylan's mom, and Everly had been so focused on her relationship with Rylan that she'd almost missed how much of a mother Lian had been to her, too.

How there was always a place at their dinner table

when Everly's own mother had neglected to keep any food in the house. How Lian accidently bought a pair of shoes in the wrong size for Rylan that managed to perfectly fit Everly when the soles had come off hers. How Lian had her over for sleepovers on nights when Everly's mom had male guests in the house.

But the truth was Lian had an entire life she'd lived before Everly ever showed up on her doorstep. This Lian was older physically, but with all the secrets out in the open, she seemed ... freer. Younger at heart, maybe, though she still carried an undercurrent of sadness from the tragedies she'd experienced.

The trees thinned, and the castle-like building of Darkfrey Estate appeared at the apex of the hill like a craggy mountain, dark and imposing, casting a long shadow over the rolling lawn.

A chill raced up Everly's back as Lian's SUV rolled into the circular drive before the main building.

An unfamiliar shadyr with a bald head approached and opened Everly's door.

"Welcome to Darkfrey Estate," he said in a monotone. "I'll be escorting you to Master Darkfrey's office."

"For ghast's sake, Bob, you know I know the way," Lian groaned from the driver's seat.

"Just following orders, Lian."

Everly noticed that Bob didn't look right at her. His

gaze locked over her shoulder on the upholstery, and she wondered if he knew about the light. Word traveled fast around Darkfrey Estate. She unbuckled her seatbelt and exchanged nods with Lian, then exited the vehicle.

Lian grabbed the large canvas tote from the back seat and put it over her shoulder, patting the side.

As they fell into step behind Bob, Lian leaned in and muttered, "Don't eat or drink anything he gives you."

Everly raised her eyebrows but nodded. Her skin chilled even more, and she tugged her jacket tighter around herself as they walked into the building.

She'd followed this same path before with Lian when they were trying to find out what had happened to Rylan, so she was familiar with the suits of armor, the oppressive entombment of the dark stone walls and floors, and the cage elevator that led to Mordan's office.

She'd been excited to see the inside of Darkfrey Estate that day. Now, she was nervous. Nervous that Mordan was dangerous. Nervous that he intended to uncover her secrets and use them against her.

What if he already knows what I am? What if it is something terrible? What if this is a trap?

When they walked into his office, Mordan immediately rose from behind his desk and straightened the lapels of his smoking jacket. The fabric was maroon and embroidered with golden threads that looked like stars. His tight-lipped smile seemed a little too wide.

"Miss Boderleth. Welcome," he said grandly, sweeping out from behind his desk to offer his hands. "I'm delighted you could meet with me."

Everly hesitated, but she didn't want to be rude, so she lay her hand in his. He clasped her fingers with smooth, cold hands and kissed her knuckles. Everly shuddered but kept her mouth firmly shut. It was agreed Lian would do the talking, and Everly didn't think things would start off well with her declaring how grossed out she was.

When Mordan straightened, he didn't immediately release her.

He studied her with shrewd gray eyes. "Such a lovely girl, aren't you?"

His unnecessary assessment of her physical appearance made her squirm, and Everly glanced at Lian, begging for help.

Lian leaned forward and batted Mordan's hands off Everly's, putting out her own in replacement. "Hello, Mordan. Don't you think I'm lovely, as well?"

Mordan glared at her hand for a few seconds too long. The two stared at one another with such open enmity, Everly could feel the tension rippling across her skin and filling the office like the charge in the air before a thunderstorm.

"Lian," Mordan said stiffly. "When I invited Miss

Boderleth, I didn't know I was inviting you, as well."

"What kind of person would I be if I sent a friend into danger on their own? But you wouldn't know anything about that, would you? You refuse to do the very things you send your charges to do."

"I did my time on patrol, as you well know," Mordan said, an edge to his voice. "And this is hardly a dangerous situation. Please, have a seat. I'll send for our tea service."

"Cut the shit, Mordan," Lian said, dumping her tote bag beside her and slouching lazily in her chair. "We both know you didn't ask Everly here to serve her Earl Grey and scones."

Everly took a seat beside her, trying not to smirk.

Mordan didn't reply right away as he settled behind his desk. His thin, craggy face was an emotionless mask, but a glint of irritation flickered in his gaze. Lian seemed to know all his buttons and how to push them, though whether doing so was a smart idea, Everly couldn't say.

"Indeed," Mordan relented. "Since you'd like to dispatch with the pleasantries, yes. My team returned from Rooks Hotel with the most intriguing tale. As such, I'd like to know more about Miss Boderleth's powers."

"Sadly, your team is woefully misinformed," Lian said, opening her palms to the ceiling in a loose shrug. "All they saw was the result of a conveniently timed gas explosion that caused an intense electrical surge, killing the vasmires."

Everly had to work hard to keep her expression from changing. They hadn't discussed what would be said beyond Lian's directive to let her do the talking, so this cover story was news to Everly. Whether it was believable was beside the point. Lian clearly wasn't handing over a scrap of truthful information.

Mordan's eyes narrowed. "A gas explosion electrocuted the vasmires. To death."

Lian shrugged. "Great timing, too, as we were admittedly struggling, what with there being two of the huge beasts. Meanwhile, your people just stood by and watched. Is that a new course here at Darkfrey? 'How to watch other shadyrs die'?"

"I'm sure had the 'gas explosion' not happened, you and your *team* would have had the situation well in hand," Mordan said dryly.

"Perhaps!" Lian said brightly. "But it all worked out for the best. Everly narrowly escaped getting hurt in the explosion. The only power she has is good luck."

Mordan huffed and directed his question to Everly. "That's really what happened?"

She shrugged, innocently. "How else would you explain it?"

"How indeed."

Mordan didn't believe her. Everly could see it in the tight lines of his face. But it was also clear he didn't have answers either.

She imagined he was weighing his options of whether to argue with Lian and demand she tell him the truth. Everly didn't know anything about their past together, but there was certainly no love lost, and neither of them had a problem goading one another into a fury.

But Mordan's gaze slid to Everly, and he straightened, seemingly coming to a decision.

"What news of Rylan?" he inquired.

The smile fell off Lian's face. "Don't pretend you care about him."

Mordan's eyebrows furrowed and his hand fell limply onto the table with a thump. "Of course, I care. And if you'd only let him be brought here, he'd have every resource available to us to treat his condition."

"Or make sure he never wakes up," Everly countered.

"I don't know what lies the Howells have poisoned your mind with, but we aren't a den of monsters trying to kill our own. We only do what must be done to keep our world safe. Rylan knew that more than anyone. He understood the nature of sacrifice."

Everly shivered at the word. "You aren't making a great case for his safety."

Mordan sighed, running a hand down his chin. "I truly do care for him and his health. Rylan is one of my favorites. A great soldier, one of the best. He's like a son to me."

"A son?" Lian leaned forward and smacked both hands down onto Mordan's huge timber desk, rattling the lamps. "A son you stole from *me*."

"Rylan and Callan wanted to be here. I could never have made them stay otherwise," Mordan snapped. "We've been around and around with this, Lian."

"They were *children*. Their actions were a direct result of your manipulation, your, your ..." She waved her hands, her eyes as wild as her gestures. "Your *brainwashing*!"

"This isn't a cult, Lian," Mordan said stiffly, leaning back in his chair away from her.

"Isn't it?" she shrieked, tugging at her gray hair.

She stood abruptly, snatched her tote bag up, and glanced at Everly. "Come on. I can't even stand to look at this man!"

Mordan reached to an antique-styled phone on his desk. "Let me get you an esco—"

"I don't need a ghast-damned escort, Mordan! Or are you trying to hide something? Well? Are you?" She turned her scathing glare on him, swinging her bag like a weapon.

He put his hands up, away from the phone. "Lian—"

But she didn't let him speak, howling into the room, "If I find out that Rylan's situation had *anything* to do with you, I'll kill you!"

Lian grabbed Everly's arm, dragging her from the office.

Mordan stood motionless behind his desk, glaring

down his nose at them. "You and the runts you surround yourself with? As if you ever could."

CHAPTER FIFTEEN

The moment the rickety elevator was in motion, Lian unzipped her tote bag and whipped out the two Darkfrey jackets from within, loaned to them from Callan and Cherry.

"That was close." Lian stripped off her long cardigan, swapping for the disguise. "Sorry you had to witness that. I knew we wouldn't get out of there without an escort if I didn't distract him. He freezes up when confronted with a hysterical woman."

Everly took the second jacket and grinned in appreciation of Lian's ruse, but even if it all was just for show, her mind was still on the idea of Mordan "stealing" Rylan and Callan.

Everly remembered as a teenager being surprised when she learned that custody of both Lian's boys had been granted through the courts to Mordan, but she figured she just didn't understand the legal system.

Rylan and Callan had seemed like they wanted to leave. Like they were just going to a full-time boarding school, where they were too good for those they left behind.

And Rylan wanted to leave everything in his life behind to come to this estate. Especially me.

The elevator rattled around them as Everly took off her faded-red jacket and replaced it with Callan's Darkfrey one. It was a little tight, and there was no way she'd be able to zip it up, but it would serve its purpose.

Everly said in a low voice, "Can I ask, what really happened to bring Rylan and Callan here?"

Lian let out a short, bitter chuckle as she slipped into Cherry's jacket easily, the fabric swimming around her tall, thin figure. "You didn't hear that I was an unfit mother?"

Everly nodded slowly. She'd heard that rumor when her own mother, in one of her rare lucid moments, had questioned Everly about whether or not Lian Howell had ever hurt her. Even then, Everly had been aware of the irony of her questioning. Janey Boderleth was the only unfit mother in her life.

"I did. Didn't believe it then, definitely don't believe it now."

Lian's eyes glittered, and she cupped Everly's cheek for a moment before she sighed and got to work stuffing their jackets into the tote bag.

"My boys ... I tried to raise them in such a way that didn't *hide* what they were, but that would allow them to have a normal life, too. I didn't want them to be mindless soldiers like the shadyrs here at the estate. Just bodies used up in the service of Mordan's war on the Everdark. Kids come here, and they just ... they stop being kids."

The elevator groaned to a stop. They both flipped up their hoods, and Lian opened the gate, ushering Everly out and to the left—the opposite direction from the door they'd entered upon arrival.

In silence, Lian led Everly down several halls, moving with a sense of purpose and an uncanny knowledge of the mansion's layout. Lian clearly wasn't a stranger to Darkfrey Estate.

They passed a few other shadyrs—groups of children and teenagers—but with their Darkfrey jackets on, the pair didn't get any double takes.

Lian darted into an uncomfortably narrow side hallway and slowed down, her gaze raking the wood-paneled walls.

There were only three dull globes set in the stone walls to light the way down the windowless hallway. The few visible doors lining the short hall were closed tight, and the thick floral carpet beneath their feet looked like it got a lot less traffic than other areas.

Everly stuck close to Lian, half of her attention on the

larger corridor behind them. If a Darkfrey student showed up and saw them loitering weirdly, they were sitting ducks down there.

Lian halted suddenly and grinned, then reached over her head to press against a carved nodule in the wood.

A hidden door sprang open.

Everly quelled a startled gasp.

Secret door, secret door!

Its very existence delighted her, calling to mind every adventure movie she'd ever seen, and every ghostly, gothic novel she'd ever read. The fact that a *real* secret passage existed made her grin from ear to ear.

Harper was already annoyed she couldn't do the heist with us. She's going to flip that she missed out on this.

Lian ushered Everly through the dark opening, then slid the door shut behind them, cutting off what little illumination there had been. A moment later, Everly had the flashlight on her phone turned on, casting pale, colorless light over their surroundings.

The secret passage was even narrower than the hall, though the ceilings were still just as high, disappearing into darkness overhead. The belly of the building was all exposed beams and dense shadows, reminding Everly of ribs and blood. Her boots scuffed the stone, but the cocoon-like area muffled the sound, almost like the hushed atmosphere of a snowfall.

"I was out one night," Lian said softly.

She motioned with her head for Everly to follow her, and they moved off into the gloom, their phone lights barely chasing away the darkness.

"An eidolghast showed up, attacked my family. The boys shifted. They defended themselves as best they could. But they were so young and untrained. That was my fault. Not theirs. None of it was their fault." Lian shrugged helplessly. "My husband, he wasn't a shadyr. He knew about us, of course, but he was human."

Annabeth's words about how she and Rylan had ended up as Darkfreys the same way came back to Everly.

"That was the night your husband died," she whispered.

Lian nodded. "He called me, as soon as he saw the boys had changed, he knew something was nearby. I got back as fast as I could. My boys, they fought so hard ... but ..."

She trailed off and it was a while before she spoke again, leading in with a long, exhausted sigh. "Mordan got to them, put it into Rylan's head that if he and Callan had been better trained, perhaps they could have saved their father. Once they started thinking that way ... I don't think they've ever forgiven me for keeping them from being fighters."

"So they left to come here."

"To be monster hunters through and through," Lian said. "I wished ... I wanted them to know that even the best fighters in the world can't shield themselves entirely from tragedy."

Everly hugged herself, remembering how broken Rylan had been after his father died.

"That it wasn't their fault, or mine either, really. That terrible things just happen sometimes and can't be prevented, and that's awful, but they didn't have to give their lives in the pursuit of trying to stop it happening again." Lian's voice broke, and they moved along in silence.

When she spoke again, her voice was soft and apologetic. "I think, maybe, that's why Rylan pushed you away too. To protect you from all of this. I hated seeing him do that to you. It wasn't your fault."

Everly's cheeks flushed and her eyes stung.

It wasn't my fault?

She'd spent so long believing that she'd wronged Rylan after his dad's death, that it was the reason he'd left her behind. If it weren't, that could change everything.

Everly wasn't the only person Rylan shut out though.

"I'm sorry, that Mordan made them think they had to leave you," Everly offered, feeling as though it wasn't even close to enough. "That they did, leave you."

"I tried to win them back." It almost sounded like an apology. "When I tried to use my parental rights to force them home, Mordan used his power with the town justice system to take me to court for custody. I'm not the first mother he's done it to, and I certainly wasn't the last."

"How can he get away with that?" Everly's own mother probably deserved to lose custody of her early on, but nobody batted an eye when she was found to be drunk or high with a five-year-old around.

How could such a bad mom have no repercussions for her actions, while Lian lost her kids to a stranger?

"Mordan Darkfrey operates under his own set of rules. All the Darkfreys consider themselves above human law, and they've built up a support system in town to make sure they stay that way."

Lian paused as the passage hit an intersection, then looked both ways before choosing to turn right.

"We're talking generations and generations of wealth and influence controlling this region and everyone in it. Nobody stands a chance against them. Even with my Pimey heritage, my family's power is nothing compared to the Darkfreys. It's just enough to keep them from running me and mine out of town entirely."

Everly thought of Tammy, Cherry, Rushelle, even Denny, all outcast for one reason or another. If Lian hadn't taken them in and given them her protection, what would their lives be like now?

Callan left the Darkfreys of his own choosing, and Everly got the impression he'd be welcomed back, but after recent events, him returning seemed highly unlikely.

Everly asked, "Has it been good, having Callan home again?"

"Hmm. He's a grown man now. I missed out on so much. But yes. Yes, it's wonderful."

Lian stopped and turned to the wall, running her fingers over a crack in the plaster. The barest hint of light seeped through a slim rectangle, and when Lian found the catch and depressed the button, the crack became a door.

Everly watched the web of wrinkles around Lian's shrewd eyes, sparkling with the effects of her shadyr night vision, and maybe something more. Everly nodded to herself, making a small, silent oath. She'd do anything to bring Rylan back to his mother as well, so she could have both her sons with her again.

The room beyond the secret passageway was dim and empty of occupants. Glass cases lined the walls, each illuminated by warm amber lights sparkling down from overhead. On the shelves inside, trophies and plaques gleamed like flame beneath the lamps.

Several freestanding podiums throughout the middle of the room held plaster busts of people—presumably shadyrs who had once walked these halls and done something noteworthy. The wood floors were laid out in a geometric pattern polished to an unnatural sheen.

"There are secret routes all over this estate, but they aren't all connected in an easy path," Lian explained. "We're going to have to cut through some areas. Keep quiet and inconspicuous, okay?"

Everly nodded under her heavy hood.

Lian strolled out into the room, moving with the speed of purpose. Everly kept to Lian's side as she glanced around for surveillance cameras from the corner of her eye, trying not to reveal too much of her face.

She couldn't spot anything. Maybe Mordan's traditional values extended into also being a luddite. She had noted that his desk only ever had papers on it, no computer. Or maybe he was just so sure of his control over his shadyr army that he didn't think interior surveillance necessary.

"That's my great, great grandad," Lian whispered as they passed one of the busts, who looked as precisely old-white-guy as the rest of them.

Everly raised her eyebrows, feeling out of her depth in all this shadyr history. "Oh. Cool."

On the opposite wall, Lian found another notch and toggled it, then they slid back into another hidden passage. It seemed older than the last. Strange lichens and soot marked the ancient stone walls.

Lian seemed to know every secret of the sprawling manor.

"How long were you here before you left?"

Lian spoke softly, although the solid rock walls blocked all sound. "Until I was twenty-two. Long enough to learn the ropes, be assigned to a brace, get into a bunch of trouble. It was Mordan's father who was in charge back then, but things were much the same. Some stuff happened … and I decided this wasn't the life I wanted. I left, met Quinn Howell, and tried to live as much of a normal life as Shroudhaven allows."

The winding passageway seemed to lead them down into the earth and back up again. "Why didn't you leave town?"

"There's something about this place. When you're a shadyr, it's like it calls to you. Maybe it's the shroudpools, connecting this dimension with the one the original shadyrs came from, or the sense of duty so many of us are indoctrinated with. I don't know. But leaving just felt too hard."

They exited and re-entered the passages three more times, and each gave Everly a glimpse into life at Darkfrey Estate. Beyond the trophy room, they passed through a quiet study where only one student worked, headphones looped over bright auburn hair and her nose in a thick textbook.

Is that Annabeth?

Everly's nerves went on high alert, and she and Lian hid behind tall bookshelves until they reached their tunnel re-entry point. The red-headed shadyr didn't look up once, and they passed out of the room without her notice.

They skirted down a long, more modern, hallway where Everly caught glimpses of small lecture rooms.

Projected onto their screens up front were things like "Anatomy of a Nyevmer", "The Coruscare and Pre-Transition Mythology", and "Serving your brace."

Farther down was a rec room with a dark flat-screen television and multiple cushioned armchairs and couches—mostly empty, since it was the middle of the school day for the estate shadyrs. The most occupied area they passed was a training room where a dozen grunting students were sparring and throwing each other onto thin mats.

A few times Lian had to turn them away from their chosen path to avoid passing a group of Darkfrey shadyrs head on, but she seemed to always know another route to take in the labyrinthine building. Everly was utterly lost when Lian stopped at yet another hidden door and reached for the release.

She paused to glance at Everly. "This is it. The archives are accessed through the armory."

Everly nodded with a rush of excitement. But a strange sensation that they were being followed left a curling tension in her gut. She glanced back and around but saw no one nearby.

The door opened on silent hinges, revealing a pitch-black room beyond. Lian lifted her flashlight to light the way, and Everly fell into step behind her. She couldn't see much beyond the dim glow of the phone until they entered an aisle flanked by two tall metal shelving units loaded down with weapons, extending into the distance.

Broadswords, pikes, vicious daggers, modern compound bows and antique longbows, a range of deadly tools Everly imagined a ninja would use—every possible type of historical weapon that existed was represented on the armory shelves. Guns and more modern weaponry were sparse.

"This is some collection," Everly puffed under her breath.

If the Darkfreys had to go to war, or if the apocalypse came to Shroudhaven, they'd certainly be in a good position to defend themselves.

"Shadyr's shifted forms come with their own inbuilt weapons, and most are happy to rely on them alone. But sometimes it's good to have more options."

"Like a sword?" Everly asked.

"That's my preference," Lian agreed lightly.

Everly eyed a rack of handguns. "I haven't seen any shadyrs carrying. Do bullets not work on eidolghasts?"

"Oh, they work well enough. It's more of a secrecy issue. Can't be going around firing off automatic rifles and RPGs around town every night and expect people not to notice."

Lian and Everly walked all the way across the room, their footsteps eerily loud. At the end of the main aisle of weapons, a set of wooden double doors was inset in the stone wall, secured by a high-tech fingerprint lock.

"Won't they know we were here?" Everly asked, eyeing the keypad.

"They would," Lian agreed, "if I tried to get through those doors. But we aren't using that entrance."

She led Everly a few feet away, reached her arm through to the back of a weapon rack, and tugged gently. The whole shelf pivoted forward in a wide arc to reveal a plain metal door, half an average adult's height.

"Does *every* room have a secret passage?" Everly whispered, amused.

Lian shrugged. "Probably. My older brother showed me the most. I think Dad showed him. And I had fun trying to find even more myself. This place has been here in one form or another since shadyrs first came through from the Everdark. It's a building built around another building on top of ten other buildings."

Crouching low, they entered the claustrophobic space behind the walls. Lian left the door open behind them, and Everly wondered if she did so in case they needed a quick getaway from the archives room. That sent a shiver of terror streaking up her spine.

Pipes and cables filled the space, perhaps some sort of maintenance access. They weaved between them slowly, hunched over.

They seemed to reach a dead end and Lian pushed on the pock-marked brick wall. It rolled slowly, crunching dust and debris beneath hidden wheels, and revealed a room filled with a strange, blue glow. A puff of cool air met them as they stepped inside.

While the rest of the estate was old-fashioned, channeling a medieval castle's aesthetic, this room was something out of a sci-fi movie. Glass-encased metal podiums scattered the room like trees, each illuminated by its own little spotlight. There were dozens of them, each occupied by some kind of artifact. The podiums connected to the ceiling on a series of tubes and cords, and a low-level hum echoed through the room.

"Each case is vacuum sealed and climate-controlled," Lian explained. "Most of these artifacts are several thousand years old, at least, brought over from the Everdark."

Everly followed her through the sea of narrow cases, too busy peeking inside the glass to pay attention to their path.

Some cases held statues so old and worn by time and weather damage that she couldn't make out what they'd once represented. Others held strangely shaped weapons, formed from the same black material as Lian's sword.

There were also books made from thick sheets of carved bone, a black-glass orb that glowed inside like molten lava, and all types of jewelry, from archaic metal pieces clearly wrought by hand to thin, crystalline objects more likely to have been woven by some otherworldly spider.

A few cases held skeletons, and Everly knew at first glance that they weren't human.

Lian stopped abruptly and Everly slammed into her back. The older woman had enough inner balance in her wide stance that the hit barely nudged her. She was staring into an empty case, a concerned wiggle between her brows.

"What's wrong?" Everly asked.

"There are artifacts missing," Lian said. "This is the third empty case we've passed."

"Do you think they were stolen?"

Lian blew out a low breath. "I don't know. These were all filled last time I was here, but that was a long time ago."

With her brows still pressed together, Everly continued searching. Lian was right—there were *a lot* of empty podiums.

Lian halted again and let out a low moan of distress. "Dammit!"

The case she stared into wasn't empty. A sheet of crumpled parchment lay across the white satin cushion, stained with a rust-colored substance. But Everly could see the rough outline on the parchment where something heavier had sat, its diamond shape marked by blood.

Something that was now gone.

"This is it," Lian murmured. "It should be here."

The Bane of Teeth and Stars was gone.

CHAPTER SIXTEEN

*G*one. Everly stared at the bloody parchment. A light-headed queasiness swelled through her, then drew together into a hard lump in her throat.

They hadn't known *for sure* that the Bane of Teeth and Stars held the answers they needed regarding Everly's powers. Maybe the name of the artifact had been a total coincidence. Maybe the vasmire's dying words didn't mean anything at all. But this artifact was the only possible lead they had.

In its absence, Everly watched all her hopes for figuring out how to deal with the dragon fade away.

She couldn't live like this, in this constant state of worrying that she'd slip up and kill someone else.

Nell's husband may have been some kind of resurrected zombie, but he'd been a moving, breathing person when

Everly's light ended him. He'd saved her, led her to Rylan, showing a heart that was still good, a mind that still comprehended the world around him.

And the thing inside Everly destroyed him with glee. The guilt of his death still hummed like a swarm of hornets inside her.

The thought of anyone else getting hurt by her ... Lian, Callan ... Harper ...

She swallowed past the lump in her throat. "Are you sure this is where it's supposed to be?"

Lian nodded and pointed to a small bronze plate on the side of the podium, engraved with the name. She then pressed her palm against the corner of the glass. The case popped open and released a blast of cool, dry air, smelling faintly of old meat and loose change.

"This is the place. And whoever took it left this behind. It belongs with the Bane." Lian reached inside and grabbed the parchment.

Small flakes of dark red crumbled and fell from the ancient material.

Everly turned on the spot, seeking any available answer. "Could it just be, I don't know, out for maintenance? Getting repaired or cleaned? Or being used or something right now, by someone at the estate?"

"The things in here, they don't get used. They're considered too precious, but mostly, no one actually knows what to do with them." Lian shook her head as she pulled a clean square of canvas from her tote bag and wrapped the bloody parchment in it. Up close, it looked like soft leather made of a dull, pale skin.

"Nobody studies them?" Everly thought about Annabeth with her head in a book.

"They've been looked at in the past, sure. But they aren't in any kind of regular use. Plus most of these are just basic relics, kept for their historical, not magical, value. Others may have special magic as yet undiscovered, but it takes a bit of trial and error to work that out, and Mordan doesn't like sharing his toys."

Lian glanced warily around at the sea of illuminated podiums. "It is weird, though, how so many artifacts are missing from their cases. Maybe you're right. Maybe someone has taken them out for some reason and we just have bad timing."

Everly nodded, but there was little hope to be found.

Lian tucked the wrapped parchment into the waistband of her jeans at the back.

"What are you doing?"

"If we find the Bane, we'll need this," Lian explained, releasing her jacket so that it fell over the parchment, hiding it from view. "It's somewhat disturbing that it's not with the Bane now."

Everly closed the glass case, the lock clicking as it closed.

"We're still going to try to find it? How?"

Lian shrugged. "I don't know. Having the wrapper is a start though. Maybe whoever has the Bane will come to us to get it. Otherwise, things will get pretty messy."

Everly's forehead wrinkled. "Messy—?"

A hint of movement in her peripheral vision caught her attention. She whirled around, her heart leaping into her throat. She was not prepared to have to fight their way out of there if they were caught.

In the shadows, a figure moved. One in a beige cardigan, with neat black hair.

Jasper?

The moment Everly spotted him, he turned on his heel and disappeared through the room, vanishing like a wraith beyond the glow of the cases.

"Busted," Lian muttered in a low voice. "We better make a speedy exit before he tells Mordan where he found us. We stand a better chance facing the master's wrath *off* his property."

Lian took the lead, rushing them out of the room with Everly close behind. They took a different path out of the estate than they'd taken in, using secret doors and hidden passages only until they were away from the archives room.

Then Lian led Everly at a swift pace in the most direct route toward the exit. There was no point hiding anymore. They hurried down large hallways and through open courtyards. Neither woman spoke as their shared sense of urgency kept them moving and alert. Everly's anxiety peaked with every person they passed, with every voice that drifted their way, waiting to be called out, captured. She didn't want to think about what their punishment might be.

But if Jasper was loyal enough to the Darkfreys to give up his relationship with Cherry, he definitely wasn't going to hold back tattling on them for breaking into the cursed archives.

They could be ambushed at any second. Expedience won out over remaining hidden.

They were ten steps from the exit of the main building when a sharp, commanding voice called out, "Howell!"

Lian waved toward the voice without looking. "*So sorry, can't stop, just leaving.*"

Two bodies moved in from their side and came to a halt in front of them like a wall, blocking their path.

Everly's heart was already beating at a rapid pace, and it shuddered into overdrive as she sized up the Darkfrey shadyrs in front of them.

She recognized Vonny from multiple run-ins with the hard-faced shadyr who led Rylan's old brace, but the muscular man beside her was a stranger. He had long blond hair slicked back over the crown of his head—milkier than Vonny's golden bob, but nowhere near as colorless as Everly's own white hair.

Age-lines marked his furious, red-veined eyes. His long-sleeved button-up shirt stretched so tight over his muscles the fabric was tortured, sitting strangely against his body, lumpy in places that didn't seem right.

"So close," Lian murmured to Everly, before plastering on a fake smile. "Vonny, lovely to see you again so soon."

"Can it, Howell," Vonny snapped.

She crossed her arms and her gaze shifted between Lian and Everly, the pinched expression making it no secret that she wasn't happy to see them. "What in the Everdark are you still doing here? You left Master Darkfrey's office almost an hour ago."

Lian's eyes snapped across to Everly, then blinked to cover the silent message.

They don't know.

Had Jasper not told anyone yet, or had the news just not reached the two in front of them? Either way, they were on borrowed time. The doorway lay right in front of them, standing open, their car still parked just out the front.

"Oh, I was just feeling nostalgic, felt like taking a little tour. But we really must be going now," Lian said pleasantly. "Don't want to overstay our welcome."

"Why are you both wearing Darkfrey jackets? Those don't belong to you. Especially not to a bliv." Vonny's eyes narrowed on Everly.

Lian drew her attention back. "Oh, this? It's my son's. I thought I'd borrow it, to fit in. Isn't that what you Darkfrey are all about?"

Vonny scoffed. "You never understood what it means to be a Darkfrey."

"You're right. I never did get the Darkfrey lifestyle. Which is why I left, and why we're leaving again now." Lian took hold of Everly's jacket sleeve and tugged, edging around from the couple.

"Don't walk away from me!" the man roared.

His shout was loud enough to shake the delicate chandelier over Everly's head. She glanced up at the shivering crystal pieces, then turned her wide eyes to Lian.

Lian left her fingers on Everly's sleeve and they both turned back.

"Kole. Sorry I didn't acknowledge you there. Everly, this is Kole Mesman, Vonny's husband."

Everly knew this would normally be the point some hand-shaking would be done, but no one moved.

Lian continued, "It's been ages. How long has it been since you left the estate and saw the light of day?"

Kole only snorted in response, like a bull about to charge.

Lian eyed the man up and down, her smile becoming crisp. "You're looking ... *bigger*."

Veins pulsed around his bulging eyes as he glared

down at them. His gaze was disturbingly both fixed and distant at the same time. Filled with simmering violence and something inhuman.

"You ... *you* ..." he growled.

"Kole," Vonny said under her breath.

Though her empty expression indicated boredom, there was an undercurrent of warning in her words, laced with fear.

The massive man stepped closer to Lian, his giant, ham hock-sized fists clenched at his sides. "You don't get to leave here without answering for what you've done."

Everly shot Lian a worried look. Maybe they did know after all.

"And what, precisely, have I done?" Lian asked coldly.

"You took in that ... *cursed girl*. After what she did to us."

Everly's thoughts whirled, confused for a moment that he might mean her. But whatever her dragon was, whatever curse was going on inside her, she'd never done anything to the Mesmans.

"Tammy?" Lian's shoulders lowered with a long breath. "She's suffering enough for what happened. I'm not going to leave the poor kid out on the street. You know what happened to Blaise wasn't her fault."

With an animalistic growl, Kole launched for Lian, his fingers curled into claws.

Vonny stepped between them in a flash. She placed a hand on each side of his face, drawing him down to look at her. Still growling and breathing hard, spittle flew from the corners of his mouth, but he stilled.

Vonny's fingers stroked his jaw lovingly. "Kole. It's not the time. We don't want to get on Mordan's bad side. Not now. These are his guests today."

Lian's hand which had remained clinging to Everly's arm released, and she took a single, tentative step toward the shadyr couple.

"I know what it's like. How hard it is." For the first time since the Mesmans had arrived, Lian's tone sounded sincere. "I lost my children, too."

"Oh, like that's the same." Vonny whipped around, her face twisting with hatred. "Your boys only left you for a better home."

"Excuse me?" Everly's temperature spiked, and her hands balled into tight fists, fingernails digging into her palms.

How dare they say that.

Lian, however, remained calm. "I know it's not the same. But it still hurts. It still gives me perspective. If my sons had died—"

"He's. Not. Dead!" Vonny hissed, her voice going low and hard.

"You will never be able to move on until you accept

that." Lian raised both hands up in front of her, stepping back again. "You have to let go, one day."

"Never." Kole snarled, pupils jittering against wide, white eyes. "I should kill you right here, so you can't protect that cursed girl a day longer!"

Vonny pressed a hand against his chest. There was no way she'd have the physical strength to hold the huge man back, but the gesture slowed him down.

Vonny glared at Lian and her lips twitched. "Just get out. Both of you. Go!"

Lian grabbed Everly's hand, and they fled the hallway for the cold, misty day outside.

They remained silent as they buckled into the SUV and sped down the shadowy drive.

Everly watched the trees thicken out the window, and breathed easier as they passed the threshold of the gates that took them off Darkfrey property.

But not even leaving behind the walls of Darkfrey Estate could make Everly forget the unstable fury and murderous glint in Kole Mesman's eyes.

CHAPTER SEVENTEEN

Standing in the shadows of a large tree, Jasper watched as Cherry and the new bliv girl sat in the open side door of a baby-blue campervan.

They chatted in hushed whispers, sipping from steaming Pimey's Diner paper cups.

Are they talking about me, about us?

Except there was no *us* anymore, Jasper reminded himself. Still, Everly and Harper knew what he and Cherry once were to each other. They may have been the only people who did.

Callan and Tammy were there too, leaning against the back of the van. Jasper was pretty sure they didn't know, yet. And he was going to make sure no one else knew.

After seeing Everly and the Howell woman snooping

around where they shouldn't have been, he'd followed them until they went right into the most forbidden and sacred part of the manor. Then he'd hurried down to the gates of Darkfrey Estate. He'd planned on confronting them on their way out, but then he saw the small squad hanging around out front.

What are they supposed to be here for, back up? What were the four of them going to achieve against all the shadyrs of the estate?

So he hid, and waited, and watched.

He tried not to notice how Cherry's fire-engine red hair dye hadn't been refreshed recently. Or how his lips met the coffee cup and blew out steam after sipping. Or how Harper wrapped an arm around his small waist, and squeezed, and Jasper immediately knew exactly how that waist felt.

It was a relief when Lian's SUV finally pulled through the gates. He wouldn't have to watch anymore. He wouldn't have to worry.

Lian parked behind the camper and opened her door to get out, though she left the engine running. Everly followed suit, shoving her hands into her pockets against the chilly morning.

Jasper slipped through the gates before they closed and approached the chatting group. He took in what he could of their conversation along the way.

"I can't believe I missed out on secret passages! You owe me, big time."

Callan laughed at the bliv. "They're lucky they weren't caught and locked away in the dungeons."

Harper's jaw dropped. "There are dungeons?"

"Especially lucky since we were seen," Everly added, looking at Cherry. "I think it was Jasper."

Cherry's lips pursed tightly. "Guess the whole estate will know soon, then."

"And we didn't get what we were after. It wasn't even there." Lian sighed. "There were quite a few missing—"

Callan barked, "We've got company."

They all quieted and turned to Jasper. He stopped a good distance from them, looking over their group. They were such a mess. Borrowed, ill-fitting uniforms, slack stances, none of the precision and strength a team of shadyrs should have. But the way they stood together against him sent a chill across the back of his neck.

A rotation of strong emotions crossed Cherry's face before he settled on pinched irritation.

He crossed his arms and vibrated with tension. "What do you want?"

"Come to drag us in yourself since the Mesmans didn't do it for you?" Lian accused, hands on her hips.

Jasper blinked. "I don't know what you're talking about."

Everly frowned at him. "You didn't tell them to stop us on our way out?"

"I didn't tell anyone anything."

Everly eyed him warily. "You saw us in a place we shouldn't have been and didn't tell anybody? Why?"

Jasper took a shaky breath. His gaze slid past Cherry for the briefest moment before he looked Everly in the eye. "Because now I know a secret of yours. Much like you know one of mine. I want to make sure neither gets out."

Lian shot Everly a questioning look, as did Callan and Tammy. Even mentioning that there was a secret was risky. But no bigger than the risk of Cherry or the other two using that secret against him.

He needed some assurance, a deal made so he wouldn't have to spend every moment worrying he'd lose his place at the estate, and today had given him just what he needed.

"I won't tell anyone where you were, what you were doing, or what you took," he said. Then he directed his words at Everly, Harper, and Cherry. "And you all keep quiet in return."

"You're blackmailing us?" Cherry spat. "Of course you'd think that way."

He crossed the wide distance between them and huffed quietly. "Jokes on you because you should know I would never, ever do that to you. You could break my heart ten times over, and I'd still never do that to you."

Jasper's cheeks flushed with heat, and he broke eye contact, too uncomfortable under Cherry's dark-eyed gaze.

"Come on. This fool is wasting our time," Cherry grunted, spinning around and marching back to his team.

"Wait." The word came out unbidden.

Cherry stopped, but didn't turn around. "What don't you get? We promise your secret is safe. I know that's all you care about."

Harper and Everly closed ranks around Cherry, staring Jasper down.

"I ... I know you didn't get what you were after today. You were looking for an artifact that's missing, right? I know what happened to them. All of the missing ones." The saliva in Jasper's mouth dried up.

What am I doing? Sharing information is a betrayal of the Darkfreys.

But he owed Cherry and his friends something more. He could never stop owing them.

Everly raised a pale eyebrow. "And what will this information cost us?"

"Nothing."

Cherry half-turned, but his lips remained pressed tight in a crooked line, and his narrowed eyes darted, scrutinizing, burning Jasper down to his core.

Whatever. It's not like I'm trying to win him back. It isn't worth the risk.

"What do you know?" There was an eager edge to Everly's voice.

Jasper fixed her in his gaze, trying to block away the view of Cherry beside her. "All of the missing artifacts disappeared ten years ago. Around the same time the Gorhanmere group split off from Darkfrey Estate."

"Gorhanmere," Lian mused. "I heard about them incorporating their own shadyr group. Thought it was weird Mordan would let them out from under his control. Weirder still if he let them run off with the artifacts."

"Some odd rumors have been coming out of Gorhanmere since then," Callan said, frowning as though filling in the blanks. "That they've become extra powerful."

Jasper nodded. "From what I've heard, Mordan didn't think the artifacts were worth starting a war over."

"No, maybe not," Lian agreed offhandedly.

"Thank you," Everly said. "That's helpful."

Jasper's eyes were on Cherry again, who still hadn't turned around.

His heart shrunk painfully. "Just keep your promise."

Callan and Lian still looked confused, and Tammy seemed like she couldn't care less about anything going on around her.

With a few waves and goodbyes, they headed over to the SUV, and the two new girls and Cherry headed to the campervan. He hadn't said goodbye, hadn't even glanced back, and a rush of yearning filled Jasper just to see his beautiful eyes one more time.

"Hey," Jasper called out, halting their climb into the van.

Cherry's gaze met his then, and Jasper's breath hitched.

He swallowed nothing, dry mouth sticking as he found his words. "If you go after them ... be careful. The Gorhanmere shadyrs aren't just powerful, they're dangerous, even a little unstable. Whatever it is you're after, try not to get yourselves killed."

Everly and Harper spent most of the day at Howell House, eating, planning, and lounging around with the team.

It was comforting to do something so innocuously normal for a few hours, despite the fact that they were talking about infiltrating a supposedly "dangerous and unstable" group of shadyrs in between snacks and video games.

By late afternoon, they had a basic plan. Rushelle and Denny would remain behind to look after Rylan, and the rest of the team would leave bright and early the next day to travel to Gorhanmere.

They would pose as shadyrs dissatisfied with the Darkfreys—not a stretch—who were looking for a new group to join, and see what they could find out from there. Once that was decided, Lian sent everyone off to rest up.

If Jasper's warning about the Gorhanmere shadyrs was legit, they'd all need it.

The sun had already dipped below the mountains when Everly and Harper got back home. The backyard was deep in shadow beneath a purple sky, but Everly caught a flash of glowing eyes in the thick brush around the swing set.

Zozo.

She locked eyes with the little cougar, willing him to stay there while she went in and grabbed him some food.

As Everly unlocked the door, Harper leaned a shoulder against the aged timber and sighed. "Hopefully this trip will be good for Cherry. Poor guy is in a rough place. Can you imagine having to keep such a big part of yourself secret like that?"

Everly shivered. "Yeah, that must be hard."

"I might run a bath and soak for a while. My pores need to steam. Do you want to grab a shower first?"

Everly shoved the door open. "No, you go ahead. Just going to grab a drink and then I'm keen to get to sleep."

"Bet you are." Harper flashed a cheeky smile and then veered off up the staircase.

"If I could go back in time and never tell you Rylan was

in my dreams, that would be a secret I'd be okay keeping!" Everly yelled after her with a laugh.

Harper ducked back down to peer at her through the railings. "But you wouldn't keep secrets from me, would you?"

Her cheeky smile remained, but there was a slight edge to her tone.

"Of course not," Everly replied, chuckling as though the idea was ridiculous. "Goodnight."

Harper blew a kiss and disappeared up the stairs.

Everly's smile faded as she continued down the hall toward the kitchen.

The fog filling the house was lighter than it had been, and the kitchen cabinets were all blessedly closed. Everly hoped it meant that the beshadowing effects were dying down as the vasmire pieces decomposed, though the faster they broke down, the sooner the team would have to find more to keep Rylan going.

How long can we keep this up?

This town felt like it was dragging her down into darkness. Since being here, there had been too many secrets and dangers and questions she wasn't sure she was going to like the answers to.

She extracted a fresh tray of ground beef from the fridge. Even just trying to focus on one thing at a time left her feeling overwhelmed. They couldn't keep following an endless cycle of killing vasmires, stocking Rylan's room, and just hoping he'd wake up.

At some point, Callan's warning about the beshadowing effects on the two of them would come to pass, and if Everly herself was beshadowed, she couldn't very well keep Harper safe.

Everly tucked her chin into the collar of her bomber jacket, warding against the cold as she skipped down the back stairs. Shroudhaven's nightly mist had filtered into the backyard, turning the shadows heavier and more menacing outside the small globe of light from the porch.

She kept her gaze trained on Zozo, studiously ignoring the idea that there could be other things roaming in the dark.

"Hey, Zozo," Everly cooed, stopping a couple of feet away on the cracked and mossy path.

She sat cross-legged on the concrete and slid the styrofoam tray out for him.

"Dinner?"

The cougar dipped his nose to the beef, sniffed at the meat, then started chowing down.

"Why do you keep coming here?" Everly asked him. "I know Nell is gone, but you were wild before, weren't you? I can't keep feeding you forever."

Everly wasn't sure if Zozo was lingering nearby because of the food or something else. But she liked being able to feed the big cat. Even with all the madness of the situation, helping Zozo made her feel more like herself, like she was doing something good, and less like everything in her life had come untethered.

She reached out carefully and ran two fingers down the cougar's silky forehead, across a carefully stitched scar. A low rumble emanated from the young cat, and her adrenaline zinged through her veins before realizing it wasn't a growl.

Zozo was purring.

Warmth tingled through her, and she added the rest of her fingers, smoothing her palm over his head.

The click of a door opening echoed through the backyard.

Zozo lifted his head, his ears flattening as he zeroed in on the house. His purring ceased, and Everly yanked her hand away before he got spooked enough to bite her.

She craned around to glance back at the house, her heart racing.

Harper stood in the glow of the porchlight wearing her fluffy pink night robe.

Everly scooted to the right in a vain attempt to hide Zozo from sight. "I thought you were taking a bath."

"Thought you were going to bed." Harper folded her arms, squinting into the darkness at Everly. "That's one awfully big stray cat. Is that one of Nell's rescues?"

Everly frowned at her casual tone. As though finding a zombie animal in their backyard was no different than spotting a sparrow on the fence. "I, um, didn't really see him until tonight. This is the first time he's come up close."

"Come on. You two are far too familiar for that. Why have you been keeping this cutie from me?" Harper put her hand on the railing and started down the short staircase in her bare feet.

Zozo growled at her approach.

Everly snapped, "No, don't come down here! It's not safe."

Harper paused mid-step. "I'm confused. Safe for you, but not for me?"

"It's complicated—"

"Then why don't you explain it to me?" Harper asked, her voice growing louder. "Because it seems pretty basic to me. You're keeping secrets and then having double standards. It's okay for you, but never for me."

Amidst the raised voices, Zozo's growl rumbled. The cougar sprang forward and landed on the path between the two women. His shoulders and head were down, teeth bared, and haunches tensed as though ready to pounce.

"Zozo, no!" Everly yelled.

The cougar looked back at her, a question in its ghostly blue eyes.

Is he trying to protect me? From Harper?

Harper remained frozen in place, her hands out in a calming gesture and eyes darting back to measure the distance between her and the back door.

"Leave her alone, she's not an enemy." Everly moved to her feet in a slow, smooth motion, making calming sounds.

The cougar's pose softened, tail twitched, and it circled back around behind Everly where it kept her friend locked in its vision.

Harper's face was scrunched up. "What is going on with you? Secretly training zombie cougars to attack your friends?"

The accusation made heat sting through Everly's eyes. "It's not like that."

"Then you'd better tell me what it is like."

Everly rubbed her eyebrow, chasing away the growing tension. "I'm not sure. I think there's some kind of connection between me and this cougar."

"Clearly. And maybe if you'd let me do some of the night-time feeds, I could have had my own attack cat, too."

"It's not just that."

"Then *tell* me. Stop keeping secrets!"

Zozo growled again, and Harper lowered her voice, almost pleading. "You can tell me. Whatever is going on, I'm here for you if you're just honest with me."

Everly shook her head. Harper was right, but that didn't make it easy. She swallowed, her body wanting to chase away the words as they rose from her.

"Remember when we ran over something on our way into Shroudhaven?"

Harper hugged herself and nodded.

"But we didn't find a body or evidence we'd actually hit something? That's because Nell got to him first. This is the cougar we hit. And I've been dreaming about it too, ever since."

Harper's face softened. "Like Rylan?"

"Sort of. But not as strong of a connection. But that's why I think Zozo is safe for me and not for you."

Harper nodded.

Her lips were tight and voice hard when she asked, "Do you know how you're making these connections?"

Everly opened her mouth, ready to deny knowing anything, but Harper's gaze pierced deep, as though waiting and watching for any sign of something withheld.

"I think it's the dragon," she mumbled.

"Your powers?" Harper urged.

Everly lifted her hands, staring at them instead of making eye contact. "I think it has somehow absorbed some, or all, of the cougar and Rylan's spirits. When the light comes out of me, it doesn't just attack. It's not just hitting things. I think ... I feel like it's also absorbing them. Like it's *eating* them. Eating their lifeforce."

Harper just stared, and Everly's voice shook as more

words tumbled out of the broken dam. "And I can't control it. Not always. It does what it wants, and what it wants is to eat things. It wanted to eat you, at Rooks Hotel. And at Nells ..."

Everly's voice shuddered to a halt with a sob.

Harper stepped forward, moving closer despite Zozo's soft rumbling. "What happened?"

"It wasn't a Darkfrey who killed Nell's husband. It was *me*. Can't you see now why I'm worried about you? This whole place is dangerous. *I'm* dangerous!"

"No, you're not."

She sounded so certain it made Everly gasp, her sobs drying up.

Harper continued her steady pace up the path to her. "Whatever is doing those things, it's obvious now that it's not you. *You* would never have done that. You wouldn't choose to murder someone! That light power you have is something, but it's not *you*. And if you'd told me all this bloody sooner maybe you wouldn't have been going around thinking it was all this time!"

"I don't want to hurt you," Everly whispered.

"I know you don't. That's why I trust you." Harper stopped right in front of her and eyed her for a long moment, then her shoulders slumped. "But you have to stop keeping secrets from me, Ev. I never thought you would ..."

"I'm sorry," Everly murmured.

Zozo nudged her arm with his nose, and she put her fingertips on his head, reassuring him that everything was okay, that she didn't need his protection. He pressed back against her hand for a moment, and then backed away, vanishing into the long grass.

Harper stared at where the big cat had disappeared, then shook her head and leaned into Everly, giving her a tight hug.

She mumbled into Everly's ear, "We're a team. We're together in all this weirdness. Stop trying to shoulder the burden alone."

Everly nodded back into Harper's silky hair. But it didn't matter whether Harper wanted to share the weirdness or not. As soon as Rylan woke up, they were leaving the weirdness behind. Because every day they remained in Shroudhaven could be their last.

CHAPTER EIGHTEEN

Rylan opened his eyes in a gleaming shopping mall. Stark, bright, and as unnerving as any dream he'd shared with Everly so far.

Shroudhaven, as small and undeveloped as it was, only boasted a dinky little strip mall. The only actual mall was two hours away, outside of the larger Shroudhaven region.

But this wasn't any mall he'd ever seen in real life.

Rainbow lens-flares sparkled, obscuring the details of cotton candy-colored shops. On the other side of the frosted glass in the ceiling, vivid sparks ebbed and flowed like fireworks, blurry and abstract.

Maybe this was based on a mall in the city where Everly had lived after leaving, or maybe it was purely her imagination, but at least some parts seemed familiar.

A bright, upbeat J-Pop song played loudly throughout

the space. The singer's sweet voice was mournful and yearning, contrasting with the energetic metal guitar riffs and electronica beats.

I know that from somewhere.

Rylan frowned, unable to remember why. The lyrics were all in Japanese.

He stood on an escalator, taking far longer than was realistic to get to the next level. As he climbed, the stairs flowed downward beneath him, twisting into a dizzying illusion that threw him off balance.

Not that Everly's dreams ever made him feel any other way. Her presence had the same effect on him, making everything upside down and confused.

He was supposed to protect her. It was what he'd always wanted, why he'd made the decision to push her out of his dangerous life, keep her as far away from the world of monsters as possible. But with all this time together in her dreams, all he could think about was holding her near.

If I can't do anything anyway, if I might be stuck here forever, would that be so wrong?

It sounded like Lian, Callan, and the others at Howell House were doing their best to keep Everly safe, which offered him some comfort. But as long as his body was still out there, and he was in here, he knew Everly would keep putting herself in danger to fix it.

Maybe it was worth trying to get her to give up.

Rylan turned a circle on the moving staircase, searching for her. If he was "awake," it meant she was here, too.

The mall was unoccupied, all the stores were gated, and interiors were obscured by a blurry swirl of glow and darkness.

When viewed from the corner of his eye, he saw familiar shapes moving behind the locked shutters—like monsters walking in the depths of the Wyrdwoods, just out of sight. He shivered and hoped the rickety metal would keep the monsters in.

As he got closer to the second-floor landing, he caught sight of Everly's striking pale silver hair sparkling in the overhead lights. She stood with her back to the escalator and her hands clenched into fists at her sides. Her body vibrated with tension.

When he crested the top of the escalator, he hopped off onto smooth white marble floors and walked over to join Everly. He was used to coming up against weird things in her dreams, but he wasn't fully prepared for what he found this time.

Dolls. Dozens of creepy, broken dolls.

They were arranged on tables at differing heights, like they would have been displayed for viewing in a toy store. Except rather than being locked away behind a store's gate, they were in the middle of the landing, all of them facing the escalators and the second-floor balcony, the latter of which didn't have a safety railing.

The dolls were ... *wrong.*

Many were missing limbs, or had battered, bloody clothes. Several of the porcelain dolls had gaping, jagged edges where their faces should have been.

Rylan side-eyed the creepy display and swallowed hard. The dolls stared back at him.

"Taking inspiration from classic horror tonight?"

Everly made a small sound of agreement.

"They're moving," she muttered without turning to look at him. "The one in the purple dress with the shattered arm blinked at me."

"You're dreaming," Rylan reminded her.

She rolled her eyes. "Yes, *I know.* That doesn't make them any less terrifying."

Near the front of the row, a black-haired, porcelain doll with a too-wide, crooked crack where her mouth should have been, turned his way.

Rylan's heart hammered. Dream or not, Everly was right—they were terrifying. He stared at the now-unmoving doll, calculating his options. If it moved again, he was going to break it limb from limb. Was he imagining a soft giggling coming from that direction? If so, it was swamped beneath the song playing throughout the chamber.

"Does the music have to be up so loud?" he asked.

Everly winced, keeping her eyes on the dolls. "Sorry,

it was stuck in my head when I went to sleep, like, really locked in there. It's going to be a hard thing to change."

Rylan listened again, the chorus somehow taking him back to his childhood. "What song is it? It seems familiar."

She cleared her throat—*embarrassed?*

"Closing credits of *Akima and the Animatrons*, season three." She smiled bashfully in a way that brought an automatic smile to Rylan's lips, too.

The sense of nostalgia the song filled him with suddenly became a clear memory. Him, Everly, and his brother, bundled in blankets on the living room floor in front of the TV, binging their way through the neon-bright animation.

When they had run out of episodes, they'd play acted their own stories as the characters. "Oh yeah, we used to watch it all the time when we were kids, right?"

"Before you left home."

Home. That was a place the Darkfrey estate never felt like. There were no lazy morning cartoon marathons there. He'd left so much behind.

Still turned away from him, Everly's voice sounded small. "I know why you left. I know about your dad. Is that why you pushed me away?"

Rylan huffed. "Mom's been talking, huh?"

Everly nodded, her eyes shifting briefly to his then back again to the dolls. But not fast enough that Rylan didn't notice the pain there.

He scrubbed the back of his head with his hand. "I just ... wanted you to be safe."

Everly's shoulders dropped as though letting out a breath she'd held too long. "The *Akima* poster is still up on the wall in your old bedroom. It's all the same in there, from before you left."

"I haven't been back there in so long. I've almost forgotten what it's like."

Everly turned to him properly then, locking his eyes with hers. "We'll get you home soon."

Rylan returned his gaze to the demon dolls and tried for an easy tone in an attempt at levity. "So, what's the news from the real world?"

"Not anything good." Everly jolted as another doll near the highest of the display tables stood up with abrupt, jerky movements. "The Gorhanmere shadyrs took off with a bunch of artifacts from the Darkfrey archives, including the one we wanted."

Rylan blew out a breath. "Well, that sucks. What's the plan now?"

"We're going to Gorhanmere to follow up. The Bane is our only real lead. If we can figure out what I am, maybe we can figure out how to free you from ..." She waved a hand vaguely in the air. "This."

The standing doll hopped off her display square onto the marble floor and began to hobble toward them. She was missing half a leg, which gave her a swaying, uneven gait. Her eyes were black and hollow, and her frilly pink dress had been slashed to ribbons. She left a smeared trail of red blood behind her on the pale floor.

Rylan glanced back at the escalator. The first floor had moved farther away so that it was more like ten stories down instead of one, and the escalators stretched and narrowed until they were as thin as ropes.

Everly's breaths came fast and her eyes were so wide the whites were visible all the way around. "No way down."

Everly usually seemed calm and collected in her dreams—at least the ones that were recurring. She'd mastered what to do to stay sane during even the worst of them. But now ... Rylan realized that she was legitimately frightened and without a plan.

"You haven't had this dream before," Rylan guessed.

Everly shook her head, biting her lips.

More dolls clambered off their pedestals and began to jitter stiffly across the smooth marble.

"I don't know what to do," Everly whispered.

"They're just dolls." *Bloody, terrifying dolls.* "How bad could it be?"

Everly raised her eyebrows over fearful eyes, expressing how bad she thought it could be.

"Okay then." Rylan stretched out his arms and cracked his knuckles.

He stepped in front of Everly, ready to fight the miniature army.

"Hang on, I want to try something." Everly searched about until her eyes landed on their target.

The ghostly cougar that was also trapped in her dreams, skirting around near the closed shopfronts.

"Zozo?"

It paused, turning to her voice.

"Get them!"

With a growl, the cougar changed its path, slinking toward the dolls in a low-bellied trot. Once it was near enough, it put on a burst of speed, sprinting in and pouncing into the thick of them.

"Huh, how about that." Everly didn't seem entirely happy about the outcome.

Rylan's lip quirked up. "You named it Zozo?"

"Not really, it's just short for Zombie Cougar." Everly shrugged as she watched it dismembering the dolls.

Despite the carnage in the main huddle of demon dolls, a large number still dragged themselves closer.

Everly pointed beyond them to a long corridor. "Come on, it looks like there's an exit over there."

The first doll reached them. Rylan kicked it viciously in the head. The doll sailed away like a football and careened over the edge of the balcony.

It hit the ground, smashing far louder than something

its size should.

"We're going to have to go through them."

Everly nodded, smiling grimly.

Together, they waded into the ambling dolls.

"So, no luck with the kiss?" Rylan asked, in an effort to pretend they weren't fending off possessed toys.

"No luck," Everly agreed, her voice shaky. "I tried, though."

It had been a silly idea to start with.

I don't know why I even suggested it.

The fact that it didn't work left Rylan with a dull hollow in his chest. Or was it the way he was now imagining Everly leaning over his motionless body, kissing cold lips, and suddenly, bizarrely jealousy of himself? She'd kissed him. And maybe he'd never know what that was like. And why did that hurt so bad?

Rylan sent two more creepy dolls sailing off the landing. "What else can we try? I'm out of ideas."

"We'll work it out. The Bane could still be something, or I'll convince Crowea to touch me and give us answers, or we'll try every other fairy tale cure out there if we have to." Everly's eyes glistened fiercely.

They dodged the worst of the dolls, Rylan booting away the ones that reached him. He was happy to have something to take out his frustration on, and he searched for more. They seemed to be avoiding him, trying to circle around him, only one target in their sights.

Everly lifted her heavy work boot to kick the one closing in on her. But it moved in a flash, leaping over her foot and latching onto her thigh. Two more joined it, rushing up at startling speeds.

Rylan grunted. They didn't care about him at all. They were putting all their energy into reaching Everly.

The doll on her thigh plunged its jagged mouth deep into her flesh. She cried out, sending Rylan's pulse into overdrive.

Rylan grabbed the monstrous toy and tore it off her, throwing it back toward the cougar. The other two dolls clambered like spiders around Everly's body, biting chunks as they went. She stumbled.

Wrenching the dolls off her, Rylan scooped her up into his arms and charged through the remaining toys and down the corridor.

She wrapped her arms around his neck, helping support herself as he ran. Her warm blood seeped through his clothing. His heart hammered.

It's just a dream.

Ramming the exit door with his shoulder, they burst out into a parking lot that extended into eternity.

Above them, a bright magenta aurora shimmered, and the dragon swam amongst it, shimmering and sparking as the two came into contact. Everything was a warm, purple tone and smelled of the candy aisle at The Boutique All.

Everly shivered against his chest, her arms tight around his neck.

The door slammed behind them, and no further sound of scraping porcelain or J-Pop music followed them through.

"Are you okay?" Rylan's whisper cracked in the silence.

Everly nodded, shifting her weight as a signal to be let down. He placed her back onto her feet, but wasn't ready to let her go. As his fingertips drew away from her, they felt somehow hollow.

"I'm sorry about that," she said, head hung and cheeks pink.

Although she didn't appear to be in pain, she still bled freely.

Rylan groaned, running a hand over his mouth. "I know it's not real, but it *feels* real. The danger feels real. Your *blood* feels real. And the worst part is knowing you're out in the real world doing even more dangerous stuff trying to keep me alive. I hate that so much, you can't understand."

Rylan's heart continued its raging beat but did nothing to shake off a sense of finality that was settling upon him. Maybe it wouldn't be so bad, if he no longer had a body to go back to. He could imagine a lifetime with Everly in her dreams. "Maybe you should just let my body go. Cut the life support."

Everly's plump lips widened into a circle. "You can't give up. Just because the kiss didn't work, doesn't mean nothing will."

"It was a dumb idea anyway," Rylan huffed, failing to turn his gaze away from her lips, once again imagining them pressed to his. "I mean, how was a sleeping beauty kiss supposed to work if I wasn't even there to experience it?"

Everly frowned, questioningly.

"I mean, when you're awake, it's like I don't even exist, so if it took any effort on my part to get out of here, how could I know what was happening enough to get back into my body?"

"It's not like I can kiss you while I'm asleep."

Rylan's heartbeat pounded in his ears, so deafening he couldn't hear his own words. "What if you did?"

"Sorry, what?"

Rylan focused on keeping his expression unchanged, as though he was asking for something perfectly rational. "What if we tried the sleeping beauty kiss here? Now?"

Everly turned scarlet, her cheeks burning against the white of her hair. "I guess. Yeah, I mean, we could do that. If you think it could help."

Rylan licked his lips, his head shaking. It was a stupid suggestion. The logic for how it would work was a stretch, at best. But what else was there?

"If there's even a small chance it will work, we should,

shouldn't we?"

"Oh. Yeah. Of course. We should." Everly took a deep breath and let it out slowly.

"We should," Rylan echoed, and stepped slightly closer.

"Just in case." Her voice was a breathy whisper.

Rylan bent toward her. He swallowed against the thud of his heartbeat in his throat and pulled her into him.

The moment Rylan's lips pressed against hers, he knew it was a lie.

If the sleeping beauty kiss was going to wake him up, it would have done so in reality. This wasn't going to wake him. That wasn't why he'd asked for it, why he wanted it.

He just … wanted it.

Her mouth was soft, lush. She tilted her head back and her lips parted ever so slightly, maybe even unconsciously. But Rylan took it as an invitation, deepening the kiss, opening her lips with his, his tongue teasing hers.

Even though they were in a dream, he felt everything— the curves of her body pressed into him, the warmth of her, the satin touch of her skin beneath his fingers as he cupped her face and then slid his fingers into her hair.

He was fairly certain sleeping beauty hadn't been kissed quite like this.

She turned him mindless. He wanted to soak in every part of her, run his fingers over every full curve. This was the moment, the dream he'd denied himself his whole life. He was lost in every sensation, every touch, wishing for more.

He'd missed their first kiss, in the real world where his body was numb and unconscious.

Here, though ... He could touch her here. He could kiss her here.

Here, maybe he could admit that he wanted her.

And she'd agreed. She wanted this too. Desire rose inside him and he squeezed her tight.

Her arms entwined his neck, pulling him toward her. Did she want him too? Or was she doing this only to try to help him wake up? The thought that she might was like a stab to his chest.

The pain shot his mind back to reality with the force of whiplash. The words he'd spoken to himself for years shouted through his mind.

You can't want her. You can't love her. You can't be with her. Not if you want to keep her safe. Keeping her safe is all that matters.

He pulled away abruptly.

Everly stared up at him, chest heaving and cheeks pink. He wanted to reach for her again, but he forced his hands to his sides.

"It ... didn't work." His voice came out low, husky.

Everly blinked three times and swiped a finger to the corner of her eye in a swift motion.

She smiled on shaky lips. "Don't worry. We'll figure it out."

Rylan turned his face to the unnatural sky above them, trying to calm his body.

And if they didn't … He'd have to convince Everly to let him go.

If keeping her safe was the last thing he ever did, it would be worth it.

Chapter Nineteen

He kissed me. We kissed each other.

Everly pushed away the memories of last night's dream as they interrupted her for the millionth time that morning. It was just a test, an attempt to wake Rylan up. It didn't mean anything. But the sensation of his lips on hers had felt so real, still haunted her, made her feel drunk and woozy and wanting to return to sleep forever. The way he had kissed her ...

Doesn't mean anything if I can't wake him up.

Everly sat near Callan, both of them anchored to the hand railing as the campervan bounced along the rough road. She'd driven past the highway turnoff that led to Gorhanmere a dozen times or more in her life while heading in and out of Shroudhaven, but she'd never taken it. Never actually stepped foot in the nearby town.

For good reason, clearly. No one in their right mind would have wanted to travel this way.

The road twisted up the side of a mountain, cutting through a thick tunnel of dark evergreens. The fall off on one side was vertigo-inducing. There were times Everly held her breath and prayed the van wouldn't tip backward off the steep road. Through the gap in the front seats, she could see Harper's knuckles turning white on the wheel.

Everything outside was dusky and silent. Glimpses of a churning gray sky could be seen through the forest canopy. Everly hadn't spotted a single bird or hint of other wildlife since Harper had turned off the main highway.

Something about their surroundings felt ... wrong. Like they'd left safety behind and driven into madness. The farther they continued up the winding road, the worse Everly's sense of foreboding.

In the passenger seat, Lian hummed, breaking the charged silence. "There it is."

Harper slowed and curved to the right onto a dusty one-lane road.

The small town appeared up ahead. Gorhanmere sat on the banks of a wide lake, with water so dark it was like a bottomless hole in the earth. From afar, the village was picturesque—a grouping of half-timbered colonial cottages with low gables and aged sandstone walls, surrounded by thick forest and backed by the mountain's craggy peak.

But as the van skirted the edge of the lake and drew closer, it wasn't quite so vacation perfect. The cottages had weathered to dull grays and off-whites. Weeds rambled, leafless and thorny over fencing and walls.

Many of the exposed timbers were crumbling away, bits of wood sticking out like broken bones. Several windows had cracked panes or lacked glass entirely, like gaping, soulless eyes.

"The village continues into the trees," Lian observed, pointing at a few visible rooflines between the thick pines.

Everly squinted through the windshield, noting the hanging signs on the nearest buildings. A bakery, town council, and a farm supplies shop, where they seemed to have selected all the deadliest looking farm tools—scythes, pitch forks, huge, toothy saws—to line the display up front. But the place seemed deserted.

"Where is everybody?"

"There's a car behind us," Harper said, leaning to get a better view of the side mirror. "A dark minivan."

In the back, Tammy and Cherry turned to look.

Lian checked in the passenger side mirror. "They weren't following us on the way up?"

Harper shook her head. "They popped out of the trees after we turned off the main road."

Lian sighed. "Everybody on their guard. We don't know what to expect. Harper, the motel's down that way.

Take a right here."

The campervan trundled over a sparsely graveled road toward a long, low building shielded beneath overgrown trees. Harper pulled into the parking lot and chose a spot near the door marked *Reception*. Like every other building they'd passed, the place looked deserted.

The other van pulled in a few spots down.

Cherry whistled. "Isn't that a coincidence. It's a Darkfrey van."

"Just what we need," Callan said as he reached for the door handle.

When he opened the door, a brisk, mountain wind blustered through the vehicle. They were quite a bit above sea level, and the temperature had dropped dramatically.

"You think they're here for us or something else?" Everly shivered and zipped up her jacket before she followed Callan out.

She hopped off the staircase onto dry dirt, and dust billowed beneath her boots. The Darkfrey team unloaded out of their van at the same time, the two groups sizing each other up.

"Hey, man!" Callan held out a hand toward one of the new arrivals. "Long time, no see."

"Look what the ghast dragged in," the guy replied with an open, honest smile.

The two men clasped hands and did one of those manly

back-clapping, single-armed hugs, then stepped away to appraise one another. The Darkfrey shadyr was tall and thin like Callan, but older, with a hard glint to his eyes and buzzed strawberry-blond hair.

Callan motioned to the man. "This is Lucas. I trained under his brace."

"You and your brother. I still say Darkfrey's worse off without the two of you," Lucas said, his grin widening.

He nodded to the rest of them, eyes passing over Tammy and Cherry without acknowledging them, then lingered on Lian. "What brings you lot to Gorhanmere?"

"Thought we'd have a weekend getaway," Callan replied, smoothly.

"Ha, sure. No one comes out here unless they're looking for something. Normally trouble."

Callan smiled. "The only thing we're looking for is a place to relax. What about you? Is it normal for a Darkfrey brace to be so far from Shroudhaven?"

Lucas nodded, glancing back at his team. They were unloading equipment from the van into one of the motel rooms.

"Yeah, unfortunately. We're investigating a beshadowing."

Lian spoke up. "I thought Gorhanmere had its own group of shadyrs to look after it?"

Lucas inclined his head. "Well ... it *does*. Mordan keeps

it hush-hush, but the leader of the group here has gone a little mad, and we can't rely on them to keep the town safe."

"You know where we might find this leader? Just to steer away from that area, of course," Callan said.

Lucas frowned slightly. "We keep clear of them and they keep clear of us. We only come up every so often to clean house. Got reports a couple days ago of strange sightings. I've put my money on it being an auerdax."

Cherry gasped. "No way!"

Lian tensed, her hand twitching at her side.

"A what?" Harper asked.

Lucas frowned at her and Everly for a moment before his grin returned. "Oh, these are your new bliv friends. Heard about them."

Everly stuffed her hands in her pockets and tried to make herself small.

"An auerdax is a rare kind of eidolghast," Callan told them, his mouth thin and downturned.

"Rare and tricky," Lucas agreed. "We were out all night hunting for this thing. Came back to grab some shut eye before nightfall, then we'll head back out."

"Need any help?" Callan asked.

"Nah, we've got it. Just keep your eyes peeled so you don't end up in trouble. We can't be babysitting you lot." He still grinned widely, but the warning was clear beneath his playful quip.

"We'll be fine," Callan assured him.

"Good to see you, man," Lucas added, offering up a hand once again. "Don't be a stranger."

As the Darkfrey team disappeared into their rooms, Lian grabbed her purse from the passenger seat and shut the door. "I'll go check us in."

Everly watched her vanish through the creaky door that led to the small office, then turned to Callan. "That's two warnings about the unstable shadyrs in the area. The shadyrs we're meant to be infiltrating in order to steal from. Should we be worried?"

"*Pshh.*" Callan waved a hand. "The Darkfrey mob also call us crazy. How bad could they really be?"

"Famous last words." Tammy shifted closer to the group, her lips barely moving as she murmured, "Welcome party approaching."

Callan stiffened and followed her line of sight.

Everly did the same.

Five figures emerged from the shadows beneath the thicket of trees, ambling slowly into the parking lot with their gazes locked on the Howell team. There were two women and three men, all of them wearing stained, battered overalls and muddy boots.

All of them had clean-shaved heads, showing off the dented, scarred skin of their scalps. Dirt smudged their wide, bulging-eyed faces. Two of the men carried shotguns holstered on their backs, and one woman had a rusty machete resting on her shoulder.

Harper hissed. "Are we about to be axe murdered? Because this feels like the beginning of a gory B-horror, and I am *not* dressed for murder."

"Looks suitable to me," Tammy muttered under her breath.

"You had the option to stay behind with Rush and Rylan," Everly said.

"Together in the weirdness, Ev." Harper's expression grew serious. "Also Denny is back there too, so, ew, no."

All five of the townsfolk were covered in scars. Dozens of white lines showed anywhere their skin was visible. As the group got closer, the eldest of the men stepped ahead of his companions, eyeing the Howell team warily. His bald head peaked strangely, ovaloid, off center, and too large. He loomed over them, staring with icy-blue eyes.

"Shadyrs, or just creepers?" Cherry whispered.

"I'll check," said Callan.

He stepped forward and casually ran two fingers from the corners of his mouth, straight down his chin. He'd done the same thing to Everly and Harper when they'd first met him again after returning to town and had been questioning him about weird stuff.

He'd since explained that this was an insider symbol for shadyrs, a way to check whether someone was in on the secret without having to come out and ask. The gesture represented the growth of two sharp fangs.

The man grunted at him and casually swung his shotgun around to the front.

"More Darkfreys?" His voice was deep, with a disturbing gurgle in it.

"No." Callan gave the man a knowing look and said meaningfully, "*Independent* shadyrs."

The man's fingers danced over the barrel of his gun as he took each of them in slowly, through bloodshot eyes. His arms, neck, and face were covered completely in thin, white lines, some of them crisscrossing at junctures where the skin had knotted and bulged while healing.

The younger woman and man of the group had fewer scars than the others, but the leader looked like his skin had melted off and only been half-pieced back together.

Finally, he said, "You have no business here."

"We were hoping maybe we could." Everly used her calmest, friendliest voice.

The man terrified her. It was unlikely any level of friendliness was going to get them far with him.

Still, she tried. "We'd heard maybe there was a place for shadyrs, up here. Shadyrs who didn't want to be Darkfreys anymore."

The man spat on the gravel, then sucked at his teeth while he glared at them one by one. "I *said* you have no business here. You're not *welcome* here. New blood is tainted. Old blood is pure. Our family is strong."

"Our family is strong," the four others intoned behind him.

Everly swallowed.

Harper pressed against Everly's side, uncharacteristically silent. Everly slipped an arm around her waist, horrified to find her best friend was trembling. She'd nearly been eaten by a vasmire and joked about it later, but when it came to people—shadyr or not—Harper had a real fear.

Callan caught Everly's eye, his brow raised. He cleared his throat. "Our family is strong too, maybe we could be—"

"You've been warned." The scarred man's fingers tightened on his gun.

Chapter Twenty

The feral shadyr led his shaggy group back into the woods, and Harper watched them go with a shudder, still clinging to Everly's arm. She'd never been that close to a crazy man with a gun before. She'd been lucky not to be, the one other time. Still, the whole encounter had left a sick, sinking feeling in the pit of her stomach.

The terror it had stirred in her was *a lot* like when her ex betrayed her. She'd tried her hardest to push all those old fears and emotions down, and it was easy to pretend she was fine when she was surrounded by all this supernatural madness.

A straightforward, evil creature from another dimension was somehow simpler. But sometimes, even shadyrs and eidolghasts couldn't keep her past from haunting her thoughts.

Especially not while staring down the barrel of a shotgun.

Fear of what other humans could do, the pain they could inflict on each other, had overwhelmed her when Bryce doxed her.

Once her home address was made public, the graphic threats that flooded her inbox, the *things* she'd found left on her doorstep, and then the man with a gun the police had caught breaking into her apartment the night she'd fled to Everly's—it all taught her that real people were capable of terrible things, and it was hard to distinguish the monsters from the rest.

To have had that caused by a man she'd loved was like him saying, "I hope someone uses this information to hunt you down. I hope you die."

It had shaken her whole world.

Everly's shoulders drooped in a sigh beneath Harper's grip. "Something tells me we're not going to be making buddies with the Gorhanmere shadyrs any time soon."

"What tipped you off?" Tammy scoffed.

Cherry shuddered physically. "For me it was the intense, evil cult vibes."

Callan wandered back toward the van, hoisting out his black duffle bag. "We've got options still. It might just mean a stealthier incursion on evil cult HQ."

"Sure, or better yet, let's just frontal assault an unknown

quantity of unhinged shadyrs on their home turf," Tammy said, feigning enthusiasm and punctuating it with an eyeroll.

Harper squeezed Everly's arm again before letting her go. "Don't worry, we'll work it out."

The creaky registration door opened, and then slammed shut behind Lian. She held three keys in her hand and a perplexed expression on her face.

"Weird people," she said, passing one key to Everly and another to Callan. "The registration office smelled like mothballs, and I'm nearly certain the clerk had spiderwebs in her hair."

"We just had a run in with the locals too. Weird would be a dire understatement for them." Harper shuddered, glancing back at the woods.

She couldn't wait to get behind the protective walls of a motel room. The weight of eyes, watching from the trees, still lay on her.

"Not friendly?" Lian asked.

"I'd prefer to face the auerdax than deal with them again," Tammy muttered.

"No, you wouldn't," Callan snapped. "We all have to take the risk of its presence seriously."

"Why's that, exactly?" Harper asked, directing the question to the group at large in an attempt to distract herself from thoughts of guns, ex-boyfriends, and betrayal.

"Auerdax are a really rare, badass eidolghast," Cherry replied.

"Don't sound too excited," Callan said wryly. "Auerdax are hard to locate and even harder to kill. They're only tangible in darkness. They turn completely incorporeal in the light."

He squinted at the overcast sky, filling the parking area with an even, dull glow. "It could be here, right now, and we wouldn't even know it, until night comes and it kills you in the dark."

Lian fixed Callan in a tight-lipped stare. "Let's all just hope it keeps far away."

"Speak for yourself," Cherry said. "I've never had a chance to shift into auerdax form before. I've heard it's awesome."

"Oh yay, a chance to be a new kind of monster," Tammy groaned.

Harper's mouth opened as she processed the details. "So weroths turn you into werewolves, and vasmires turn you into vampires ... what form do shadyrs take around an auerdax?"

"Hopefully it doesn't come close enough for you to find out," Callan said darkly.

He left the conversation, shoulders hunched, and let himself into his room.

"Just wait and see," Cherry grinned at Harper, then

followed after Callan.

Lian and Tammy shared the second room, and Everly and Harper would be bunking together in the third. They unloaded their bags and went to settle in.

Lian managed to get them side-by-side rooms connected by interior doors, which helped Harper feel slightly more protected, given she didn't need to leave her room to mingle with the shadyrs.

Harper stayed behind to chat with Cherry while Callan and Everly drove back to the main strip of town to check for hot food options.

It was mid-afternoon, too late to be called lunch, too early to qualify as dinner, but most of them had skipped breakfast that morning before they set out for the mountains. After learning of the auerdax, they also wanted to have everyone behind closed doors before sunset.

When the van returned, Harper went to help unload.

"All we found were some pies and pastries at the truck stop," Everly said apologetically.

As they unpacked their make-shift feast in the middle room, Harper cringed at the warm canned sodas. "We're going to need ice."

"I'll go with you," Callan offered quickly.

He picked up the plastic bucket, holding it out for her.

Harper eyed him, concerned by his eagerness, but she accepted the bucket and headed for the door, glad she didn't have to go outside alone.

She shivered and wrapped her arms around her torso, wishing she'd brought something heavier than a distressed, off-the-shoulder sweatshirt to keep her warm. Not the first time she'd sacrificed warmth for fashion, and it definitely wouldn't be the last.

She caught Callan's eyes on her a few times, and made a quick, silent wish that he wasn't about to make things awkward. She enjoyed his company, and—minus Denny— enjoyed the company of everyone in the new group of friends they'd found with the Howell team.

Even Tammy, with her gothic nihilistic attitude, was growing on her. But she had lived enough years in her skin to know *the look* Callan was giving her, and romance was the last thing on her mind these days.

They turned into the enclosed alcove where the ice dispenser sat between a soda machine and snack machine, the latter of which had a huge *Out of Order* sign taped to the glass.

"Looks like a midnight junk food raid is out of the question." Harper shoved the ice bucket beneath the dispenser.

Callan peered into the dark machine and scoffed. "All that's in there are spicy fries and sesame snaps. I think I'm good."

He reached past her and depressed the button to

dispense the ice.

Harper tensed at the nearness of him. *Just relax. He's not one of the monsters.*

Over the racket of the ice hitting the bucket, a tinny sound system mounted in the corner near the ceiling played "There's a Mermaid in My Lighthouse."

Harper chuckled, humming to the beat then singing along. "Hungry light shines over the waves, and my merrrr-maaaaaid, she yearns. When will I return? When will I return?"

She trailed off at the intensity on Callan's face. "What? Did I get it wrong?"

Callan shook his head and blinked, focusing on her. "No. It's just ... You have a beautiful voice."

"Oh. Um, thanks." She checked on the progress inside the bucket then glanced back at him. "I took vocal lessons for years. Got to be that triple threat, you know."

"I think you've got all the threats covered." Callan's cheeks flushed. "Surprised you know the lyrics to that one though, it's kind of unique to Shroudhaven."

"It didn't take me long to pick up, they play the bloody song over and over everywhere."

Callan chuckled. "Yeah, I used to wonder if every speaker in the region was beshadowed, cursed to only play one song, because seriously, it's everywhere you go. But if you know it, that means you're a true local now."

Harper rolled her eyes. "Don't say that in front of Everly. She'd freak. She's *so* uncomfortable in Shroudhaven."

"What about you?"

Harper half-smiled and tugged the bucket out of the cubby hole before the ice overflowed. "There's a certain charm to this area, monsters and all. I mean, I'm not dumb. I know this place is dangerous. But there are monsters everywhere in this world, you know?"

Callan nodded, but she wasn't sure he really understood. "I'm glad you guys have stayed a bit longer. I wanted to, umm, ask you ..."

Harper cringed internally, freezing in place.

"You wouldn't want to ... I mean ..." Callan avoided her gaze and rubbed the back of his neck, staring at the *Out of Order* sign like it held the mysteries of the universe. "Dinner. With me. You know, when all of this with Rylan is over, and we can go back to normal. Shroudhaven normal, anyway."

Harper took a long breath, lifting her lips and putting on the picture-perfect manners she'd practiced for years as though it were armor.

She played it naïve. "Are you asking me on a date?"

"Yes. I'm doing an awful job of it, aren't I?" He laughed.

"Nooooo. I mean, yes, but no. You're adorable. Really," she cooed as if he was some unknown fan on the street asking for her number.

Callan was already nodding slowly, head hung and chin bumping against his chest.

"I'm sorry," she blurted out. "If it were any other time in my life, you'd be getting a yes, I swear. It's just … I'm not ready for another relationship. Not with anyone."

He looked up at her from under his lashes.

Harper clutched the cold bucket to her chest, and let her act drop. Callan deserved more.

"I hope you can understand that it *truly* is not you, it's me. The whole experience with my last boyfriend, it's put me in a place where I've been rethinking *everything*."

Harper swallowed, wishing she had the answers to give him, but she honestly hadn't found them yet herself.

She tried to dig out the words to explain. "I'm questioning everything, about me, what I want, what love is. I don't even know if … I don't know what I want any more."

Callan frowned. "I'm sorry, I should have realized. I knew what had happened to you but didn't think about how that could make you feel, which makes me a complete idiot. I get it, why you'd need time."

Harper's heart swelled a little, and she pouted a smile at him. "Thank you, for understanding. Friends still?"

"Of course."

Harper winced bashfully. "You sure?"

"Absolutely," he said, smiling broadly.

But she could hear the let down in his voice. She hated being the one to make him feel like that.

He turned to head back toward the rooms and she caught up to walk beside him.

"But, you know, if you are looking for romance in your life, I think maybe Tammy might be interested in a little something more," Harper pointed out with a sly smile.

"Tammy?" He raised an eyebrow and coughed a laugh. "She's more like a little sister. Like the kind of little sister who can't stand her older brother."

"Really? I got the impression there might be something there. But what would I know?" Harper bumped her shoulder against his. "The only thing I'm an authority on is what's *not* a happy-ever-after."

Chapter Twenty-One

Tammy leaned face first against the cold bricks just out of sight, fighting hot tears in her eyes as the mountain wind cut through her black hooded jacket.

Like a little sister. Great. She closed her eyes and ground her teeth.

She didn't care if Callan *liked* her. She just wanted to be taken seriously. Instead, she was treated like a child. Sure, she played into that, with the sullen teen groans and eye rolls, but it was the easiest way she'd found to get people off her case, to stop them babying her. Keep them all at a distance.

But she wasn't a child. She'd known loss. She'd known grief. She'd known death. In terms of suffering, she was just as far advanced down this pointless mortal coil as the rest of their miserable party.

And why does that infuriating influencer chick think I have a thing for Callan?

She'd been sure she hadn't shown anything—because there wasn't anything to show. It wasn't like Callan had ever given her reason to think he was interested. Even if he did, it wasn't something that could happen. Not for her.

She dug her fingertips into the corners of her eyes, annoyed that the tears wouldn't stop.

What is wrong with me?

Everything, a dark voice inside answered.

Callan and Harper's conversation continued as they left with the ice bucket, voices growing quieter as they headed back to the rooms.

The paper bag holding the veggie pie Tammy had taken for dinner crumpled in her tense hand. She'd picked it up and stepped outside, wanting to be alone after the long drive stuck in the van with everyone. Instead, she got to be the secret audience to Callan and Harper's little soap opera moment.

I should have stayed inside.

With her paper-bagged dinner cradled against her chest, she turned around, sliding her back down the wall until she landed on the concrete.

And saw that Everly was standing right behind her.

The unexpected company jolted her. She half expected

to disappear to Dark Corner but managed to keep it together. Since going on purpose from Rooks Hotel, it seemed a little easier for her to hold onto herself.

"What the ghast?" Tammy snapped. "How long have you been there?"

Everly's gaze moved over Tammy's face, where tears must have left smudgy tracks on her cheeks.

She shrugged one shoulder. "About as long as you have. Lian didn't want you to be alone."

Tammy swiped her sweatshirt sleeves over her face and looked out at the trees behind the motel so she wouldn't have to see the pity on Everly's face. "Completely defeating the purpose of why I came out here."

She kept her gaze on the dark, eerie forest as Everly came closer. If she thought the bliv would get the point and leave, she was wrong.

The white-haired woman lowered herself down to sit next to Tammy on the ground, leaning against the motel wall. She had a paper bag in her hand too, and fished a sausage roll out of it, snapping off a bite-sized piece with her fingers and popping it in her mouth.

"I don't need a babysitter," Tammy growled.

"I know." Everly dusted crumbs off her jacket.

Tammy would have never admitted it, but she liked Everly's trademark red bomber jacket. She wished she could wear red like that, but black was the only color that matched her anymore.

"But what about some company? Especially after eavesdropping what just echoed our way."

"I don't know what you're talking about," Tammy snapped, but her voice came out thick with tears.

"You don't have to be strong with me," Everly said quietly. "I've been hopelessly in love with Rylan for what feels like my whole life."

Her fingertips drifted to her lips then were chased away with a small shake of her head. "And he's done everything in his power to keep me away from him. I understand how it feels."

"I'm *not* in love with anyone."

Everly eyed her for a split second then shrugged. "Maybe not, but feeling unwanted still sucks."

Tammy sighed and opened her paper bag, pulling a bit of crust out to nibble on. "Yeah. Yeah, it does."

"You and me, team freak, and team rejected by Howell boys." Everly chuckled, lifting her paper-bagged food as though making a toast.

Tammy's first instinct was to spit another denial, but it didn't matter. Not really. Whether or not she had any feelings for Callan, Everly was one hundred percent right about the rejection part. Tammy hmphed and lifted her bag to join the toast.

Before she got close enough to touch, the strange

sensation sizzled in her fingers. She snatched her blackened hand away again.

"Team freak all right," she grumbled.

"Yeah. I felt that too," Everly agreed, swapping her food into her other hand and flexing her fingers. "It wasn't a one-off thing that happened at Crow's then."

"Guess not. Lucky you, got an excuse to keep your distance from me."

Everly shifted around, moving to sit cross legged in front of her. She reached out both hands, holding them palm up between then, a few inches away from Tammy's.

"Come on. Let's test this again. Slowly."

Tammy pressed back into the wall behind her, horrified. "Why?"

"Scientific curiosity." Everly wriggled her fingers like an invitation. "We should try and understand what is happening with this reaction, and why."

"Except that we know exactly why. I'm cursed." Tammy dropped her bag on the ground, staring at her Everdark-stained hands.

Everly caught her gaze, and her voice came out firm. "You are not defined by what happened to you. You're so much more than that."

"Speak for yourself," Tammy murmured. "Aren't you just as haunted by your past? Your curse?"

They stared at one another in silence for a long moment.

Tammy sighed and lifted her hands closer to Everly's. Their palms were only inches away from each other, and a low-level hum rose between them from the proximity.

Something supernatural was at work, something she was starting to think took *both* of them to happen, since it had never happened with anyone else. Not that many people had touched her blackened hands. But Lian had, Rushelle had, without flinching, without any reaction.

She hesitated. "You think it's safe?"

Everly's hands closed-up, pulling back toward her chest. "I ... don't know, actually. I'd probably bet that it's not. Maybe it's not a good idea after all. I just thought—"

"Whatever, let's do it."

Tammy closed the space between their hands until their fingers touched.

This time, there was no big flash or loud bang like an explosion, but brilliant sparkles did sizzle between their palms, chased by what looked like black flames.

Tammy yelped at the fiery pain in her fingertips, and the two released each other quickly. Energy hung in the air for several seconds, casting an arc of blue light around them that glittered off Everly's wide eyes.

A gray mist rolled in, and the late afternoon light grew darker. It took less than a moment for the day to completely disappear in the fog and shadows. The billowing mist thrummed around them with unnatural sounds as it heaved and churned.

They both got to their feet, to avoid being submerged entirely. The cloudy substance was thick and tangible, scraping against them like sand within waves.

"So weird," Tammy muttered, her gaze roaming the thick blanket of mist. "It's almost like a beshadowing effect."

Everly nodded, her bottom lip between her teeth.

Her voice was a tiny whisper, "Like what an eidolghast causes."

"It has to be caused by my hands. I mean, I'm *literally* poisoned by shroudpool magic."

Everly flexed her fingers as if shaking away the memory of the stinging electricity. "I don't know. I think I'm part of it, too. Whatever that light is, inside me … when I touch you, it roars."

Tammy raised her eyebrows. "Okay then. So I think we can scientifically conclude never to do that again."

A new voice cut through the gloom. "Everly? Tammy? Girls, where are you?"

"Lian," Tammy said under her breath.

Everly nodded, then called out, "We're over here!"

A few moments later, Lian appeared from the mist like a mirage. The fog parted around her, and she moved with an elegant grace that Tammy was used to seeing around Howell House, her long cardigan swirling at her ankles.

"You girls okay?" Her gaze swept around the thick fog, the cold, paranormal wind, and the static electricity on the air. "We were worried when you didn't come back."

What was with the babysitting?

Tammy narrowed her eyes. "We've only been out here like five minutes."

Lian blinked, then glanced down at the delicate gold watch on her wrist. "Sweetheart, you've been out here almost an hour."

Everly's jaw dropped open.

Tammy lifted her blackened hands, staring at her fingers in shock.

Lian crossed her arms, her expression grim. "I'm guessing then that you weren't just getting along so well you lost track of time?"

Everly shrugged. "We were testing the weird reaction that happens when our hands touch."

"You two caused this?" Lian turned slowly on the spot, taking it in. "Thought it seemed like something more than usual weather. It's almost like a minor beshadowing. Maybe that's what caused you two to lose time."

"Creepy," Tammy muttered, shoving her hands back into her pockets.

Everly did the same. "Agreed. No more touching."

Lian motioned for them to follow her. "Come on. It isn't safe out here. Especially with all of this mist dimming the lights and an auerdax around."

Tammy fell into step beside Everly as she asked, "We could beat it though. Right? I mean, especially with the Darkfrey team close by. That's what, ten of us against one of it?"

"Don't underestimate an auerdax." Lian frowned deeply as she led them back toward their motel rooms. "Though, we do have an advantage with my sword."

"Ah, the famous sword," Everly teased. "How did you get it again?"

Tammy smirked. It was an ongoing joke at Howell House that it had been stolen from the Darkfrey's archives, but Lian had always played it coy. She'd also always made sure not to let any Darkfreys see her with it, despite keeping it on her person almost constantly. It hung at her side even now.

Lian's pace slowed, and she spoke to them over her shoulder. "I stole it from the Darkfreys when I left them. More as an act of rebellion than any thought-through plan. I was young and dumb like that once."

Tammy's mouth opened, stunned. Everly caught her eye, looking equally shocked.

Lian continued. "Everyone thought it was useless anyway, a cursed weapon, which is probably why I got away with it."

"Why do they think it's cursed?" Tammy asked quietly.

"Because it blinds you as long as you are wielding it."

"What? No, I've seen you using it," Everly scoffed.

Lian looked a little farther over her shoulder, one side of her mouth pulled up. "You have. And yes, I was blind at the time."

"Why would you even use it then?" Tammy grunted. "That does sound useless."

Lian turned away from them again. "I thought so too, at first. Then came the night an auerdax attacked my home."

"You mean, the night ..." Everly's words cut out.

Lian continued. "After what it had done ... I was so desperate to kill the thing that I grabbed the sword off the display where I kept it like some stupid trophy. Hoping I could just get one good slice in. It fled into a lit room and I just lunged, blindly, furiously, and the sword impaled it, even though it wasn't really there. That's when I learned the sword's power."

Tammy blew out a slow whistle. "It can harm an auerdax even when it's incorporeal?"

Lian nodded, still facing away from them. "If only I'd known sooner ..."

Tammy shivered, and pulled her hands into her sleeves. She knew Lian's husband had been killed by an eidolghast, but she'd never known what kind. That must have been terrifying, for her, for her boys.

They reached their rooms again and Lian stopped at

the door, hesitating a moment with her fingers on the door handle. "Since that night, I've trained with it every day, learned how to fight without the use of my sight."

"That's amazing," Everly said in a hushed whisper.

It's totally badass, Tammy thought, but didn't say it aloud.

It seemed somehow strange, to praise a skill that had emerged from such a tragedy. Like the way the others had called her a hero that night she'd helped them escape Rooks Hotel.

It almost felt like they were saying, "Hooray, isn't it great Blaise died in a shroudpool so that Tammy can do this!"

A sharp pang of grief hit her chest and her face twisted. She smoothed it out again when she noticed Lian watching her shrewdly.

With a small smile, the older woman said, "It goes to show, that sometimes things that people consider cursed can prove to be the most valuable."

Tammy turned away, staring back at the mist. *And sometimes, they're just cursed.*

Chapter Twenty-Two

Everly turned on every light in their motel room. Both bedside lamps, both reading globes over the beds, the hanging lamp over the corner table, and the strip of lighting above the bathroom mirror. All the Howell team would be sleeping with the lights on that night, to stay safe from the auerdax.

The thought of a monster that would strike only in utter darkness left a cold chill running down Everly's spine. Even worse was the idea that it could be there now, lurking around them unseen and untouchable, just biding its time. For all their sakes, and especially Lian and Callan's, she hoped the thing stayed far away from their brightly lit rooms.

With a plan in place to canvass the town for intel

starting early tomorrow, they all retired for the night not long after dinner. Everly crawled beneath the covers and rolled toward Harper, who was staring at the ceiling from her own bed nearby.

Right next to her pillow, leaning on the wall, was the axe Callan had given her. She'd painted her name up the side in a flowing script with glittery pink paint.

"It's so bright in here!" Harper whined, rubbing her eyes. "I forgot to bring my eye mask. I'll never get to sleep!"

Everly squinted at the brightness too, feeling far from slumber herself. She hit the power button on the remote for the television and started scrolling through channels. Most only showed snow. The way Harper glared at her phone screen without tapping away told Everly that reception was out for everything.

She wanted to ask about what had happened with Callan. Everly had heard the end—Harper needing time, agreeing to remain friends, then her suggestion of something with Tammy getting shot down. Everly could guess what had led up to that point.

Should I confess that I overheard? Or just wait until she's ready to tell me about it?

Harper threw a spare blanket over her head and rolled over with a frustrated grunt. Everly settled on waiting. It left her uneasy, and saddened, that there was one more secret pushing in between the two of them.

She hadn't known Harper that long, but the way they had bonded quickly over their various traumas meant they'd shared everything at first. Everly didn't want that to change, but life since they'd arrived in Shroudhaven had been so volatile. She didn't know where it would leave their friendship.

Taking inspiration from Harper, Everly grabbed a spare t-shirt from her bag and tied it into a makeshift blindfold. Light still poked through the gaps, but it was enough to help her settle.

And then she was at Howell House.

Upstairs, in the hallway connecting all the bedrooms. The colors were dimmer, grayer than real life, and thick beams protruded from the woodwork into the hallway at strange angles, making it hard to move along the space without ducking and weaving.

"I'm dreaming," she said out loud.

A reply echoed to her in return. The deep rattle of a train, combined with the howl of wind and growl of hungry wolves.

Oh no, not this dream.

She spun on the spot, eyes wide. Through a window over the staircase there was the flash of something black and twisted, shooting by like the reverse of lightning.

"RYLAAAN?" Everly screamed.

Where was he? She needed to keep him safe. What if

it had already found him?

"Down here." His voice drifted up from the stairwell.

Everly ran to the landing. "Get up here, quick!"

A second later he emerged, jogging up to her with his forehead furrowed. "What's wrong?"

"This dream. This is bad. We have to hide." Everly kept her eyes on the windows for movement.

The garden outside was ashy and swayed like seaweed in a tide under a ghostly sun.

Rylan scoffed. "Bad? I'm not sure how it could be worse than some of the other dreams you've had."

"It's worse. There's something outside ... something dark, and twisted, and ... empty. It's hard to explain, but if it sees us, if it touches us, it will turn us into nothing."

"Nothing?" Rylan's eyebrows raised and he checked the window too. "And that's happened to you before?"

"Yeah, but it's just a dream, for me. It feels awful, like what I imagine dying to feel like but worse, but I then I wake up in the real world after it happens."

Rylan stared into her eyes. "What answer did we end up landing on with the whole, *if I die in your dream do I die for real* question?"

Everly swallowed and shrugged. "Really not something I want to risk testing."

The shadowy thing flickered past a window again, a swirl of null, of void. It roared its strange, clattering sound as it brushed by an old oak, and the tree was obliterated into ashy snowflakes that faded into nothingness.

"Right. Okay, so how do we stay unseen?" Rylan grunted.

"We have to hide." Everly rubbed her forehead, trying to clear her panic and think. "All the rooms have windows."

"Closet." Rylan pointed down the hall, to the narrow door at the end.

They bolted, crashing into each other as they dodged and clambered over the uneven levels and barricades the protruding beams created. Rylan's hands pressed against Everly's waist, helping lift her over one, and Everly pulled at Rylan's arm as he ducked under another.

The shadow creature's roar grew deafening as they rushed into the closet and slammed the door behind them.

Everly's eyes spun in the darkness, seeking chinks of light that identified holes they could be seen through. It was pitch black. She sighed, relieved.

Everly had gone in first, her back cushioned by hanging jackets, and her chest pressed against Rylan. His warm breath drifted down over her, and every part of her body remembered the kiss they had shared the last time she dreamed of him.

The space was tight, and she tingled everywhere his body rested on hers. One of his knees was between her legs, entangled and trapped amidst clutter on the floor, keeping them entwined. His strong hands moved on either side of her, tickling along her waist, her arms as they searched.

There was a soft click, and a small bulb above them illuminated. Rylan's hand still rested on the pull cord. His face was barely an inch from hers, hunched close in the cramped closet.

The railroad howl of the creature sounded again, rattling the walls and coat hangers.

"Are we safe in here?" His voice was soft and husky.

Everly tried to answer but her voice got stuck. She licked her lips and nodded. It felt like the closet got smaller every time she thought about it. Knowing how her dreams liked to test her limits, it probably was.

"I think so," Everly forced the answer out. "I'm sorry. That you're trapped in here."

"It's okay. It's not so bad." Rylan shifted his weight, leaning a shoulder into the hanging jackets to one side. He brushed the fingertips of his other hand over her face, pulling stray strands of hair off her cheeks.

"Scary creatures of darkness aren't that new to me, after all. There are a lot worse places to be than in a closet with you."

His touch traced lines of fire on her skin, like she'd stood too close to a candle's flame and it would melt her. She leaned in, unbidden, wanting more, wanting him closer.

I can't do this. I can't be this close to him.

It'll break me.

Rylan dropped his hand away again, frowning.

He cleared his throat. "So, what's new in the real world? Did you guys make it to Gorhanmere?"

"Yeah, we're there now," Everly replied, struggling to get the words out.

Stop looking at his lips.

Her gaze dropped, lingering instead over the strong lines of his neck and chest.

Everly blinked rapidly then turned her eyes to the jackets beside them. "We met some creepy local shadyrs already, and there's a Darkfrey brace up here too, hunting an auerdax."

"An *auerdax*?" Rylan's body tensed, pressing Everly harder back into the coats surrounding her. "What time is it? Is it night? You need to get out of there."

"We left all the lights in the room on," she assured him. "So even if it does show up, we're safe."

"You can't be safe enough from a creature like that. You don't know …"

Everly's eyes flushed with tears at the pain in his voice. "I do. I know what happened."

Muscles twitched in Rylan's jaw. "Then you should understand how serious this is."

"I promise you I'm doing my best to stay safe. I feel like … It's not only my life at risk, you know? You're a part of me, somehow, so I have to be extra careful. If I died, maybe you would, too."

She paused, struck by a sudden thought, then laughed bitterly. "Although, for all I know, me dying might be the thing that actually frees you."

"Don't even joke about that." Rylan grabbed her, both of his hands sliding up her arms, over her shoulders, then cupping her cheeks as he glared down at her.

There was so much worry, so much pain in his eyes it made her ache.

"You are *not* going to die," he said sharply. "I don't care if that's the answer. I'll live in these dreams with you forever if I have to, as long as that means you're *alive*."

Everly shivered, unable to speak, to move, unable to do anything but stare at his eyes, his lips.

Rylan's gaze swept across her face as if he were memorizing every aspect of her. His thumbs brushed close to her mouth.

"Being freed from here because you died wouldn't be a victory. It would be a nightmare. I'd rather walk every one of your nightmares *with* you than live my own without you."

They stared at one another for an interminable amount of time. Everly was distantly conscious of the dark being roaring outside, shaking the house in its hunt for them.

But her every sense was overwhelmed by Rylan's

presence—the warmth of his hands on her skin, the intense glint in his warm-green eyes ... *the way he had kissed me.* The way she wanted more than anything for him to kiss her again.

"Evie ... I need to tell you something," Rylan murmured.

Everly's heart raced so fast, she choked on her words as she said, "O-oh? What is it?"

His gaze drifted to her lips. "Something I should have told you a long time ago. I haven't been honest with you for so long. I haven't really been honest with myself. But you deserve to know how I—"

The dream shattered.

Everly awoke with a jolt, sitting straight up in her motel bed with her heart beating out of her chest and her skin prickling with unease.

Everything was black. She ripped her makeshift blindfold off, taking in her surroundings and trying to work out what woke her. It took her several moments to surface from the dream world, to leave all her emotions surrounding Rylan behind and figure out why the room felt ... wrong.

It wasn't morning. It was still night, and everything was dark,

Everything was dark.

Panic struck through Everly's nerves like electric sparks. All the lights she had left on were out. Even the television had gone off, leaving the whole room shrouded in deep, unending shadow.

Everly blinked away the last vestiges of sleep, rubbing her eyes as she searched the darkness for danger, for a monster, waiting to attack.

Movement caught her attention.

A shimmering, translucent ghost was walking through the room—coming right for her.

CHAPTER TWENTY-THREE

The ghost lifted a hand and put a finger to his lips.

It looked like Callan.

Shock rooted Everly to the mattress as he stalked past the end of her bed toward Harper's side of the room.

Callan's a ... ghost? Her stomach flipped over inside her.

Had he died? Had the auerdax showed up and killed her friend while she slept?

Two more forms came through the walls, stepping right through the cheap wood paneling as if it didn't exist. Tammy and then Lian, who held the hilt of her sword as if ready to draw at a moment's notice. Even in their luminous, translucent form, it was clear they were all in pajamas, jackets thrown on over the top. Their faces were grim and alert.

They didn't look dead. They looked ready for battle.

It's their shadyr form, Everly realized in awe. The auerdax turned them into *ghosts*.

And that meant it was near.

A short, sharp gasp echoed through the silent room, and then a flash of light. Harper sat up in bed, shining her phone at the 'ghosts.' Her eyes were so wide her whites gleamed in the dim light.

Everly caught her friend's gaze and shook her head once, putting a finger to her lips just as Callan had done. Harper reached out with her free hand and wrapped it around the axe handle.

Lian broke away from the others and stepped between the two beds.

Her voice came out low and echoey, as if she were whispering down a long tunnel. "The auerdax is here. It must have tripped the motel's fuse box. I didn't think they were that smart ..."

She glanced at the door to the room, where Tammy and Callan were peeking through the wood.

Their heads were *outside* while their bodies were inside, as if the door was nothing but a waterfall.

Lian continued in an urgent, hushed tone. "The Darkfrey team is outside with Cherry. They're going to distract the ghast. We need to get you out of here to safety."

Everly shoved the covers aside and rooted around

blindly on the floor for her shoes. "What do we do?"

"Wait until it's clear." Lian's movements were slow and fluid, like she existed on a different plane of existence while under the influence of the auerdax. "Then run to the camper and get the Everdark out of here. Go into town. Find light."

"We have some light in here," Harper said, shaking the phone in her hand.

"It's not strong enough. Even when partially corporeal, the auerdax can kill."

Everly helped Harper find her designer sneakers in her mess of a suitcase, and they both tugged sweatshirts on over their pajamas, anticipating the cold outside.

Near the doorway, Callan's head popped back into the room. He motioned to them, his ghostly face grim.

They tiptoed silently to the door and stood behind the three shadyrs. Callan raised his hand again, signaling them to wait.

Seconds trickled into minutes. Everly shifted on her feet, her heart like a frightened bird in her chest. She could hear *nothing*. No sounds of battle. No creaks or groans of a large monster sliding past their motel door. Just empty silence.

Then Lian pulled back into the room and snapped, "Now. Run."

Everly didn't hesitate. She slipped the bolt and snatched

at the flimsy doorknob, throwing the door open to the inky night.

Outside in the motel's parking lot, the Darkfrey brace had surrounded something, as far away from the building as they could get without disappearing into the trees.

Everly glimpsed Cherry a few doors down, evacuating a sleep disheveled family from their own room, and one of the Darkfrey girls was doing the same with a young couple even farther down the sidewalk.

"Go!" Lian snapped.

Everly startled, then clasped her fingers in Harper's and yanked her in the direction of the campervan. Lian, Tammy, and Callan sped the other way to join the Darkfrey team.

Everly's feet pounded on the asphalt. The shadyrs were shouting in strange, echoing voices. Harper screamed.

The auerdax appeared before them, blocking their path.

It loomed out of the shadows with an unearthly growl that shook the ground.

Everly skidded to a stop, stunned by the sight of it.

She hadn't known exactly what to expect, but anything she could have imagined wouldn't have come close to the truth.

In the meager light of Harper's phone, and no moon above, it was almost completely solid, with only a hint of blurry translucence.

Of the eidolghasts Everly had seen so far, it had the most humanoid form, but could never be mistaken for a person. It towered over her, three times her height, with a massive, asymmetrical torso.

It had no head, no face, but dozens of empty eyes stared back at Everly. Skulls. Its chest area was full of them.

Bones, black as the night sky, filled the monster, as though all that made up this creature was the gruesome skeletal collection and the strange, sickly goo that held them together.

Like a malformed blob of melted flesh and shadows, with uneven, lumpy legs, and whip-like arms with deadly talons at the ends.

It seemed as if someone had created the beast from all the world's night terrors.

Fear come to life.

"You ..." the auerdax hissed and growled, but Everly understood its meaning.

Every skull in its torso turned to track her, jaws opening in time. "You I know ... familiar essence. Loathsssssome light. Desssstroy ... Again!"

The tendril of bones and slime protruding from one shoulder whipped out, rocketing toward Everly's head.

With a loud cry, Harper swung her axe. It shimmered in the night, slicing through the mishappen limb. A harsh screaming sound filled the air, as though every bone Harper had broken cried out in pain. Pieces fell to their feet, still jiggling.

Harper beamed. "Yes! Did you see that?"

The auerdax wobbled and morphed, bones crunching as it reshaped itself, growing a new arm.

Harper's smile dropped. "Oh shit."

"Get out of here!" Cherry yelled, catching up to them.

The rest of the shadyrs arrived too, a crowd of ghostly shapes flanking them, and the fight began in earnest.

The auerdax lashed out again, and Everly ducked the new bony arm. Harper hoisted her axe over her shoulder, and Everly grabbed onto her. She hauled Harper along with her, making a beeline for the van.

"We need more light!" an unfamiliar voice called out. "It's too strong when it's this solid!"

An answering reply got lost on a brisk wind that rolled off the mountains and buffeted past Everly's ears.

They need more light.

If they could get to the van, they could turn on the headlights and point them at the auerdax. She and Harper couldn't really do much to help fight the monster, but they could do that.

They reached the van, and Harper threw open the driver's side door and clambered into the cab.

Everly leapt into the passenger seat. "Turn it on! We need to light up the parking lot!"

Harper dropped her axe into the seat well and stabbed the keys into the ignition.

The van rumbled to life. Harper jammed it into reverse, spinning around to light up the battle.

Something large slammed into them, rocking the camper almost off its wheels. There was a *bang* as one of the tires blew, and the side window cracked like broken ice.

The auerdax had landed on the driver's side. With the headlights so nearby, it was faint and ghostly, but still strong enough to shake the whole vehicle. Slippery, barely there, it oozed slowly right through the driver's door of the van. Harper shrieked and slid across the front bench toward Everly's side.

"Teeth and starssss. Mussst ... dessstroy!"

It wants me.

If she ran, she could keep Harper safe. It was a risk, for her, and for Rylan, but the auerdax was a claw's reach from Harper.

Throwing open the door, Everly leapt out of the van.

"Everly!" Lian cried. "What are you doing?"

Everly ignored her and raced past the group of shadyrs surrounding the van and the eidolghast. She headed for the opposite end of the lot, praying that the monster would take her bait and get the hell away from Harper. Then she'd do whatever she needed to do to keep herself safe.

Shouts filled the air, and a scuffle broke out behind

her. Everly whirled around to see the creature had turned away from the van to her direction, fighting through the shadyrs blocking its path.

Lian took a blow from one of the monster's semi-solid, bony arms. Her wiry body hit the ground. She sprawled out on the concrete with her sword thrown out of reach. Everly's breath caught, but Lian was already getting back to her feet.

Tammy kicked the sword back to her and Cherry helped to extract Harper from the van.

Lucas leapt, landing on the auerdax's bulbous top. It didn't seem substantial enough for him to stand on, but his own partially-intangible shadyr form was designed just for that, somehow on the same wavelength. Lucas tore into the beast with his bare, ghostly hands, flinging handfuls of bone and gooey flesh away into the surrounding darkness.

Another Darkfrey shadyr and Callan joined him, clinging to the monster and tearing it apart.

The auerdax gurgled and grated its bones, moving straight into the beam of the headlights.

Then it was gone, and the three shadyrs fell to the hard ground.

No, where is it?

A second later it reappeared on the other side of the light, rushing straight toward Everly. The shadyrs cried out, trying to surround it, hold it back, but as it moved out of the light it seemed to grow stronger.

And it only had eyes for Everly.

Light, we need more light, she thought, glancing around at her surroundings.

The best opportunity for the shadyrs to destroy the thing was to have it in a semi-solid state. Too bright, and the being disappeared entirely. Too dark, and it outmatched them for strength. A medium level of light was the Goldilocks zone, the one the shadyrs' ghost forms could fight it in.

At this end of the parking lot, there had been a streetlight, but Everly glanced up at the backdrop of swaying trees to find it was dark and useless now. A trail of white smoke still seeped from it and glass glittered on the ground below.

The auerdax charged, railroading every last shadyr in its path to reach her.

There was only one source of light left for Everly to use.

Her shock at the auerdax's presence and disturbing appearance had overridden all her other senses. But as her anxiety grew, her dragon began to awaken, too. She felt it stirring inside her, felt the light pressing against her skin and bones, stretching her until her body felt detached from her own mind.

Her dragon was made of brilliant, blinding light. It should be enough. Or maybe she could take out the monster entirely.

She set the dragon free.

Pale blue light burst from her like a waterfall of exploding sparks. Her feet left the ground and she soared into the air as the motel parking lot lit up, bright as day. The dragon roared inside her, and hunger swept through her like a sickening tide.

Everly fought to surface from the light's sudden takeover, determined to keep it at bay. She refused to be just a passenger, unable to control her own body, much less anything the dragon did. If she let the dragon have that level of control, it would do whatever it wanted.

Including consuming her friends.

Everly's gaze swept the parking lot for the monster and found nothing. Shadyrs, wispy and ghost-like, moved around her, but the auerdax was ... gone.

Horror grew in the pit of her stomach. She was giving off *too much* light.

"Find the monster!" Everly pleaded with the dragon. "Eat the monster!"

The dragon purred at the idea of a meal, and hunger rumbled through Everly's body. But on the heels of the hunger, a new sensation—confusion. The dragon couldn't see or sense the auerdax either.

Dammit!

They were safe from the auerdax as long as she kept

the area lit, but she didn't know how long she could keep the others safe from *her*. The dragon surged against her attempts to control it, bellowing its frustration.

It was hungry now, and it had been promised a meal. If it couldn't find the ghast, it wanted something else instead. Or someone.

"Back down!" Everly bit out through her teeth, shoving with all her might against the dragon. It was a battle of wills, and the dragon was strong enough to win if she dropped her guard for even a second.

Then, finally, the dragon relented, withdrawing into her. Instead of letting her down gently, it dropped her like a kid throwing an unwanted toy. She crashed back onto the parking lot, her knees buckling beneath her, landing across the asphalt in an inelegant sprawl.

"Ow," she groaned, shoving up to her elbows.

She'd taken the force of the fall on her knees and right hip, and all three throbbed in agony.

Someone yelled, and she glanced up to see the auerdax—visible again in the dark—across on the far side of the lot. The Darkfrey girl who had evacuated the couple knelt on the ground below it, bleeding from a gash in the side of her neck.

Everly couldn't guess the ghast's intentions, whether it had fled there from her light, or had pounced on the chance to take out a shadyr isolated from the rest of the group, but the girl had clearly been caught unawares. The other Darkfrey were all too far away.

The auerdax whipped a violent tendril of bones, spear-like talons shooting at the girl's back.

Callan appeared, flying through the air in a spin. He grabbed the arm across his chest and brought it into the turn of his body, wrenching it free from the ghast's shoulder. It howled and turned from the girl to him, the skulls swiveling in unison.

Callan dropped the dismembered limb, scattering the bones across the ground. They smoked and melted under his feet. Everly could make out the shadows of the motel straight through his semi-translucent form, and his skin was luminous. Pale. With his battle face on, he looked so much like Rylan.

He put himself between the auerdax and the girl, and yelled across at Everly. "Take Harper and go! Find light and stay there!"

Tammy appeared at his side, lifting the injured girl and scurrying with her to take cover in the van's headlights.

Everly launched to her feet, limping as she regained her footing. She fought past the bruised ache in her limbs.

Harper stood at the back of the van, watching wide-eyed as the shadyrs descended on the eidolghast once more. She clutched her axe in front of her, looking ready to run back into battle.

Everly didn't slow. She linked her arm through Harper's and yanked her away from the camper, into the night. Behind them, the shadyrs swarmed the creature, like ants on a carcass.

Lian stood before the auerdax, her hand on her sheathed sword and a grimace on her face. She couldn't risk swinging at the monster with the other shadyrs attacking it. She yelled at the Darkfrey to get clear, but they ignored her.

Everly and Harper bolted down the drive from the hotel, around the corner onto the main road, leaving the skirmish behind.

There was a streetlight on the corner not far ahead. A quaint, black iron lantern-styled light that beckoned them like a sanctuary.

Everly's bruised knees ached and her footsteps landed unevenly. Anxiety tangled like a knot in her throat, and the dragon's hunger was all-consuming.

She focused on just her next breath, her next step, surviving the next ten seconds of pain. But she didn't breathe easier until they left the darkness and reached the comforting glow of the streetlamp. The cries of battle reached them dimly through the trees.

They leaned against the ornate lamp post, catching their breath.

"Are ... you ... okay?" Harper huffed out between breaths.

"A few bruises, you?" Everly panted.

She put her back against the pole, using it for balance. Her knees and hip trembled. Shooting waves of pain left her nauseated.

"I'm only hurting for my poor van. My baby was mint condition." Harper smiled wryly, but her voice shook.

Everly eyed their small circle of light on the ground. The brightest part seemed to barely cover their bodies where they huddled in the center. It dropped off quickly around the edges.

"Hey, listen. The auerdax, it wants me. Or rather, the beast of teeth and stars. If it comes after us again—"

"What? No! Don't even suggest what I think you're getting at," Harper snapped.

"I just—"

"No! I don't want you to martyr yourself for me. You think I'd be happy living with myself after that? Hot take, but I feel like that wouldn't be fun. If it does come back, you can use your light powers to glow this place up and we'll *both* be fine."

"I told you, it's not safe for you."

"I trust you," Harper said.

Maybe you shouldn't.

Harper lifted a finger and tilted her head. "You think they're okay back there?"

Everly paused, listening. Things had gone silent.

"Is it over?" Harper whispered.

With a crash and crackle of bones, the silence broke apart around them.

The auerdax charged through the trees, toward their small sanctuary of light.

Chapter Twenty-Four

"Just stay in the light. It can't touch us in the light," Everly said, as much to herself as to Harper.

Harper hoisted her axe, ready to swing. "Yeah, and we can't touch it either."

The auerdax barreled toward them, shadyrs trailing in the distance. It moved *fast*, its body of bones and fleshy ooze somehow as fleeting as shadows.

Everly latched onto Harper's wrist, worried her friend was about to charge forward and play chicken with an eidolghast. "What time is it? We just have to make it to sunrise."

Harper rested her axe on her shoulder and pulled her phone from her pocket.

With a groan she said, "Three a.m. Look at that thing!

It's already grown back everything the shadyrs have done to it."

The ground shook as the auerdax reached them, halting beyond the sphere of bright, clear light that came from the streetlamp. With a growl like scraping gravel, it lashed at them. Everly winced, but as its whip-like arm moved into the light, it vanished. Claws that could have shredded them to bits harmlessly passed right through.

Everly gasped. It couldn't touch them. The shadyrs were on their way, if they could just hold out—

In an explosive crash, shards of glass and rocks rained down over them.

Harper shrieked and darkness fell like a cloak.

No, how did it do that?

"Run for the next light!" Everly screamed, fear for her friend stronger than any fear she had for herself.

She launched into the shadows, following Harper's silhouette for the next sphere of light about twenty feet away. The ground shook. The auerdax was right behind them. Halfway along, Everly veered, away from the light and her friend. Harper's hand shot out, latching onto her arm, her sharp nails digging in, dragging her into the glow.

"Don't do that!" Harper growled. "We stay together."

"It's too fast, we can't keep outrunning it!" Everly panted, wincing at the pain in her legs.

A glance back confirmed they'd only made it because

the first of the ghostly shadyrs had caught up. The auerdax shook them off as if they were nothing more than annoying fleas and barreled toward the two women.

"Desssstroyyyy ..."

It swiped a boney arm along the ground then flung a hailstorm of gravel at them. Everly shielded her face from the pelting stones, and the lamp above them shattered.

Not again. Her whole body ached as she pushed it to keep going.

By some miracle they reached the next streetlight, only to have it shattered before they could catch a single breath. The monster cackled inhumanly, relishing how it whittled away their protections.

They ran again, Harper's hand still tight around Everly's arm. Ahead, there was only one more streetlight at this intersection, then a huge gap of darkness before the light of the town.

Everly's anxiety peaked. When the auerdax took out that last light, they'd have nowhere else to go.

They couldn't make the next gap. Her fear mounted until she couldn't breathe, couldn't see. Her hands began to shake, and the trembling moved into her arms, her legs, her body.

Still she ran for the final light.

Harper's fingers detached roughly from where they held hers, followed by a thump, and a scream.

Everly stopped running, staring back with pure, abject terror.

"No!"

The auerdax had Harper's leg wrapped in one whip-like arm, reeling her in. Harper twisted and turned, trying to get a hit in with her axe, kicking with her free foot.

Everly released a feral growl. The only way to save Harper was to let the dragon loose. But as soon as she did, the auerdax would vanish, leaving Harper as the only edible soul within striking distance.

A ghostly figure broke ahead of the rushing shadyrs, sprinting at breakneck speed.

It was Lian. "Let your light out, Everly. Do it!"

She did.

The dragon roared happily as it was given free rein once again. Its hunger had grown exponentially, and it took every inch of Everly's will to keep the light from reaching for Harper.

Gorhanmere lit up as if a new day had dawned. The light washed over the auerdax, and it vanished from sight, turned completely incorporeal by the illumination. Harper stilled on the ground, set free from the dragging grasp of the auerdax. She quickly rolled over, scrambling away.

"Hold it steady!" Lian called as she bound toward the place where the auerdax had vanished, then leapt high. Mid-air, she unsheathed her sword, and struck.

A screeching cry pierced the night.

Lian hung there above the ground, gripping the handle of the sword which seemed to float, stuck into nothing.

With a victorious grunt, she yanked her sword free, landing on her feet, only to slice the sword again in a wide arc in front of her. Again it made contact, the momentum of her strike lost as the blade passed through the invisible monster. It gurgled and hissed.

"I've almost got it!" Lian yelled. The other shadyrs reached the boundary of Everly's light, hanging back, unable to strike the incorporeal auerdax.

Everly was losing her tenuous hold on the dragon. The light hungered, cataloguing every living soul around her, trying to decide which it most wanted to eat.

Every time, it went back to Harper, who crawled toward her as though she were safety.

"Not going to happen!" Everly snapped.

She couldn't last any longer. With a battle cry, she jammed the light back down inside her, ignoring the dragon's irritated squeals, ignoring the debilitating hunger that clung to her, the ringing agony in her head. Each breath raked across her throat, painful and insufficient.

I'm. In. Control! She crumbled onto her hands and knees, gritting her teeth for one final shove.

The light finally relinquished, slithering back inside of her.

All illumination winked out, and the auerdax reappeared.

Broken and oozing from its wounds, it raced off into the trees.

Lian sheathed her sword, blinked, and watched it go, looking almost as though she were ready to make chase.

Harper offered Everly both hands and helped her to her feet.

"I knew you could do it. When are you going to stop doubting yourself?" Despite the encouraging words, Harper's expression was icy.

Everly sighed. Hunger sat like a brick in her stomach, so strong her whole body shook. She could feel the dragon's fury at how she'd shoved it back into its cage.

The Howell and Darkfrey teams circled up around the two girls. It was strange to see ghosts panting, doubled over while catching their breath. In a cascade of shadows and sparks, one after another swirled with shadyr transformation magic, returning to their human forms.

"You going to go after it?" Callan asked Lucas.

"Ghast no." He laughed, then switched quickly to a frown as he took in his team.

The girl with the gash in her neck had kept fighting, but looked woozy, skin pale against her jet-black hair. She'd lost a lot of blood, if the amount on her clothes were any indication. Lian had a cut and bruise blooming across her temple, and Callan had sustained several scratches on his arms and chest, shredding his pajama shirt. He didn't have his armor on underneath.

The Darkfrey team were in a similar state, clothing ruined and lacking the protection of their armor. The auerdax's ambush caught them all unawares.

Only Tammy and Cherry seemed to have made it out mostly unscathed.

Lucas shook his head. "I told Master Darkfrey this was at least a two-brace job. We were lucky you guys were around."

The Darkfrey girl put a hand gingerly to her neck, wincing. "Very lucky. Thanks. Pretty sure you saved my life."

Callan shrugged bashfully. His battle face was gone and suddenly he was back to his gawky self again.

"Happy to. Anytime. I mean, not that I want another chance to."

She chuckled, watching him as she tucked her hair behind her ear. Everly shot a glance at Tammy, but she was looking the other way, scowling.

When Everly turned back, Lucas was staring straight at her. "Having someone around who's a walking daylight source came in handy too. What's the deal with that?"

Everly wrapped her arms around her middle, swallowing away her hunger. "Still trying to work that out."

"And our business, either way," Lian added, eyes narrowed.

"No problem. Not like we haven't seen weirder in this line of work." Lucas gestured to his team. "Come on. Let's get back and patch up."

With groans and sighs, both teams turned around to trudge back toward the motel.

Everly stumbled, and Harper looped her arm around her waist, taking some of her weight, but didn't look at her. Callan and Lian took position in front of her, with Tammy and Cherry at the rear.

The injured girl and two other Darkfreys took the lead, but Lucas hung back to walk with the Howells.

He elbowed Callan softly. "Hey, I really do appreciate your help tonight. Molly only just joined our brace, and it would have been terrible to lose her, especially so soon after Adrian."

Callan said, "I thought she seemed fresh. I'm sorry."

Lucas's shoulders dropped. "You know how it is."

Everly frowned. How often was it that Darkfreys didn't make it home from a mission?

Luca lowered his voice. "You're here looking for the stolen artifacts, aren't you?"

Callan exchanged glances with his mother. "Why would you think that?"

Lucas smirked. "Your poor deception skills, for starters.

Look, going after them has crossed my mind a few times when we've been on missions up here, but orders are to keep our distance from the Gorhanmere lot. But I've got no such orders not to help you out. I was thinking, if I point you in the right direction, you could get what you want and maybe we can get something out of it too? Split the booty?"

"If that did sound like something we'd agree on, what direction would you point us?" Callan asked.

Lucas slapped him on the shoulder. "There's a ruined mansion out off the old mountain pass. Mostly falling apart, abandoned, but something's up. We've seen the Gorhanmere shadyrs going in and out. Haven't been able to get close enough ourselves to check it out, but I'd bet it's worth a look."

"Thanks, man."

"No, thank you. Again." The two shook hands before Lucas picked up speed to join his team.

Callan seemed to trust Lucas, but Everly wasn't so sure she could trust any of the Darkfreys. Still, they had somewhere to start looking tomorrow for the Bane of Teeth and Stars.

Everly clung to Harper on the journey back to the motel, thankful she'd been able to control the dragon long enough to keep her best friend safe. But would she always be able to? Every time she let the light take over, her hunger grew, and she knew there would come a point when the dragon demanded its meal and wouldn't take *no* for an answer.

She had to be careful. Not use the light anymore. At least, not until they could find answers and she could understand more about how to control it. On the bright side, Lian had definitely wounded the auerdax, so hopefully the beast would limp off into the woods and die.

Back at the motel, the lights burned radiantly, power restored. All except the streetlamp at the end of the lot, which had been destroyed rather than just tripped in the fuse box.

Everly knew the auerdax was smart, able to work out how to destroy the streetlights, but being smart enough to trip the fuses was something else.

She cast her eyes over the motel frontage and spotted a large metal box hanging on the wall near the office. It was partially in shadow, around the corner, but seemed too brightly lit still for the auerdax to have gotten to it.

Everly frowned, her body still rattling with nerves and hunger. The golden glow of the porch lights and the illumination behind the gauzy white curtains in their rooms sent relief rushing through her.

She never wanted to be in the dark again.

The Howell team walked into Lian and Tammy's room together, then stopped short.

Their belongings were strewn all over the floor, clothes torn, and furniture smashed.

Up behind their beds, there was writing on the wall, in thick, dripping letters that looked an awful lot like blood spelling out *LEAVE OR ELSE*.

"Someone's been in here," Callan grunted.

"Really? You don't think that wrote itself?" Cherry said.

"I mean, okay, obviously."

Tammy squeaked, holding out her blackened hands. Shadyr magic swirled around her, the black smoke uneven and thin, juddering strangely.

She was shifting, parts of her skin turning smooth and hard like in her vasmire form, while her legs grew ghostly and insubstantial. Fur sprouted on her face, and her claws grew and curved. Patches of skin were covered in scales. Behind Callan, a similar reaction was taking place for Cherry.

"Something's wrong," Tammy said, her voice coming out thick and muffled by long vasmire teeth.

Concern knit Lian's brow together, and she held out an arm, indicating for the rest of them to stay back. With one hand resting on the hilt of her sword, she stalked forward to investigate the blood.

She sniffed at the wall, her nostrils flaring. "It's eidolghast blood. But it's ..."

"A mixture," Callan finished, his gaze locked on Tammy. "It's a mixture from a bunch of different monsters."

Lian nodded. She slid a finger over the letters. The blood spread beneath the pad of her fingertip, and her form shifted seamlessly. First, ghostly auerdax, then stone cold, fanged vasmire, then dark fur sprouting and bones popping as she grew into the larger weroth form.

"Where did they get it all?"

She returned to human form. Plucking a tissue to wipe her hand clean, she continued to stare thoughtfully at the message.

Everly considered the words too. "Someone really wants us gone."

"Unless this is from the woman at reception reminding us about check out time, I'm guessing it's from our friends in the woods who are too friendly with their razors," Harper said.

It wasn't just the words that scared Everly, but the possibility that the Gorhanmere shadyrs had also tripped the fuses. They would have known about the auerdax, known how light affects it. They could have purposefully stripped them of their protection.

"I can't sleep like this," Tammy griped. "I have no control over the change. I look like a monster."

"You can have my bed," Harper said, still avoiding eye contact with Everly. "I can handle being in here."

Everly wanted to talk to Harper, apologize, explain what she was trying to do, how she was trying to keep her friends safe in the only way she knew how. But Harper had her back turned, already moving to remake the ripped off sheets of her new bed.

Tammy stared at Everly as though waiting for her approval too.

Everly worried at her lip but nodded her agreement. Regardless of bedding arrangements, something told her that none of them would be getting back to sleep, knowing the horrors lurking around them.

Chapter Twenty-Five

Everly rubbed gritty eyes as she crouched between Lian and Callan, hidden inside the tree line. Before them loomed a hulking mansion—the place that may hold her answers, or a whole heap of scary shadyr cultists.

Harper, Tammy, and Cherry remained a few steps behind them as they watched for signs of movement.

Everly felt every inch of her sleepless night. She wished she'd said "yes" to the third cup of coffee Cherry had offered her from the pot that morning. But the motel coffee had tasted like sludge and choking down the first two servings had been a chore. Considering she wasn't particularly picky about her caffeine to start with, that was saying something.

The mansion before them had been abandoned a long time ago and left to go to seed. It was three stories tall, cross-timbered like the rest of the village, and missing at least half the glass in its windows.

Two wings, tangled in ivy, angled off from the main building. The leaves blew in the wind, swirling and moving as though the vines grew before Everly's eyes. Four chimneys stuck up from the aged, moss-covered shingles, and the front door stood wide open—a gaping, screaming mouth.

"Maybe Lucas has sent us on a wild ghast chase," Callan said, glancing at his mother. "This place is clearly uninhabited."

Harper scoffed, her gaze flicking about the trees surrounding them. "Did you see those crazies yesterday? They didn't have the presence of people concerned with health and safety."

"They're exactly the kind of people I'd expect to hole up in a place like this," Cherry agreed.

Everly swallowed hard against nausea. She'd been trying to ignore the strange feeling welling up inside her from the moment they'd left the campervan back on the old dirt road. They'd walked half an hour to get there, and with every step, a sick sensation rose inside her.

"Something's there," she said, her voice cracking. "I don't know what. But I can sense it."

Callan caught her gaze, and Everly winced, touching her solar plexus where the nausea sat like a stone in her gut, right next to the hunger that remained from the night before.

Lian sucked at her teeth for a moment, then lay her fingertips on the hilt of her sheathed sword. "All right. We have to check it out. Keep an eye out for tripwires, surveillance, anything that screams we're walking into a trap."

"And hope no one is home," Harper added with a chuckle.

She'd regained some of her usual bravado, but a haunted vulnerability filled her eyes that hadn't been there before.

Everly hadn't seen that expression since Bryce had torn her world to shreds. Her hand rested on her axe head at her hip. She'd fashioned a sort of holster for it so it could hang on her belt. Everly had wanted to talk to her that morning, but she had refused any help when changing the blown tire on the van.

Everly still worried about her but had to admit she'd gotten a pretty good hit in against the auerdax the night before. It shouldn't have surprised Everly that Harper would excel at monster hunting just as she did every other aspect of her life. She just wished it wasn't a part of her life at all.

Callan took the lead beside his mother, with Harper and Everly behind them. Tammy and Cherry took up the rear. They entered the house through the open door, moving slowly and silently.

Everly noted the front door hanging off its hinges, never closed, and the severe water damage just inside the threshold that caused. She hissed a warning and steered their crew away from the worst of the rot with a hand on Callan's shoulder. Falling through decayed floorboards would be a great way to announce their presence if anyone were around.

The foyer opened on a grand staircase that had become a cascade of ferns and vines. At the top, a raven sat, pecking at something. It didn't startle or caw at their entrance, but stared at them with glassy blue eyes.

A huge hole in the domed ceiling overhead likely dumped buckets of rain on the steps every time a storm rolled through, which meant going upstairs wasn't a safe option. A glass and crystal chandelier had shattered on the wooden floors, and weeds grew around the glittering pieces.

Harper let out a long, low sigh. "This would have been beautiful in its day."

"Let me guess, you'd love to do a photoshoot here," Everly whispered back with a grin.

Harper returned a small smile, but didn't reply.

Callan peeked into a dusky doorway to the right, then called back in a hushed voice, "Clear. Living room. It's empty. Not even any furniture. Just a fireplace."

Tammy, who had crossed to the opposite archway, answered, "Clear. Dining room. With a table that could easily seat twenty freaking people. Like anyone has that many friends."

Callan turned a circle, his gaze sweeping over the broken railings and the obvious dips in the floorboards where water had pooled for decades. "Should we split up? Search the rest of this floor?"

"No." Everly shook her head and pressed her hand tighter to her belly.

The ground had a heartbeat. One that thrummed through the soles of her feet.

"It's below us. Whatever I'm feeling, it's below us."

Lian nodded, her gray bun swinging. "A place like this probably has a basement. Let's check the kitchen for stairs."

They moved in single file through the darkened dining room. Splintered chairs lay in cross-hatched piles in the corners. Tammy had been right; the massive mahogany table was a little worse for the wear, but in its heyday had been capable of seating more than twenty guests.

Everly could almost sense their specters hanging around, a dinner party of the dead. The memories of every person who had once lived within these walls.

Shadows flittered in the darkest parts of the room. A gilt-framed painting of a man on horseback seemed to move. The horse's nostrils flared. Blood dripped from the man's eyes. Everly blinked and it returned to normal.

"You guys see that?" Everly asked, hoping she wasn't

going crazy.

"Yeah," Callan said. "There's some weird stuff going on here."

"A beshadowing?" Harper asked.

"That would be my guess. But I can't sense an eidolghast nearby." Lian turned her eyes to Everly.

Because I'm sensing something.

Down another short hall, filled with dust motes and cobwebs that seemed to reach out like tiny hands in the dark, they found the kitchen. It hadn't fared much better over the years.

All the appliances were still in place—a stove, fridge, dishwasher, fancy coffee machine, all relatively new. The place hadn't been abandoned too long, despite the accelerated takeover by nature. The tile floors were cracked and moldy beneath timber cabinet doors that hung crooked on their hinges.

Out of nowhere, the faucet gurgled and coughed out black ooze. Tammy jolted and flickered out of reality for a moment before stabilizing herself again.

"You're getting better at stopping yourself dissappearing," Callan noted with an affirming nod.

"Also getting better at not shoving my fist in the face of people who patronize me," she muttered.

"Over here." Cherry stood in the corner of the room. He'd opened one doorway through to an empty walk-in pantry, and then next to it a second door with stairs leading down into darkness.

Everly flashed the LED light on her phone down the stairs. "Looks sturdy enough. Looks ... *new*, actually. There's no way these cheap pine planks are original."

Lian leaned past her. "Seems like good evidence this place isn't as empty as we thought. Careful now."

They descended into the dark bowels of the house with Everly's phone light leading the way. At the bottom of the staircase, a small, dank cellar stretched around them, bare of anything but a few empty, wooden workbenches and an ancient water heater in the corner.

The floor seemed to have been carved from one solid piece of smooth, pale limestone, and moisture dripped down the paneled walls. In places where water ran in larger rivulets, it almost seemed as though stalactites were forming, but Everly knew that couldn't be possible. They took millennia to grow.

"Nothing," Callan remarked, his sparkly shadyr eyes taking in the room despite the darkness. "A bunch of black mold, though. We shouldn't stick around here long."

"No ..." Everly let the word trail off as she picked her way across dusty, debris-strewn floors.

She circled the staircase, following the nagging feeling that something was nearby. It was like the closer they got, the farther away she wanted to be. She fought the sensation. In the corner beneath the stairs, the wall panel sat crookedly, less than an inch out of line.

Moving closer, the distinct tickle of cold, moving air flowed through the crack, and her nausea spiked.

She wrapped her fingers around the warped edge of the wood and tugged. It scraped loudly over the stone floor, and she cringed at the way it screamed through the quiet house.

On the other side, a natural, rocky tunnel curved away into the darkness.

"Whoa," Callan said softly as the rest of the team gathered around them to peer inside.

Harper squealed. "Yes! I get to do a secret passage after all!"

The shadyrs all exchanged worried glances.

"I'm not sure we should be going down there," Callan said.

Harper pouted. "Of all the crazy adventures you guys go on, you don't want to go into a cave?"

Callan shook his head. "Caves are bad, bad news. Shroudhaven is full of interconnected, subterranean caverns."

"Which we affectionately call the underdark," Tammy added.

"And they are filled with eidolghasts and shroudpools. Shadyrs lost that battle centuries ago. We just let the underdark be enemy territory and avoid it at all costs."

Everly squinted down the long tunnel, wishing she had the night vision of a shadyr. She felt so close to finding something, even if it was something the light inside her seemed to despise. Maybe that was a good thing.

She couldn't turn back now. "There's no proof that this tunnel connects all the way back to Shroudhaven though, is there?"

Callan shrugged.

"And are you sensing any eidolghasts nearby yet?"

Lian wrinkled her forehead and closed her eyes for a moment. "There's something ... You're right that there's something nearby. But no, not eidolghast. Not exactly."

The others shook their heads too.

"Then I'm going in."

"If you're going in, we're going too," Harper snapped.

Callan glanced from her to Tammy. "Maybe you should—"

The glare Tammy returned was so intense his words seemed to dry up.

Harper unholstered her axe. "Let's move."

Callan took the lead, ducking his tall, lanky form through the small door and into the cave beyond. Everly followed, praying that this would be worth it.

Whatever she sensed ahead, it was powerful. It had to be the stolen artifacts. Even if the Bane of Teeth and

Stars didn't do anything, maybe one of the other ancient shadyr items would. There had to be a solution there to what she was, how to save Rylan, how to keep the dragon under control.

She glanced back at Harper who was right behind her. She knew Harper could take care of herself. She'd never known anyone more capable than her friend. But Everly was still filled with fear that something terrible would happen to her and it would be her fault.

They moved by the light of Everly's phone, keeping it pointed low. Only she and Harper seemed to need it, the shadyrs moving confidently in the darkness. Fog drifted around their feet, and the walls clung close, pale limestone shiny with perspiration.

The tunnel twisted left, then right on a steep decline, as if they were moving toward the bowels of the earth. If the house had seemed eerily quiet, the cave was a riot of sound. Dripping water and the rushing of the wind barreling through stalagmites and stalactites made for a symphony of noise that even covered up the scuff of their footsteps.

Which was likely the reason they snuck up on a Gorhanmere shadyr without being noticed.

The man rested on a flat-topped stalagmite, staring forward into the darkness.

No—into the *light*. There was a deep, pulsing red light ahead, and the moment Everly's gaze locked onto that light, nausea rolled through her and she gagged.

Harper stepped forward, making a series of hand signals that Everly still didn't understand. Callan raised his eyebrows, and nodded, looking impressed.

The man was huge, with thick, corded muscles beneath his dirty overalls. He carried an automatic rifle on a strap around his shoulder and a vicious knife buckled to his muddy boot. In the red glow, crescent shaped scars over his arms and shaved head gave him an odd, zebra-striped pattern.

Harper silently handed her axe to Callan. He rushed forward on silent feet and cracked the butt of the handle into the back of the guy's neck.

He grunted, pitching forward. Then with a low growl he straightened himself up and turned on them. His eyes were bloodshot and wild.

"Shit," Callan muttered, before taking a swiping blow across the chest.

He was knocked backwards so fast he cartwheeled over himself and crashed into a veil of limestone. The axe clattered out of his grasp.

Lian sprinted across the space with surprising speed. Before the Gorhanmere man could get his hands on his rifle, Lian unsheathed her sword and cut through the air gracefully, severing the nylon strap and sending the gun catapulting across the ground. Lian sheathed her sword and dodged a punch.

Callan leapt back to his feet, joined by Tammy and Cherry as he rushed back into the fray.

"They aren't changing," Harper said, her eyes narrowed. "Come on, this is an even human V human fight for once."

Everly reached a hand out for balance, buckling at the waist and dry retching. "Can't."

Harper hesitated, looking back at Everly with concern.

"Except, not actually sure this guy's human!" Cherry yelled across to them.

The four shadyrs grappled with the huge man as he swung his tree-trunk arms at them. Callan and Lian grabbed for his meaty fists, trying to keep them pinned.

Tammy scrambled up the man's back, like scaling a mountain, and wrapped her blackened arms around his neck, squeezing tight. The man's breath gargled and his face turned red, but still he raged at them.

"Use your light!" Harper insisted, motioning to their friends. "That guy is like a grizzly on steroids had a lovechild with a pro-wrestler. He's wiping the floor with them!"

"I can't," Everly said, shaking her head a little too long and hard.

Between the nausea from whatever strangeness lay ahead, and the dragon's hunger consuming her thoughts, unleashing the light in this state would be a bad idea.

On top of worrying about the dragon consuming any

one of her friends in this cave, she worried about Rylan's essence being consumed, too. As though every time she refused the dragon a meal it grew hungrier, and it was starting to turn that hunger inwards, to the lifeforce trapped in Everly's dreams.

Too many unknowns and not enough answers stayed her hand. She knew the Howell team could defeat the Gorhanmere goon. He was just a man, wasn't he?

She hoped.

The battle was short but brutal. Tammy remained latched around the man's neck while the others did their best to keep his hands off her. Finally, he went down onto one knee, then the other, then face first onto the ground.

Lian checked the man's pulse and nodded. "He's out. I thought we were going to have to kill him for a moment there. Best we don't, though. There's clearly some kind of beshadowing here, so these guys aren't themselves."

Cherry brushed his fingers beneath his nose, and they came away as red as his hair. "How many of these guys do we think there are hiding out down here?"

Tammy shook her head, her normal scowl shaken off her pale face. "It took four of us and way too long to bring him down."

Twisted in unconscious slumber, the man's face wasn't familiar to Everly. "He's not one of the five who welcomed us last night."

"At least that many then, so we just need—" Cherry pretended to count on his fingers. "Twenty of us."

"And even if we're not trying to kill them, I don't think they are going to return the favor," Tammy groaned.

Harper bent to collect her axe. "That guy didn't go down quietly. If there were any more nearby, they'd be on us by now."

Callan nodded. "We've come this far. There's a light coming from just ahead. We check there, then get out."

Everly swallowed the sickness in her throat and followed on wobbly legs as Callan led the way.

"You okay?" Harper moved close beside her.

Concern seemed to have overridden any iciness or grudge she'd been holding from the night before.

"I feel like the dragon is trying to vomit itself out of me to escape this place. It's pushing so hard. I'm worried I can't control it."

"If this feels wrong, we should go. Something that is hurting you shouldn't be the answer. We can find another way."

"No. I'm fine. I can do this."

Harper just frowned in response.

The tunnel ended around the bend, opening to a large cave with soaring ceilings. Unlike the limestone tunnels that had led them to this point, the cavern was absolutely covered in giant crystals.

Bone white and glass-clear pillars stuck out all around the walls and ceiling like jagged teeth, as if the cave were the mouth of the giant beast about to swallow them whole.

The cave billowed with fog and pulsed with that strange red light, ebbing and flowing like waves between the crystal shore. The cold breeze Everly had been sensing since they found the hidden door grew stronger. The prickling on her skin that raised goosebumps head to toe told her the beshadowing came from something in this cave.

Lian's eyes gleamed in the pulsing red light. "That's it. The Bane."

Everly's heart leapt. She followed Lian's gaze toward the center of the cavern, to the source of the glow.

A black triangle stuck out of the moving clouds.

Everly forced herself toward it, each step a battle.

The fog parted, revealing a pillar, jutting out from a dark, sludgy pool.

Liquid covered the crystal podium, and the black object was wedged into the top. The triangle turned out to be a diamond-shaped item as large as a head. Made of intricate filigree black metal, it oozed red liquid continuously through the gaps in its rune-like curlicue designs.

The edges of the diamond weapon looked razor-sharp.

It was the source of her sickness. Bile rose in the back of her throat, and she stumbled away from the Bane, retching.

Harper was at her side in a heartbeat, pulling her hair

back even though nothing came up. Everly had skipped breakfast, and her coffee had long since moved through her system. She dry-heaved, dimly conscious of the Howell team gathering around the Bane.

Finally, when the heaving stopped, Everly leaned heavily against Harper, and they turned to survey the quietly chatting shadyrs.

Tammy and Cherry had both moved away from the bloody Bane in a state of semi-transformation, like what had occurred in Lian's motel room the night before.

"That damn thing is bleeding the same weird mixture of ghast blood," Cherry snarled.

The red light strobed on his face, highlighting his high cheekbones and casting the shadows of his shifting face into harsh relief.

Callan glanced down at the fog, obscuring the sludgy pool Everly had seen beneath. "Explains the beshadowing. There's so much blood."

Tammy explored the far corner of the room. "Woah. Apocalypse central over here. Road flares, canned goods, bottled water, ammunition, extra guns. It's like my crazy Uncle Teddy's doomsday bunker."

To the other side, a massive stalagmite had been sawed off, forming it into an altar-like surface stained with dry, dark splotches.

Lian moved around it, shaking her head. "More blood

here too. But it's different. Just weroth and vasmire. What dark business are they up to?"

"Business you should have kept out of!"

The new voice startled Everly so bad she jumped, and Harper tightened her arm around her waist to make sure she stayed on her feet.

"We warned you. What happens now is your own fault." It was the wild-eyed forest man.

The older, more scarred leader of the little pack that had approached them when they arrived in Gorhanmere.

He was alone, but Everly had a feeling his minions were right behind him. The way Lian caressed her sword's handle, she must have figured the same.

She spoke firmly. "We're taking the Bane, and the other stolen artifacts. You are beshadowed. If we take this away, you'll be cured."

"Cured? We are strong!" The man cackled breathily, lifting his bulging arms out to his sides and raising his hands into the air. "You arrogant Darkfreys, thinking we need help."

Lian opened her mouth as though to argue their misclassification, but the man's voice boomed over her.

"Can you not see? We have all the strength we need to cut the darkness from this land. Eidolghasts fall at our feet." He flung a hand toward the altar. "We bring a new sacrifice even now."

Everly's heart pounded as a monstrous wail echoed down the tunnel.

Tammy gasped, her hands flying up before her. Shadyr magic swirled as her body shifted into a ghostly, translucent form.

She whispered, "The auerdax."

The scarred man smiled. "It comes."

Chapter Twenty-Six

For a moment, nobody moved.

Then the Gorhanmere leader cackled like a wicked witch—high-pitched and maniacal— as he was consumed in black mist, shifting into a ghostly form.

A roar shook the crystal pillars and sent debris sifting from the ceiling. The Howell team backed up closer to each other. Tammy, Cherry, Lian, and Callan all shifted.

The auerdax burst into the cavern, rushing through so fast it slammed into the wall. Crystal shards exploded from beneath its giant, misshapen body of bones.

On its heels charged five shadyrs. They had stripped back their overalls to the waist and were painted in blood. From the wide range of strange forms they took, Everly guessed it was the blood that had spilled from the Bane.

Their twisted bodies were part vampire, part ghost, part werewolf, and part other things Everly couldn't even identify. They taunted loud cries as they clawed and lashed at the eidolghast, driving it farther into the cavern.

No ... They herded that thing here?

The man had mentioned sacrifices, but Lian had only sensed weroth and vasmire blood on the stone altar. If auerdaxes were rare, maybe they'd never killed one before. Maybe they were in for a much bigger fight than even they were prepared for.

The skulls in the ghast's chest swiveled wildly. It ground to a halt, surrounded by shadyrs on both sides, Howells at the front, Gorhanmere behind. With a shout that was part raven's caw, part thunder, it whipped out a tentacle of bones, knocking down two of the five shadyrs that had chased after it into the cave.

The red light that pulsed from the Bane didn't appear to affect the auerdax's tangibility. It was rock solid and deadly in the dim glow.

The cult leader cackled again, as though delighted by everything before him. "New blood is tainted. Old blood is pure."

The knocked down shadyrs returned quickly to their feet.

Their words echoed in harmony through the cave. "Our family is strong."

Two of them launched themselves onto the auerdax. The other four made straight for the Howells.

"Come on," Harper cried, tugging at Everly's jacket.

Everly stumbled, still nauseated and wobbly on the uneven cave floor which was obscured by the swirls of fog.

Something smashed behind them. Dozens of pieces of crystal shard rained down, hurtling toward Harper and Everly. Everly threw her arms around her best friend, turning them both away as pieces ricocheted off her back.

Edges sliced across Everly's neck, causing hot blood to well up on her skin. She hissed and put a hand to the scratches, though they were more annoying than painful. The two of them ducked behind a thick row of stalagmites.

A roar filled the cave, then the auerdax's shifty, shadowy voice whispered, "Star-teeth beast ... You are here ... Show yourself and die."

Harper straightened, brushing the glittering slivers off her clothes as she turned wide eyes on Everly. "You okay?"

Everly swallowed, glad she was the only person who spoke eidolghast. "Not great."

"That Bane thing is really doing a number on you. You need to keep safe. You're in no state to join in."

"We need light."

Harper pulled out her cell phone, but Everly shook her head. "That's not enough. Tammy said there were road flares in the stash in the corner. Come on."

The two girls ducked behind a giant pillar of crystal. Everly peered around the edge to survey the battle taking place and plan a safe route around the auerdax.

Tammy was in hand-to-hand combat with one of the cult women, mostly just doing her best to dodge her wild attacks. Three monstrous men had backed Callan and Cherry into a corner.

They fought hard to bring the cultists down, but still seemed to be pulling their punches.

The Gorhanmere shadyrs were still people, and all the eidolghast blood in the cave and on their bodies had likely made them crazy. If the Bane were taken away, they had a chance to heal and return to normal. Killing them wasn't the answer.

Unfortunately, they weren't giving the Howell team the same treatment.

One of them caught Cherry with a blow to the chin. It knocked him upwards and back, tossing him onto a cluster of painfully sharp looking crystals.

Lian, standing beneath the auerdax with her hand on her sword's hilt, grunted and ran back to help Callan. With a precise strike, she slashed her sword across the ankles of two of the Gorhanmere shadyrs, toppling them to the floor.

Everly winced. *Ouch. Survivable, but ouch.*

The cult leader and another woman clung to the auerdax, pulling at its limbs, dragging it toward the altar.

The auerdax whipped at them, shaking them off and throwing them away, only to have them pounce back on again.

With everyone's attention occupied, Everly motioned for Harper to follow her. She fell into a stooped sprint, darting from pillar to pillar, keeping her gaze locked on the eidolghast.

She wasn't certain where Tammy had found the Gorhanmere prepper stash, but she remembered her general location. Once there, she scanned the forest of small, jagged crystal pillars until she found what she was looking for: several wooden crates full of supplies. The two women began flipping off lids.

"Got them. Road flares," Harper explained, passing a red tube over to Everly.

Everly stared down at the flare. "Do you know how these work?"

Harper grabbed one for herself and popped the cap off, then twisted the striking pad open. She held it up beside the end of the flare. "Just like a match."

She struck them together, and the flare sizzled to life. Bright light bloomed from the flaming tip, sending red sparks spilling from the tube.

Everly half-smiled. "Of course you know."

Harper held her flare up with a grin. "Best thing is the auerdax can't break this like it did the globes last night."

"No, but these won't last long, will they?"

"So we have to hope the others slay the monster before our lights run out." Harper unholstered her axe again, peeking over the top of their cover. "And also deal with the army of crazy strong cultists. Easy peasy."

"Hey!" Lian circled and dodged around the feet of the auerdax, hand on her sheathed sword, trying to find an opening to strike. "Throw some of those flares over here! I can't get a hit in on this thing when it's at full strength."

Everly and Harper dug into the chest of supplies and found four more flares. One by one, they struck them to life and tossed them out into the melee. Each one made the auerdax a little more ghostly, putting him on the same plane as Lian and the rest of the shadyrs.

But it also drew the ghast's attention. Every skull in its bulbous chest turned toward the source of the glowing projectiles, toward Everly.

"Dessstroy."

Callan still tangled with one man and Tammy was busy with her opponent. Their scarred bodies were nothing but muscle, and they fought like they hadn't even lost their breath. Cherry still hadn't returned to the fight, and Everly worried, unable to see where he was.

The auerdax tried to move toward Everly, but it was held back by the two shadyrs clinging to its torso, and Lian taking neat slices at its legs.

Lian kept her feet planted, head cocked for every sound, as she turned and struck with her ancient sword. One of her blind attacks caught the lead cultist in the arm, dropping him off the beast. He rolled out of sight into the shadowy, red fog.

The auerdax growled in a way that made the crystals shimmer and sing like wine glasses. It grasped at the shadyr woman on his back again, but instead of throwing her, it gripped her in its boney tendril and slammed her straight up into the cavern ceiling.

With a sickening crunch, a stalactite impaled straight through her chest. She hung there, pinned like a fly, twitching and dripping blood.

Everly gagged and retched, tears hanging in her eyes. The shadyr numbers were dropping fast, and still the Gorhanmere group were turning against them instead of the monster.

The auerdax prowled toward Everly, out of the range of Lian's blade. Lian sheathed her sword, blinking as her sight was restored. She took in the situation—and stared upwards in horror.

Then the flare that glowed at Everly's feet began to sputter and dim.

"That's not ideal," Harper groaned.

They both watched in horror as their flare died.

Everly glanced out at the fight. "We have less than a

minute before the other four are going to go out, and we'll all be back in the dark with the auerdax."

"Ev," Harper said, her expression serious. "You're going to have to use the dragon."

"No," Everly snapped. "Bad idea. I'm not at a hundred percent, and it's already feral with hunger. I can't guarantee I could control it at all at this point."

Harper pointed at the auerdax. "I *can* guarantee that this is about to kill us if you don't."

In the center of the cavern, Tammy let out a pained yelp, and both girls whipped around to see her fall to the ground, out cold.

The Gorhanmere leader had joined the woman sparring with Tammy. He stood over the girl with an evil, victorious grin on his face.

The woman joined him in her gleeful expression and lifted a taloned claw, ready to deliver a killing blow against their downed friend.

The flares sputtered out.

There was no time left. No options left.

"Harper? Run," Everly commanded, and she let the dragon loose.

White light exploded from her body, and she shot off the floor into the air as the dragon took its form around her. Tendrils of blinding light unfurled and guided her forward, quicker than she expected, as if the dragon had just been waiting for her to free it.

One glowing thread shot toward Harper before Everly even sensed the dragon's intentions, but Harper was already on the move and darting behind a pillar. The tendril slammed into the column of translucent crystal and shattered it.

Everly opened her eyes wide and struggled to gain control of the beast inside her.

I'm in control! she roared in her mind.

The dragon didn't respond. Hunger washed over her in debilitating waves. Everly had refused its desires for too long, her body was too weakened by exhaustion and sickness. The dragon's influence was all-consuming, and it wouldn't be denied any longer. It *would* take what it wanted.

Terror shot through Everly as a coil of light whipped out toward Harper again. Harper lunged away and sprinted across the cavern, right into the battle, axe grasped in both hands.

Everly clenched her hands into fists and tried to get a grip on the dragon's consciousness, but it moved without her. She dangled uselessly, merely a puppet in its luminous grasp.

Everly's light suffused the cavern, filtering through the crystals to form an even, low glow. The auerdax had faded into a see-through ghost of itself.

Lian blocked its path, lunging and striking left and

right as it tried to dodge past her. Shattered bones and tar-like ichor spread across the floor as it backed away from Lian's deadly assault.

The Gorhanmere shadyrs stood in awe of the dragon's imposing presence. Cherry was back on his feet, a little wobbly but alive. He took the opportunity to strike, taking out Callan's opponent with a large chunk of crystal that thunked against the side of the man's shaved head. Callan turned to take on the remaining woman.

They were hurting, exhausted—the dragon sensed it like he was scenting a weakness. Its hunger had reached an uncontrollable point. Tendrils danced on the air in anticipation.

The leader of the Gorhanmere shadyrs had been distracted by Everly's light, but his attention whipped around to Harper, fleeing across the cavern to stay away from the dragon's grasp.

He rushed to intercept her.

No!

The dragon shot into motion, spurred on by the sudden rush of fear and adrenaline through Everly's body. They barreled across the cavern, Everly's only thought to reach Harper before the Gorhanmere shadyr did.

But when Harper saw the dragon's light coming toward her, she darted away again, right into the murderous man's arms.

He howled with that eerie, maniacal laughter and grasped each side of her head in his monstrous hands. Harper screamed silently as he lifted her off her feet, trying to crush her skull.

Tears streamed down her compressed face. She shifted her grip on her axe and swung. The man dropped her, dodging the sharp metal. She landed hard. He reached out, snatching the axe out of her hands and lifting it over his head, ready to bring it down.

Get him, Everly told the dragon. *You can have him!*

She let the hunger fill her every cell until she was blinded by bloodlust, and directed every part of it toward that man.

The dragon roared with glee at being let off its metaphysical leash.

The tendrils of light latched onto the man and fed.

CHAPTER TWENTY-SEVEN

The axe fell from the man's fingers.

His eyes bulged and his mouth gaped wide with horror. His body shook and shifted, his shadyr form changing through a range of shapes before reverting to a normal human. Thin tentacles of brilliant light wrapped tightly around the shadyr, like a jellyfish trapping its prey, until he vanished behind the illumination.

Harper scuttled away from the man and the dragon's coruscating attack.

The bile rising in Everly's throat no longer had anything to do with the Bane. She hated this part. Hated the strange sense of chewing and biting, even though nothing of the sort *physically* took place. She could sense the way the dragon consumed the shadyr's life force like a monster chomping on a victim.

Like the vasmire at Rooks Hotel eating that poor man in the bathrobe.

And she had sanctioned it. She had chosen this shadyr to die.

It had to be someone, she tried to justify to herself. *It was him or Harper.*

But it still left her insides twisted with guilt.

Within moments, it was over. The tendrils retracted, dropping the man. His body slumped to the floor and collapsed, still and pale with lifeless, staring eyes.

A loud, earth-shaking scream vibrated through the cavern. Everly jerked her gaze away from the dead shadyr. Lian was poised atop the auerdax, her sword hilt-deep in its center.

With a battle cry, she wrenched downwards, splitting the monster down the middle. It staggered and oozed ichor as it tried to reform, failing to reconnect its halves. Its pieces crumbled to the floor. Whatever life had animated it was gone, leaving nothing but unmoving bones and shadows.

Lian sheathed her sword, breathing hard. She looked over the dead eidolghast with hard, glittering eyes. Callan and Cherry chased off their final foe, high fived, and bent at the waist to catch their breath. Beside them, Tammy stirred.

They'd survived. They'd *won*.

But still the dragon wanted more. Before Everly had

even realized it, the tendrils had reached for another of the Gorhanmere shadyrs who was crawling across the floor with his cut hamstrings. An easy target.

No, no more!

It was too late. Everly was overwhelmed with a sickening feeling of *fullness*.

She focused all her willpower onto taking control, as the dragon turned again to take another victim. It shot toward Harper, who remained on the ground, clutching her head.

With a feral growl, Everly snatched at the light, putting a mental shield between it and her friend. *Enough! Leave her alone.*

Irritation poured off the dragon, and it returned her growl. The light coming off it surged, brightening the cave blindingly. She couldn't control it.

Bile rose again, and Everly's eyes widened. *It hates the Bane.*

Everly grunted, summoning just enough strength to force herself closer to where the diamond-shaped artifact was pierced into its crystal plinth. Nausea surged through her and the light dimmed. She latched onto the stubborn beast, dragging its tendrils back toward her body. The dragon hissed and kicked.

You've eaten! Everly yanked harder. *You're done!*

The light burned hot around her, manifesting its fury.

She clenched her teeth and closed her eyes, pushing it back where it belonged.

Or rather, where it resided against her will.

Her body absorbed the light with an audible pop, and the cavern went dark.

Prepared for the drop this time, she fell to the floor on her feet in a crouch. Every muscle and joint ached. The cave had dimmed once more, but the red pulsing flash of the Bane made her eyes burn.

Across the space, Lian helped Tammy to her feet, and Callan and Cherry fussed over Harper.

"I'm fine. I'm fine!" Harper pushed their assistance away with a grunt, standing up by herself.

Everly got up with a groan, shuffling to join them. She kept her eyes turned away from the woman impaled on the cave ceiling, the two men dead and drained on the ground. Three lives, lost. Two by her hand.

Lian caught her looking away from the dead bodies. "The other three scampered off, if that's who you're looking for. It's over."

Only me and the auerdax, the two monsters, killed people today.

In the dark cavern, lit only by the red light, the eidolghast had reverted to its corporeal state. The giant pile of bones looked a lot less deadly when it was silent and unmoving. But no less creepy.

"Do we leave it here?" Callan said, as Everly limped over to join the circle of her companions.

Lian nodded. "I think so. This cavern is far enough away from people to cause no harm in the time it takes to rot."

"Ev!" Harper shoved away from Cherry's supportive grip and threw her arms around Everly's shoulders. "I knew you could do it. I knew you could control it. You're a freaking glowing goddess."

Everly whispered into her friend's hair. "But I ... it killed them."

Harper pulled back and gave Everly a knowing look. She knew what Everly's light had done to those men. How it consumed their lifeforces.

Everly wished she could take it back, that she'd never explained how it felt like she *ate* things. But from the proud smile Harper gave her, she wasn't even entirely sure her friend believed her. To her, and the others, she was just their bright super weapon. A good thing.

But Everly felt as far from good as possible.

"You did what you had to," Harper said firmly. "You saved us."

"You still got hurt."

A bruise blossomed around Harper's left eye, and there was a split in her eyebrow above a trail of dried blood down the side of her face.

Harper grinned and probed the skin next to the cut with a grimace. "It'll make for a cool story. I was thinking—mauled by a goose in the park. My followers would love that. I can work with my graphic designer and launch some naughty goose merch."

There had been real fear in Harper last night when they'd been running from the auerdax. And again today when Everly's light had attempted to grab her. But there she was, laughing and making plans for her next publicity stunt while blood still dripped down her cheekbone.

"You shouldn't have even been here," Everly said hotly. "We should have made you stay back at the motel."

Harper's green eyes grew fierce. "I beg your pardon? 'Made me stay'? I'm not a toddler you can just boss around. I chose to come here."

"And look what that got you." Everly motioned to the cut on her face. "That's probably going to scar. How's that going to look in pictures?"

"Wow. Would you chill?" Harper rolled her eyes. "First of all, makeup companies make incredible concealers nowadays. I'll probably land a deal *because* I have a scar they want to prove their product can cover."

"But—"

"*Secondly,*" she pointed at the others, who awkwardly watched their argument, "both Tammy and Cherry got hurt, too. Should they have been left back at the motel?"

Cherry raised his hand. "I believe I win the prize for getting knocked out of the fight first. We were all getting our asses kicked."

Harper gave a sharp nod. "I had things under control. I'm not some fragile princess, and I thought of all people you'd know that by now."

Everly's emotions swirled, every thought a raw nerve. "It's not that I don't think you're capable, but you're only human—"

"You think I don't wish I was all special and magical like everyone else here? I have to work with what I've got, and I *know* I can do it. But thank you sooo much for making me feel like not enough."

Lian stepped between them and spoke up before Everly could respond. "Sorry to interrupt, but we should get what we came for and get out of here before any of our cultist friends return."

Callan cleared his throat. "And I'd like to touch base with Lucas and let him know what happened before rumors start flying."

"Of course," Harper said, backing away to rejoin Cherry.

She brushed her fingers down the fresh trail of blood on her face and turned away from Everly.

"Right then. Would you like to help me release the Bane?" Lian asked.

"If it's okay with you, I'd like to stay far, far away from that thing for now. It makes me ill." Everly stared at her feet, fighting against hot tears.

Lian crooked a finger at Callan, pulling the rolled parchment from inside her jacket with her other hand. Once the parchment was spread across Callan's arms, she climbed up onto a natural nodule in the crystal pillar, wrapped her hands in the hem of her t-shirt, and then reached for the artifact.

It made a sharp metallic scrape as it pulled free from its resting place. Then she placed it on the blood-stained parchment across Callan's hands.

The moment it touched the parchment, the continual oozing of blood ceased, and as Callan wrapped the parchment closed, Everly's nausea ebbed to a more manageable level.

"And that's why we needed the parchment," Lian said. "It's the only thing that stops it bleeding."

The nearness of the Bane no longer affected Everly as it had, muted by its wrapping. Lian climbed down, wiped off her hands, and then made a disgusted face at the eidolghast blood on her shirt.

"Take a look around," she said to the group. "See if you can find any other artifacts. Ghast knows what will happen if they're left in the hands of these beshadowed shadyrs."

Though the group searched the supply trunks and

every dark corner of the cave and ruined mansion, they found nothing else of note. Wherever the other shadyr artifacts were, they weren't in the cave, which meant the Gorhanmere shadyrs would have them for a while longer.

And as Lian had said, there was no way of knowing just what kind of damage they could do.

When Harper pulled the van into the lot at the motel, the door to Lucas's room popped open. He stood in the frame, watching the Howell team disembark. As though he'd been waiting for them.

Everly shivered as she hopped out of the campervan. The afternoon had turned cold and breezy, and a light misting rain fell from a charcoal sky.

There was something sinister about Gorhanmere that sent chills up her spine. She'd be glad to see it in the rearview mirror. All they had to do was pack and go, but the way Lucas eyed them left her worrying that wasn't going to go smoothly.

The Darkfrey shadyr approached, his hands shoved into the pockets of his cargo pants like he was just out for a stroll. His blue gaze cast over their general sense of dishevelment and injuries, then landed on the blood-stained parchment bundle clutched in Lian's hands.

"Seems like you found what you were looking for," Lucas remarked, catching Callan's eye. "But you know that's Darkfrey property, right?"

"Finders, keepers," Cherry jeered, and Lian shushed him with a glare.

Callan squared up against Lucas. "It *was* Darkfrey property, before Mordan allowed it to be stolen by someone else. Now it's ours, because we fought for it, risked our lives, and won it."

"We had a deal, that you'd hand over what you found."

Callan scoffed. "The deal was we'd take what we needed and share the rest. There was nothing else. Go look for yourself if you want."

"Really? Maybe we will go and check. But still ..." Lucas folded his arms and raised his voice. "We really can't let you leave here with that."

The rest of his brace filtered out of the motel room and took up stances behind him. Everly wasn't sure if they meant to look so menacing, or if that was their standard appearance, but it set her heart racing.

She had no misconceptions that she could take a Darkfrey shadyr in a fight.

Not without using the dragon, which was something she wanted to avoid again for a long, long time.

Callan leaned around Lucas and smiled. "Hey, Molly.

How's your neck?"

Everly recognized the girl who'd almost died the night before. She looked fresh-faced today with only a small, raw scratch where the ghast had almost slit her throat.

Molly tucked her hair behind her ear. "Oh, um. Great. All healed up. Thanks again."

"Wonderful." Callan cut his gaze back to Lucas and his smile fell away. "It's so lucky you're alive, Molly."

"Touche," Lucas murmured, a sly grin turning up one corner of his lips. "I get the point. We owe you. Fine, keep your ill-gotten goods. But you know I'll have to report it to the estate."

Lian scoffed and brushed past him on her way to the rooms.

She tossed her final thoughts over her shoulder. "I can handle Mordan. You go ahead and tell him we did something he *couldn't*. I'll celebrate that victory. Also, the auerdax is dead. You're welcome."

Lucas raised an eyebrow at her retreating back, then looked at Callan. "Your mom's kind of a badass."

"I only recently figured that out myself," Callan replied wryly. "If you want the auerdax body for a safe cleanup, you'll find it in the cellar of that abandoned mansion. Little triangular door under the staircase leads to a cave."

"Will we find more than just a dead eidolghast body?"

Callan shrugged. "Maybe. Maybe not."

Lucas sighed. "I should make you do the cleanup."

"That's one of the advantages of not being team Darkfrey anymore. You can't make me do anything." Callan's grin widened. "It was good to see you, Lucas. Keep in touch."

"You know I won't." Lucas saluted him, then turned around and ushered his minions back toward their room.

Everly took a few steps forward to stand at Callan's side.

Under her breath, she asked, "Is Mordan going to be a problem? Once he knows we got the Bane?"

Callan's gaze turned troubled as Lucas's door closed behind him. "I don't know. But I'd venture to say we're going to find out."

Chapter Twenty-Eight

Everly sat in the passenger seat, all too aware of the Bane's closeness. Even though it was at the back of the van with the others, the sick, dark energy it spilled that made her want to roll down the window and puke.

The Howell team passed the artifact between them, examining it, trying to form any understanding or meaning from the runes and shapes etched into its sides. The only thing they knew for sure was that it made Everly sick.

They'd chosen to stop and see Crowea on the way back to Howell House. They'd been able to shower and get into clean clothes back at the motel, and they were all in need of a solid meal. Dinner at Crow's was a unanimous vote, and Lian wanted to touch base with the old witch and see if she knew anything about the Bane.

The street outside Crow's Nest was quiet for a weekend night, which was probably explained by the heavy, driving rain that soaked through Shroudhaven. The storm had started not long after they left Gorhanmere, and their trip home had been fraught with slippery close calls on the mountain descent.

Harper pulled the campervan up across two parking meters, clearly unconcerned about tickets at that point. She'd barely spoken to Everly since their fight in the cave.

They'd have to talk eventually, but Everly had little hope of trying to fix their friendship when she couldn't even fix herself.

Everly slid from the passenger seat and shoved her hands into the pockets of her jacket, walking quickly away from the van before the others.

She didn't want to be anywhere near the Bane.

She squinted against the downpour and jogged toward the lit door to The Crow's Nest. The door opened on a wave of sage-scented heat mixed with the smell of fried foods. They were early enough for Crowea's nightly dinner special, and it smelled divine.

Crowea sat at the bar with a paperback in one hand and a coffee mug in the other. She glanced up when Everly stepped inside, shaking her silvery hair free of raindrops.

"Blown in on the storm, I see," Crowea drawled, setting down her mug.

Everly gave her a wan smile. "You could say that."

Crowea placed her book face down on the bar. Her lone eye traced the edges of Everly's face with a concerned look.

"Oh no, what's wrong, baby? You need to chat about it?"

About how her only hope to discover the source of her powers was a dark, bleeding weapon that made her sick to her stomach?

Or how her relationship with her best friend was falling apart because of this horrible, dangerous town? Or how she'd taken lives that day, *chose* them and allowed them to be taken? Everly swallowed hard, tears sitting along her lower eyelid.

She was saved from having to respond when the door whipped open behind her, and the rest of her friends piled into the bar, carrying the scent of wind and rain with them.

Lian greeted Crowea with a hug. "Dinner special all around, please. Got some tired and hungry shadyrs here."

Crowea smiled, crinkling her eye. "Sure thing. Go on and sit. I'll get the kitchen started on your order and make sure they pile the plates up good."

Lian hovered a moment longer. "Think you could come sit with us for a bit?"

Crowea nodded, her good eye flicking toward Everly again. "I'll do what I can."

Joining the others, exhaustion washed over Everly as

she sank into a comfy armchair and let her limbs melt into the cushions.

Even though they'd only been in Gorhanmere for a day, so much had happened that she felt like she'd run a marathon. For the first time in forever, she was actually looking forward to returning to Boderleth Antiques.

While everyone else chatted in a somewhat subdued manner, Everly closed her eyes and drifted in a place between sleep and wakefulness, wishing she could let herself dream.

Wishing she could dream of Rylan.

But her over-stimulated mind only served her visions of the Gorhanmere leader's face contorted in dread as he died. And other strange flashes of the Bane. Like distant memories, too hazy and ancient to view clearly. Just sensations of closeness, of cutting, of falling apart.

"Hey," Callan murmured, nudging her shoulder. "Food's here."

Everly blinked open her eyes. Not only was there now a pitcher and several full glasses on the table, but a meal waited for her, as well. There was a pile of crinkle cut fries on her plate, and a golden-brown stuffed pastry.

When she bit into it, the buttery crust flaked away, and the concoction of veggies and spices exploded inside her mouth.

Hints of curry, thyme, and dill, and some kind of

yogurt sauce. But Everly's stomach churned, too close to the Bane, still feeling too *full*, to enjoy the food.

Crowea was settled in a chair beside Lian with her coffee mug, now steaming with fresh brew. Her expression was stern as Lian muttered to her between mouthfuls of chips.

"All right. Let me see it then," she said.

Lian reached down near her feet and her hand returned with the Bane, still wrapped in its thick, blood-stained parchment. Crowea made no action to take the bundle from her.

She sucked in a breath and put her mug aside. "I can already feel magic."

Lian nodded. "It was with the Darkfreys for a long time. It's called the Bane of Teeth and Stars."

"Isn't that lovely and ominous," Crowea murmured.

"It's almost the same name a vasmire called Everly," Lian added. "The beast of teeth and stars."

"Speaking with eidolghasts now?"

Everly shrunk into her armchair. "I can understand them, sometimes."

Lian's voice became strained. "The similar name is why we thought it would give us some clue about her. But we can't work anything out about it ourselves. We were hoping—"

"That this old witch would place hands on a thing obviously corrupt and dangerous in order to answer some questions for you?" Crowea's eye was wide and her lips pursed.

Everly should have known this would come to nothing. Crowea had also refused to use her psychometry on her.

Does that mean I'm something corrupt and dangerous, too?

She didn't want to believe it, still hoped there was some other answer, but everything kept pointing that way.

Lian's voice trembled. "This could be what wakes up my son. What saves him. Please."

Crowea lifted her face to the ceiling, and her gaze flickered lightly over Everly. "Very well. I'll see what I can see. But I do not like this."

Eating around the table ceased, and everyone watched as Crowea peeled off her elbow length gloves and reached for the parchment.

She paused, her fingers hovering over the weapon as she gave Lian a pointed look. "Safe to touch?"

"We've all handled it. Just avoid the sharp edges."

Crowea pinched the edge of the flimsy parchment and unwrapped the Bane as carefully as if she were unswaddling a baby. She inhaled sharply.

"My, my, my." Crowea tugged aside the second flap of the Bane's stained wrapping, her one good eye raking over the weapon beneath a narrowed brow. "Powerful. Deadly."

Everly gagged at the sight and presence of the Bane.

She tossed the remnants of her veggie pocket onto her plate and curled back in her chair.

"What can you tell us about it?" Lian asked.

Crowea took two deep breaths, letting them out slowly and deliberately. She closed her one eye, then she placed her fingertips on the black metal, well away from the sharp edges of the diamond's sides.

Her eyeball could be seen flickering and rolling beneath its eyelid, and from her other eye, dark liquid started oozing from around the edges of the eidolghast tooth. She sucked in a breath, snatching her fingers away from the Bane. Her one eye fluttered open, bloodshot and dilated, zeroing in on Everly.

"You." Crowea returned her gaze to the Bane, her fingertips bouncing lightly in the air above the artifact. "Oh, this thing knows you, baby. Intimately."

Everly opened her mouth to ask more, but it had dried up entirely.

"So they are connected?" Lian urged.

"It remembers ..." Crowea muttered, closing her eye once more. "That *thing* ... The thing inside the Boderleth girl is only a piece. It's not whole."

She tilted her head, wincing painfully, and her wild gray curls shivered. "So, so many destroyed ... It was this weapon that broke that *thing* into pieces."

Everly wrapped her arms around herself, trying to hold

off a chill that had formed deep in her chest.

"But what is it, Crow? What is in Everly?" Lian urged.

Crowea's eye shot open. Her pupil narrowed and focused on Everly.

Don't say it. Don't say it. Please don't say that I'm a monster.

"Soul eater," Crowea whispered.

Every eye at the table turned on Everly then, staring with a mix of pity, awe, horror. Everly's head shook, wanting to deny it. But what could she deny?

Into the absolute silence that fell after Crowea's declaration, Callan asked, "Is that some kind of eidolghast?"

Lian shook her head. "Not one I've ever heard of. Though there is always the chance a new one has ventured through a shroudpool to wreak havoc on the world without us knowing about it. Can you tell us anything else, Crow?"

Crowea shook her head. Her skin had paled, and she stood up, shaky on her feet.

She slipped her gloves back on. "No, I can't. That's all I've got. That is all I'm willing to bear."

Lian placed her hand on Crowea's covered hand and squeezed with a kind smile. "Thank you."

Crowea left them to their meal, and Lian wrapped the Bane back up. While everyone else brainstormed what this could possibly have meant, Everly stared blankly at the bundled weapon, too upset to finish her food. The one theory that kept returning and coming back around was that Everly was possessed.

Possessed by a "piece" of an eidolghast that ate souls.

And just like that, her absolute worst nightmares were confirmed.

By the time they left the bar, the rain had slowed to an annoying trickle—enough to wet eyelashes, but not enough to justify an umbrella. Everly and Harper walked out of the pub last. Harper tapped away at her phone even though Everly doubted she had any service.

It was just an excuse to ignore Everly.

The rest of the team climbed into the camper, still talking about the artifact and Everly's supposed secret identity.

Everly grabbed Harper's arm and tugged her around. "Hey. Talk to me. I know you're mad."

"Oh, I'm not mad." Harper hit the button to turn off her screen. The ambient glow cut off, leaving them in the dark. "I'm upset. There's a distinct difference."

"Why don't you explain it to me then?"

"You really don't get it? You can't see how it would be upsetting that my best friend thinks I'm so useless that she has to act like a damned *martyr* to save me?" Her tone was harsher than anything she'd ever used with Everly before, and it stung no different than if she'd slapped her.

"And you know what? It does suck that I don't have all the glowy swishy powers the rest of you have, but that doesn't mean I'm worthless. But everything you've been doing is making me feel that way. You're shutting me out, lying to me, leaving me behind. I had to bust you with your freaking pet zombie before you'd even open up to me a little!"

"You think it was easy for me to tell you that stuff? That I like being this *thing*?"

"Of course not! But it's the difficult things we should be telling each other, otherwise how are we supposed to survive this? But any time the issue has to do with this place, all the supernatural woo woo, you ice me out and remind me that we're not staying, like you have every say in the matter." Harper waved her arms wildly as if to encompass the whole town.

"Because it's not safe here. There's no reason for you to still be here."

"No reason? How about being here for my best friend?" Harper jabbed a shiny-nailed finger toward Everly's chest.

"What happens when Rylan wakes up? Are you coming home with me, or are you going to ship me off alone, get rid of the useless human? I don't know what weird entity has latched on to you, but in case you need a reminder, you're human, too, Ev." Harper's voice had risen during her tirade, echoing through the rainy street.

"Beg pardon. I don't mean to intrude." Cardboard Box Barry appeared beside them.

He wore his usual uniform of holey jeans and heavy metal t-shirt, but he'd covered his arms with a stained, khaki jacket. His long white beard dangled in a smooth, freshly woven braid down his chest.

Everly stared at him, astonished. She couldn't remember a time he'd ever approached her or any group of people she'd ever been with. She'd never even heard his voice before, which didn't match his appearance at all. Smooth, cultured, and a deep bass tone.

Barry glanced at the camper, where the shadyrs were watching the exchange through the windows. Then he sized up Everly, before his gaze slipped away to settle on Harper.

"Are you all right, little lady?" he asked gently.

Harper huffed. "I'm just *fine* apart from being called little lady."

Barry shifted back and forth on his feet a couple of times, his gaze marking the shadyrs and Everly. "I just thought, maybe you need to get away from this lot?"

"No. No, these are my friends ..." Her expression softened. "I'm fine. Really. Thanks."

Barry shrugged. "Suit yourself."

Everly watched him disappear back into a nearby alley, stunned by the exchange.

Harper pointed after him and whispered, "Did he just try to save me from you?"

Everly shook her head. "No idea. That was so weird."

Harper grunted a frustrated squeal. "Why does everybody think I need saving?"

Everly snorted a laugh, and Harper joined her, shaking her head. For a moment, it was just the two of them again. No anger. No frustration.

Then Harper sighed and looked up into the drizzling rain. Her smile fell away, and she put her hands on her hips. "What do you have to say? I talked to you. Now talk back."

"I'm sorry," Everly said without hesitation. "I don't think you're useless. You're on the entire other end of the spectrum from useless. But you don't *have* to add monster hunter to your resume. You don't have to excel at every single thing in this world."

Harper laughed again, but there was no humor in it. "If you think that then maybe you don't know me at all."

"I just ..." *I want to keep you safe.*

Everly exhaled and looked over at the van, thinking of Lian, her husband, what had happened to the Howell brothers.

Even the best fighters in the world cannot shield themselves entirely from tragedy. "And I just realized I'm doing to you exactly what Rylan did to me. Shoving me out of his life to keep me safe. That's not fair."

"You're right. It's not. Because we're a team," Harper reminded her.

"We are. A damn good one."

Harper stepped forward and hugged her. "So don't do it again, okay? Promise?"

"Promise." Everly squeezed her back.

As they released one another, she was struck by an idea. "Hey, I'd like you to be the one who looks after the Bane. We need to keep it from ending up back with the Darkfreys, and I know you can do that."

"Seriously?"

"Seriously. Considering what it is, how its connected to me, there's no one I'd trust more to keep it safe." Everly glanced at the van, then lowered her voice. "But there is something I want to try before you put it away."

Chapter Twenty-Nine

The back porch globe couldn't dispel the gloom behind Boderleth Antiques. The small, square yard pressed in on the ambient light like it was nothing more than a candle flame in the void of space. Shadows turned the overgrown weeds and the ancient swing set to monsters, and to Everly that felt too soon. Too raw. Monsters *were* real, and they were everywhere.

Even inside her.

"Is he here?" Harper asked quietly, her voice stealing through Everly's dark thoughts.

Everly nodded, motioning to the darkness beneath the broken swings. Zozo's reflective eyes blinked at her, then glanced warily at Harper.

"Are you sure about this?" Harper's knuckles had

turned white on the parchment-wrapped Bane.

Misty rain clung to her long, dark eyelashes. True to form, though, her mascara wasn't running at all.

She clutched the artifact to her puffy pink jacket, her face pale. "This thing is dangerous. Look what it did to those crazy people in Gorhanmere."

"That was the eidolghast blood. Not the Bane." Although the blood did come *from* the Bane. Everly frowned. "I think."

"Always fun to play with ancient, cursed artifacts we don't understand," Harper said, laughing nervously.

Lian had handed the Bane over to them in a gesture of trust that left Everly teary. It had been scrubbed and disinfected, and they worked out that as long as one part of the Bane was in contact with the parchment, it didn't bleed. So that was one more thing they knew about it.

As Harper slowly unwrapped it again there in the backyard, Everly gagged.

Harper blanched, folding the parchment closed again. "How is this supposed to work?"

"I get sick when I'm close to the Bane, but I think it's the dragon ... the soul eater"— the name was bitter on her tongue—"that's reacting to it. I don't understand the thing inside me, but I can sense how it feels."

The dragon roiled within her.

"It wants to *consume*, and the Bane makes it want to

vomit. I think I ... *it* somehow partially consumed Rylan and Zozo. And it doesn't want to let them go. I want to try and release Zozo first because he's only partially trapped inside me. It might be easier to get him out."

"So what? You think the Bane will help you vomit them out?"

"Maybe?" Everly tugged up her hood against the rain. "Or maybe it will help me get enough control over the dragon to set them free. I know it's a long shot, but I have to try. Rylan can't stay inside me forever."

Harper flashed a sly grin. "Oh, I bet he'd want to try."

Everly groaned and punched her lightly in the arm. "Inappropriate."

Harper adjusted her grip on the Bane. "Right then. Do we just hold the Bane near you while you toss your cookies and hope for the best?"

Everly winced. "I think it needs to be more than that. We know the Bane can hurt the soul eater, that it can, and has, even broken it apart. To get it to lose enough control, I think we need to hurt the dragon."

"Hurt the dragon. Like ... we use it to hurt *you*?" Harper shook her head. "Nope, we've reached bad idea territory now and I'm not keen to trespass."

"You can either help me, or I'll do it myself."

Harper's gaze grew fierce. "I don't like either of those options. You're being a wannabe martyr again."

Everly rubbed the rain off her face and sighed. "Please. This has gone on long enough. Zozo and Rylan both deserve freedom. I want to do this for them, and I want you by my side while I try."

For a long moment, the two women faced off on the backyard path. The rain continued to mist down, coating everything in a glossy sheen. The porch light gleamed off the sprinkling rain like there were thousands of tiny diamonds falling to the pavement. Beyond the creaky wooden fence at the back of the property, the trees shifted and swayed in a whispered lullaby.

Harper groaned. "Fine. What kind of friend would I be if I let you experiment with a dangerous weapon from the Everdark alone?"

Everly put her hands on Harper's arms, squeezing them through the puffy pink fabric. "Thank you."

Turning away, she rolled up her sleeves then knelt on the concrete. "Come here, Zozo. Come see me. Don't mind my friend, Harper. She won't hurt you."

Although, she was driving the van when it hit him. Luckily, he didn't know that.

Zozo came out from under the swing set timidly, his eerie blue eyes bouncing between the two of them. He nudged Everly's hand with his nose and let her pet the top of his head. A strong purr rumbled inside him, though it stopped when Harper kneeled next to them.

"It's okay," Everly soothed the skittish animal.

"What now?" Harper whispered.

Everly kept one hand on Zozo then offered her other arm to Harper. "Cut me."

Harper made a slashing, stabbing gesture in the air above the bare forearm. "Just like ... do it?"

"Did you want to say a few words first?"

"Should I say grace or give your eulogy? 'Cause we have a wide range of potential risks here."

"Sorry. I'm nervous, too. But I have to know if this will work. Can we just get it over with?"

Harper sucked in a breath and unwrapped the Bane without releasing it entirely from the parchment. Her hand shook as she brought the sharp edge of the artifact over to Everly's arm.

Everly swallowed down the urge to vomit and braced herself for the slice. She had a high tolerance for pain, mostly, but there was something psychological about knowing what was about to happen that made it hurt much, much more than when it was an accident.

"I'm sorry," Harper whispered.

The Bane's sharp edge bit into Everly's forearm, and fire licked up her skin.

Light flared, though the dragon itself didn't manifest. Sickness overwhelmed her. Then Everly felt a huge expulsion of energy, like some part of her had been torn asunder and tossed aside. Lightning crackled between her hand and Zozo's fur where they touched.

Everly screamed, overwhelmed by the pain and illness raging from the cut in her arm, and the violence of having a piece of her ripped away. She collapsed sideways onto the concrete, her bleeding arm twisted beneath her chest. She flushed hot from head to toe and grew lightheaded. Disoriented.

Everything seemed to dim.

"Did it work?" The words were a mere crackle in Everly's throat. She curled on her side, and her eyes sought the dark space for the cougar.

Zozo snarled and backed away, his tail flicking irritably.

She reached for him. "Zozo?"

He growled and snapped at her fingers, and she pulled her hand back quickly. The cougar backed away several steps, then he turned tail and sprinted away.

"Ev?" Harper's voice shook.

"I think it worked," Everly whispered.

Then she launched to her knees, crawled to the grass, and emptied her stomach.

She lost track of time for a little while. Fever wracked her body, and nausea ebbed and swelled. The dragon howled and swam within her, charging the walls of her mind, a wild, wounded beast. It was furious.

Everly was too weak to move her arms and legs, so

Harper had to support her and drag her into the house. There was a bit of confusion where Harper couldn't carry her up the stairs to a bedroom, and then Everly was on a fainting couch in her father's antique shop. Her eyes closed, then opened again to Harper's distant voice and the press of ibuprofen in her palm.

Everly managed to choke down the pills. At some point, Harper had removed her shoes and covered her with a blanket.

"We need to go free Rylan," she murmured, nearly dropping the glass of water Harper had given her.

She closed her eyes, more comfortable in the darkness beyond. Her head felt like it was splitting in two.

"No, you need to recover." Harper's voice rose, strained. "Rylan isn't going anywhere."

"The dragon is angry. About Zozo. Rylan isn't safe."

"Tomorrow, Ev. Please. For me. Just rest."

Everly made a small sound of disagreement, but sank deeper into the cushions, unable to hold her train of thought, let alone a conversation.

Harper's fingers entwined with hers, and they both fell silent. Everly drifted somewhere between sleep and waking for several long moments, until Harper must have assumed she was asleep.

Because the last thing Everly heard before she finally passed out was Harper saying, "Lian? I need your help."

Everly was back in the crystal cavern, surrounded but jutting outcrops of shimmering stone.

She couldn't remember how she'd gotten there. They'd driven home from Gorhanmere. Stopped for dinner at Crow's Nest. Left this cave far behind. Plus it looked ... different.

The clear and translucent crystal pillars were red now, all of them pulsing with an inner light. So many flashes at once made the whole cave look like a blood-tainted ocean reflecting moonlight. The Bane was gone.

But there were padlocks. *Everywhere.*

Ancient, heavy, rusted ones. Clinging to the crystal pillars. Hanging from stalactites. Cemented into the floor beneath her feet. Even locked onto small, broken chunks of crystal scattered across the ground.

Padlocks everywhere she looked. Some of them were broken, but most of them were locked up tight with no keys in sight. Something scintillated softly in the far corner, growling in a low rumble. The dragon, knotting itself into a tight glowing ball, sulking.

"I'm dreaming," Everly muttered.

Rylan's gruff voice echoed through the chamber. "Boderleth? You in here somewhere?"

She stepped out from behind a larger pillar that blocked her view.

Rylan stood near the entrance to the cavern, lips twisting into a half-smile when he saw her. "Is this place some kind of metaphor?"

"I wish," Everly said with a shudder. "This is where we found the Bane in Gorhanmere. It was just like this, but without all the padlocks. They're new."

"You found it?" Rylan rushed forward, halting just a step away from her. "Have you worked anything out yet from it?"

The Bane, the blood, her plan, and the slice down her arm all rushed back into her memory. Along with the name. *Soul eater.*

"Yeah, I've learned some not great things." Everly's voice wavered in a way that she hated, and tears sprung up in her eyes.

"Hey, it's okay." Rylan stepped closer, pulling her into his arms.

Everly sank into him, her face pressed against his shoulder, trying to hold down a shaking sob. She breathed deep, surrounded by the scent that was so singular to him. A scent that took her back years and years to a happier time. That took her back home.

Her *real* home—the one she'd made with him and the Howells, not the broken mess that her mother had created around the hole where her father once was.

"It's okay," Rylan repeated, stroking her hair. "If it doesn't work, if you can't put me back—"

"No. I think I can. Maybe." She released him. "Hang on just a second."

Rylan arched a dark brow in question, but she ignored him and wandered off through the pillars.

"Zozo?" Everly searched among the red columns, looking for the little cougar.

He was always nearby in her dreams, even if she only caught a glimpse of him. And he'd come to her when she called, when he'd pounced on the creepy dolls in the shopping mall for her.

But he didn't come this time.

His ghostly form didn't stalk the edges of the dream space.

She could feel his absence.

He was gone. Whatever part of him, his soul, that had been trapped in her dreams had been expelled.

"It worked," she said out loud, astonished. "It actually worked."

"What worked?" Rylan had followed her and spoke over her shoulder.

Turning back to him, it startled her how beautiful he was. The red light glittered off his short hair and his warm green eyes. His jaw tensed as his lips pressed together then parted in a way that brought back every single sensation from the kiss they'd shared.

Whether Rylan cared for her or not, whether he wanted her near or not, he was and always would be an anchor in Everly's life. One solid point in a world that too often felt like a tumultuous ocean. He was the embodiment of *home* Everly had never found anywhere else.

Now it's time to bring him home.

Locking her gaze with his, Everly's smile wavered. "Do you remember that game we used to play when we were young? The one where we'd get every kid in the playground who would join us, and all hold hands in a huge ring. Then we'd run around like crazy, all linked together, tugging and shoving at each other."

In a mirror to her words, faceless, silhouetted children appeared around them, skipping together in a wide, jostling ring-a-rosy.

Everly lifted her hands between her and Rylan, palms up and waiting in invitation.

Rylan frowned but took her hands in both of his without hesitation, sending a jolt of warmth through Everly's chest.

"Yeah, I remember. If you fell over, or let go, you were out. But what does this have to do with anything? *What worked*?"

Everly shook her head and continued, "As kids got out,

the circle got smaller and smaller. There was that one time when it came down to just you and me. And we just, stood there, holding hands."

Rylan's frown morphed into a smile and he chuckled. "Oh man. How could I forget? It was so awkward. But I didn't want to drag you over just to win."

Everly was sure as well, even back then, that he could have if he wanted to.

She squeezed his hands in hers. "And I ... I just didn't want to let you go."

Rylan's smile faded and she could see him swallow.

"But now I have to. I have to let you go." Everly let Rylan's hands fall from hers. "And I know how. I know how to put you back in your body and get you out of this nightmare."

Rylan covered his mouth, his voice muffled beneath it. "How?"

"The Bane can help free you. If I cut myself with it while touching you, you'll be free."

"Wait, what? Cut yourself with the ..." Rylan's teeth bared. "No. Do you realize how bad that sounds? There has to be another way. Don't go doing anything dangerous for me. How many times do I have to beg you not to?"

He reached for her, and Everly backed away from him, shaking her head. "It's what I did for Zozo, and I'm ..." She remembered vomiting, collapsing, burning up from the inside. "I'm fine."

The unlit children ran faster, spinning hectically around them, a dizzying chaos of ghosts.

Rylan's gaze pierced straight through her. "Evie, no—"

"You can't stop me." She had to do this for him. She had to free him.

She had to let him go.

"I'm dreaming! Wake up!"

CHAPTER THIRTY

Everly sat up with a sharp inhalation. Her heart raced and a cold sweat covered her skin. Goosebumps ran up her arms and the back of her neck.

The antiques store was quiet, lit by a stained-glass shaded floor lamp that sat next to the fainting couch. She felt disoriented for a moment, then remembered Harper half-carrying her into the house and getting her settled in there.

Being in the antiques store after dark with only a single lamp to chase away the shadows and ghosts sent a chill down Everly's neck. She shivered and stretched, trying to rouse herself and push away the pain and wooziness that overwhelmed her.

She rubbed the sleep from her eyes, but she couldn't do anything about the flu-like symptoms that had begun after she'd released Zozo with the Bane.

Leaving her shoes where they lay, she quietly left the store, passing through the frosted-glass door, which Harper had left open. She heard voices from the doorway to the kitchen and the sound of the coffee machine running. A quick glance showed Harper and Lian over by the sink, hands waving animatedly and conversing in harsh whispers.

Only snippets reached Everly's ears.

"... he's my son."

"And she's our Everly. We can't ..."

"I know. *I know*. Ghast damn all of this."

The Bane didn't seem to be with them.

Where is it?

Everly blinked her sore eyes and narrowed them as she searched. The candle-shaped bulbs were dim, and the doors to the laundry and basement stairs were closed as usual.

But one of the drawers of a small buffet-and-hutch by the back door was slightly open, a pale shape jammed in the closure. It looked like the parchment the Bane was wrapped in. Harper must have shoved it in there between moving Everly inside and calling Lian.

Holding her breath, Everly crossed the open kitchen doorway in one swift step, hoping they wouldn't see her.

Their conversation continued without interruption, and Everly gingerly opened the drawer. As it edged open, her sickness increased. It was the Bane.

Reaching for it, a wave of guilt caught Everly's hand back. She'd promised. She promised Harper they were a team, that she wouldn't keep any more secrets or take risks on her own. And here she was, stealing the Bane in secret, after giving it to Harper as a gesture of trust.

What if they try to stop me?

The way they were arguing, Everly worried they might not give her another chance to do this. And she had to. For Rylan.

She couldn't leave him trapped inside her with something that ate souls for a moment longer.

She snatched up the Bane, wrap and all, and headed for Rylan's room.

Everly tiptoed up the stairs, carefully avoiding the warped boards that she knew would creak under her feet, then passed down the upstairs hall in the dark.

Inside her old bedroom, she eased the door shut behind her. She flipped the light switch. Nothing happened. The vasmire pieces were still doing their level best to beshadow the space.

Sighing, she turned and carefully worked her way across the room to the window. In the pitch black, she could sense the vasmire parts billowing with power, and cold fog parted around her bare ankles as she skirted the bed.

It smelled horrific, like a slaughterhouse in high summer. Coupled with the proximity to the Bane and her leftover illness from earlier it left her wobbly and weak. But she pushed on.

At the window, she ripped open the curtains. The glow of moonlight filled the room, illuminating the body on the single bed with silver light. He lay exactly as he had since they brought him home from Nell's laboratory. He looked gray and ghostly pale, like a colorless statue lying atop the mattress.

Everly's heart was in her throat as she sat on the edge of the bed and rested the Bane in her lap. She touched his face, his skin frigid beneath her warm fingertips, then she slipped a finger beneath his nose to reassure herself that he was still breathing.

The tickle of his breath on her skin reminded her of all the times they'd been close in her dreams. All the times she'd wished it had been real.

Could it be real, once he's awake again? Will he treat me the same?

Everly didn't give her questions time to search for answers. She had to wake Rylan up for *him*, not for any of her own desires.

She unwrapped the Bane and stared down at the weapon in the dim light. For such a dangerous creation, it was quite beautiful. She wrapped her left hand around Rylan's, their fingers intertwined, and rolled up her sleeve.

Hefting the head-sized object in her right hand, she

positioned the blade over her left forearm. She would have matching cuts on her arms—one for Zozo, one for Rylan.

And they'd both be free.

Then another thought emerged. Maybe, if she cut deep enough, could she cut the *thing* out of her? Expel the soul-eating dragon from her entirely? It would be worth it, to not be a monster anymore.

I could be human again. Just human. In control of myself.

Everly lingered on the thought, torn between hope and the fear of hoping. Her hand shook, unwilling to cause self-harm. She felt frozen in time, willing herself to act, but afraid of the consequences.

The door slammed open.

The light switch clicked loudly in the silence. The bulbs, which hadn't worked for Everly, snapped on, flooding the room with harsh yellow light.

"Ev!" Harper snapped, looming in the doorway like an avenging angel. "What the hell are you doing?"

It has to be now. Everly gritted her teeth, looked back at Rylan, and plunged the Bane deep into her arm.

Harper was across the room in a split second, frantically yanking the diamond-shaped blade out of the wide wound it caused. She cried out as the sharp edge tore into her fingers, and Everly watched, mind blurred by agony, as blood welled up on Harper's hand.

Then everything splintered to shards.

Everly wandered a world of dark, shattered glass.

She found nothing and no one but herself. It didn't even seem like a dream. Just empty, unending black, the vastness of the universe, broken by the glint of sharp edges as crystal broke and fell like rain around her. Over and over. Endless sparkling shards in an eerily soundless deluge.

She was alone. No Rylan. No Zozo.

Is the dragon gone, too?

Her heart clenched as a shimmering ribbon of pale light flashed by her field of vision.

No. NO!

Everly crumpled. She couldn't remember a life without Rylan in her dreams. Even before he'd become trapped there fully, he'd always been around.

She'd lost him. An empty pit opened in the center of her being.

But that thing, that soul eating *thing* was still there. She felt shattered and lost, and no matter how many times she demanded to wake up, she couldn't. So she walked. She cried. She screamed at the emptiness, at the terrible creature that swam like an aurora around her, and she begged for mercy.

Until finally, her eyes opened.

Early morning daylight filtered into the bedroom. She recognized the off-white plaster relief ceiling, the brown, floral wallpaper, the chest of drawers directly across from the bed, and the bookshelf beside it which they'd loaded down with vasmire pieces.

Except … The crates were gone. And the room smelled like disinfectant, not rotting eidolghast.

Everly sat up with a start, throwing her arm out to touch the other side of the mattress, where Rylan had lay lifeless.

He was also gone.

Everly pushed back the covers and put her bare feet on the floor. But as she stood, a wave of dizziness washed over her, and nausea ripped through her guts. Her skin flushed hot, too hot, and her legs wobbled underneath her. She keeled over and hit the rug on her hands and knees, knocking everything off her bedside table in an attempt to catch herself.

A glass of water and bedside lamp crashed to the floor. Loudly.

Racing footsteps echoed in the hall, and a moment later, Lian barreled through the door, her gaze scanning the room.

When she saw Everly on the carpet, she *tsk*ed. "Got up too fast?"

Everly nodded, tears blooming as pain roared through her arm. "Rylan?"

Lian smiled. "He's awake."

Everly closed her eyes and let out a single, thankful

sob. The pain in her arm, the sickness in her body, none of it mattered if Rylan was back.

Lian tucked her arms under Everly's shoulders and hauled her back to sit on the bed. "You need to rest. You were in really rough shape last night. There were moments we were worried you wouldn't pull through."

There were times Everly had also wondered, in that world of darkness and shattered glass, if she'd already died.

Lian's smile fell away. "That was a stupid, dangerous thing you did."

"But it worked," Everly pointed out weakly.

Lian's eyes turned glossy and she pulled Everly in for a hug. "It did. Thank you."

Everly's head swam, trying to grasp onto reality. She worried about Harper being angry with her, and how she'd been cut with the Bane too. She worried about the throbbing pain in her arm, and how long she'd been out. But only one thought kept emerging to the surface.

She needed confirmation, she needed to see with her own eyes. "Can I see him?"

"There were some ... complications." Lian fluffed the pillows up, avoiding Everly's gaze. "I'll ask him if he feels up to it."

"Complications? What complications?"

Lian shook her head. "I'll let him tell you."

After she disappeared through the door, Everly leaned

back onto the pillows for a moment, working through a breathing exercise to fend off what felt like a killer panic attack. Voices sounded from downstairs, too many to be just Lian, Rylan, and Harper. It sounded like the whole team was down there.

He's awake.

Everly lifted the hem of the bedsheet, intending to dry the tears from her eyes. Pain lanced up her left arm and traveled through her body, making her momentarily blinded from the agony.

She grunted painfully under her breath as she lifted the sleeve of her sweatshirt.

Her arm had been bandaged where the wound was, but there were marks on her skin, extending out around the edges of the dressing.

She was cracking apart. Like the glass in her dream.

The damage was faint. Paper-thin, jagged red lines showed beneath her skin, spider-webbing outwards. She pressed a finger to the cracks and stifled a scream as it felt as though glass shattered beneath her skin. The cracks grew darker and spread farther.

That can't be good.

Heavy footsteps filtered through her despair, and she yanked her sleeve down. If they hadn't seen it when treating the wound, then no one needed to know.

It'll heal. It'll go away, Everly assured herself, watching the doorway in breathless anticipation.

Rylan stopped outside the threshold to the room, his warm green eyes latching onto hers.

Everly let out a breath she'd been holding since the night he was attacked. All that they'd been through since that moment felt insubstantial, unimportant. The goal had always been to bring him back, and here he was. Whole again. Whole and beautiful. And angry.

"Hey," he said, voice gruff and eyebrows low.

"Hey," Everly replied, cheeks flushing hot. "Come in."

His gaze flicked away from hers and latched onto the floor. "I can't."

"What do you mean?"

He scrubbed at his face, then ran a hand over his short hair, blowing out a breath. "I don't know how to explain ... I ... Just watch."

Rylan took a single step into the room, and immediately began to swirl with black, sparking shadyr magic.

His body juddered and twitched. He sprouted fur. His limbs lengthened and hardened, and vasmire fangs grew past his lips, then retracted again, reforming into a wolf-like snout. His clawed hands turned milky translucent until the wall appeared behind them.

It was the exact thing that had happened when Tammy and Cherry came in contact with the eidolghast blood mixture that had once covered the Bane.

"Oh, no." Everly's good hand fluttering to her mouth. The wound in her left arm ached and throbbed. "I don't understand ... We cleaned the Bane."

Rylan backed out of the room, stopping a few steps behind the threshold. His body contorted and with an almost painful groan, the shifting magic ended, and he returned to his human form. He still hadn't looked at her again.

"We're not sure what's causing it. For some reason my shadyr form is reacting to you. Or more likely the soul-eating being inside you. Maybe there are still some essences of the eidolghasts it's consumed in there."

"But it doesn't affect anyone else." Everly's voice cracked.

Lian had sat right next to her, held her. If the Bane had changed something, why was it only happening to Rylan?

Rylan shrugged. "I'm free now, but my spirit spent a long time in there, caught up with you and the dragon. Maybe that changed something. I don't know. I just can't be close to you right now, not without becoming a monster. But it doesn't matter ..."

He trailed off and cleared his throat. "Because you're leaving."

Everly's heart froze in her chest. "What?"

"You should never have risked your life the way you did," he snapped, finally meeting her eye. "I told you I didn't want that."

"But it worked!" Everly said desperately, feeling as if her entire world were turning upside down.

She tried to stand up to move closer to him, but didn't have the strength, didn't want him to feel as though she made him a monster.

"I don't give a damn! I woke up to see you lying lifeless on the floor, blood everywhere, Harper screaming. I thought ..." His tone was cold and remote. "You shouldn't have had to do that. You shouldn't be *here*."

Where was the Rylan from her dreams? The one who had so casually chatted with her? Who had touched her like old friends, who'd laughed with her, fought by her side, comforted her ...? The Rylan who had kissed her until the world fall away.

"I don't understand," Everly said in a small, devastated voice.

But she did. It had been too much to hope that any of the closeness they'd shared in their dreams would continue into the real world.

Rylan had become himself again.

He half-turned away from her, staring again at the floor. "You did what you said you were going to do. There's no reason for you to stay."

Everly swiped at the tears in her eyes before they could fall. "No reason? None at all?"

She wanted to beg him to stop acting like this. Rylan

was every reason in the world she wanted to *stay*.

All along, she'd said over and over that when he was safe, she would go back home. But a part of her had always known that it wasn't the truth. It was a pretty lie she'd told herself to make it easier to walk the halls of her haunted home.

Leaving him wasn't what she wanted.

She wanted *him*. It had always been Rylan. It would always *be* Rylan.

But clearly, he didn't feel the same way about her. He looked at her like she was a monster. And maybe she was. She was possessed by a monster, after all.

Of course Rylan didn't want her. Of course he'd only want her to be gone.

Rylan turned away. "Go home, Everly. Before you really get hurt."

She took a shuddering breath, praying she could hold it together until he left. "If that's what you want."

"It's what you need," he replied, and then he was gone.

The day outside the back door was blustery and gray, and a heavy fog had rolled in off the mountains. Everly couldn't even see the swing set in the backyard for the

thick clouds.

Lian stood on the warped boards of the back deck, looking in the door at Everly, who leaned heavily against the doorframe, panting with the exhaustion of just getting downstairs.

The rest of the Howell team had come up to the bedroom to check on her before heading home. Rylan had already left without even a goodbye. But Everly insisted on getting up to see Lian off.

Lian cupped Everly's cheek in one hand and smiled sadly. "I wish you'd stay."

Everly fought against her rising emotions. She refused to cry in front of Lian. If word got back to Rylan that she was emotional about leaving, she'd have been humiliated.

So she lifted her chin and said, "There's nothing left for me here."

"That's where you're wrong." Lian patted her cheek. "You will always have a home here with me."

Everly blinked back tears and stepped away from Lian's hand. "I appreciate that. But I have a new home now, one that it's past time I got back to."

Lian stared at her for an interminable moment, looking as if she wanted to say something else.

Instead, she just smiled again, even more sad than the first, and said, "Well. Call me and let me know when you get home safe."

With tears finally cresting over her cheeks, Everly watched Lian disappear around the corner of the house.

Her own mother had never once requested such a thing.

Closing the back door, Everly gingerly hobbled up the hallway, doing her best to seem fine and not pass out at the same time. The only person she hadn't seen yet that morning was Harper. That was the other reason she'd worked up the strength to get out of bed.

Everly found Harper bent over the table in the antiques shop, her camera beeping as she took photos of a jewelry box with a delicate, dancing ballerina inside.

"Hey," Everly said.

The camera beeped again and Harper didn't look up. "I'm glad you're alive but I'm not talking to you."

She certainly seems okay, other than angry.

Everly sighed and slumped onto a small two-seater couch beside her. "I just wanted to know how your hand was."

"My what?" Harper glanced up.

She was in full makeup this morning, her thick dark hair down in the kind of messy curls only girls like Bellsy could pull off. She was wearing soft pink overalls with gold buckles that hugged her hips and a baby doll tee that said *Ask me how much I care* in gold letters.

"Your hand," Everly repeated. "You cut it on the Bane last night."

Everly was ninety-nine percent certain the strange reaction taking place beneath her skin had to do with the soul-eating beast inside her, but a small part of her had been worried about Harper ever since she woke up, despite reassurances from the others that she was fine.

Harper shook her head and returned to her photos. "I didn't cut my hand. You must have imagined it."

"No, I saw—"

Harper let the camera hang from the strap around her neck and lifted both hands. She wriggled unmarred fingers at Everly. "No cuts. I promise. I'm perfectly fine. You, on the other hand, look like you need about five months of sleep."

"Feels accurate," Everly said dully.

I must have imagined it. Everything is so blurry. Pain lanced through her arm again and her face crumpled.

Harper straightened and set the camera down next to the light box she had built on the table. She sat on the couch beside Everly, her expression soft and understanding.

"You okay?"

"Yeah. Everything is good. Everything is done." Everly looked away as tears spilled out of her eyes.

She swiped at them and shrugged. "It's time to go home."

"What? We have so much to do here!" Harper swung her arm around, gesturing at the mountains of antiques.

"We'll hire someone, send a moving company to pack it all up," Everly murmured. "Your last sale was huge. I've got more than enough to pay for it. We can get a storage unit back home and work out of there. Or not. You can go back to your normal work and I'll go and beg for my job back. Whatever. But we don't have to stay here."

"What about Rylan?"

"What about him? He's awake. It's over." Everly couldn't see Harper's face through the blur in her eyes. "He made it pretty clear that he didn't want me here."

"Well screw him then." Harper rested a hand on Everly's. "Forget him and what he wants. Do *you* want to be *here*?"

Everly shrugged. "I didn't think so ... No. It's better this way. Maybe away from Shroudhaven, I'll get a better handle on the dragon, like I did before. We can get back to normal."

Harper pouted and leaned her head on Everly's shoulder. "I'm sorry, Ev. I really thought there was something between you two."

"There was never anything there. He's just some kid I used to know, grown up into a man I don't know. Any feelings were probably just the weird connection caused by the dragon. And that connection is gone now."

Harper brought her head back up and looked at Everly with piercing green eyes. "I think you should talk to him—"

"There's nothing else to say," Everly said. "We pack up and we go. That's that."

"Okay, Ev. If that's what you want."

The mirror of what Everly had said to Rylan almost sent her over the edge into full-on, heaving sobs. But she'd spent her entire life mastering her emotions, learning to function even when everything seemed too hard to carry on. She'd mastered the art of surviving trauma much earlier than most.

"When will we leave?" Harper asked.

Everly straightened and took a steadying breath. "Tomorrow. If that's all right?"

"Of course. I go where you go."

Everly smiled, though even she could tell it didn't meet her eyes. "Where's the Bane?"

Harper's expression hardened and she crossed her arms over her overalls. "Hidden where only I can get to it. Because clearly *you* can't be trusted."

"But it worked!" Everly waved her hands wildly in the air, feeling like a broken record. "Not to mention, it's not like I have another soul inside me still to remove. It's just me in there now."

Wandering through a dark and broken emptiness.

"Regardless," Harper said firmly. "The Bane is my responsibility. You stay away from it."

"Fine." Everly glanced around her father's store.

A hint of bittersweet sorrow filled her bones. She had grown to love this space. She wanted to stay. She'd enjoyed building a fledgling business side by side with Harper. She wanted to get to know more about this store and what it held, to be close to the spirit her father had left behind in his beloved antiques.

Leaving meant giving up the friendships she'd formed with Callan, Cherry, Rush, and Tammy. Even Denny. It meant turning her back on a home with Lian and dinners at The Crow's Nest. No more Cardboard Box Barry sightings. No more Zozo. No more "There's a Mermaid in My Lighthouse." No more coffee on the back porch as the sun rose over the misty mountains.

No possible future with Rylan.

But leaving was her only option. Staying would only hurt more.

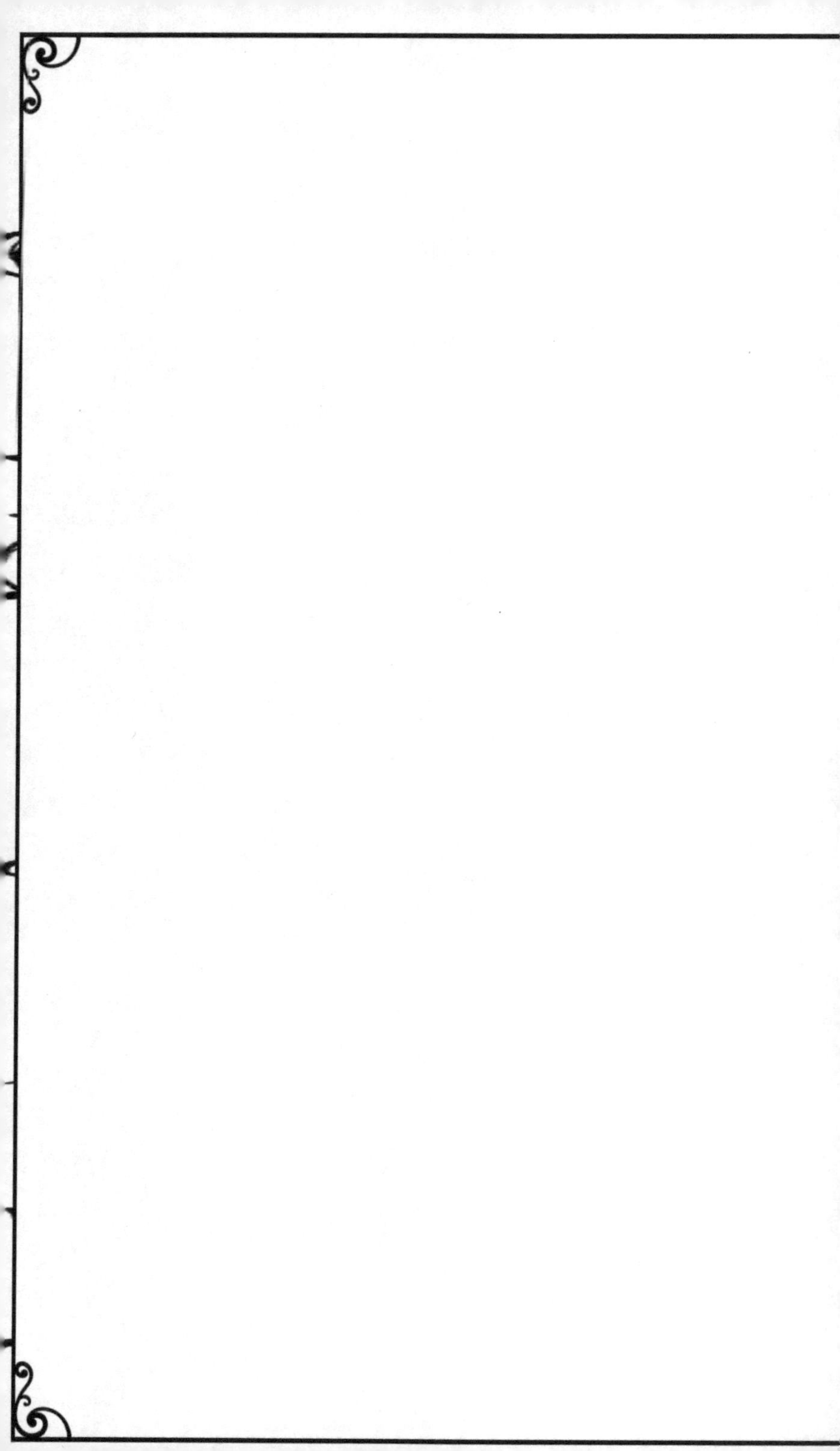

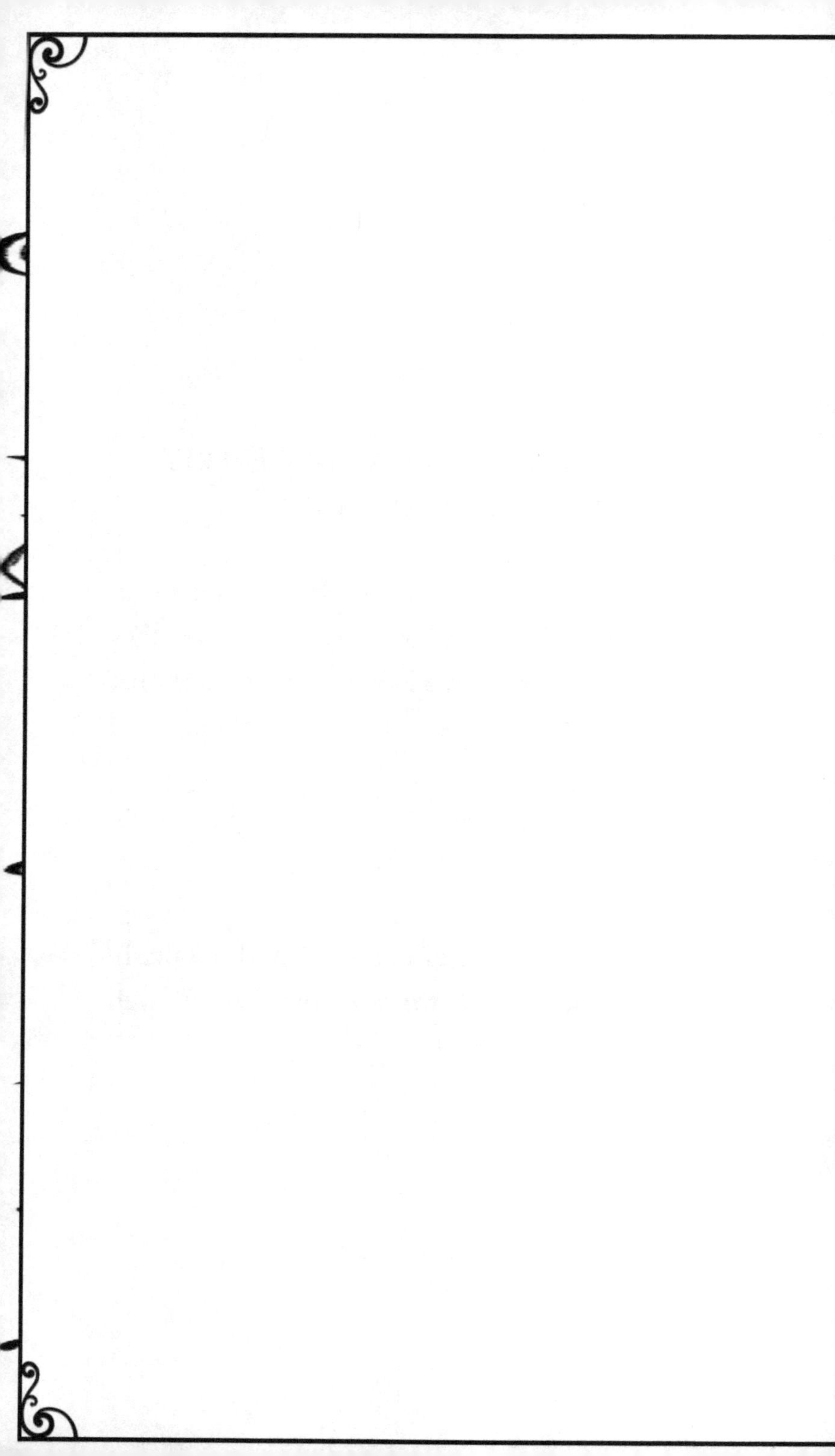

More Books by Selina A Fenech

Shadow Dragon Saga

Into a haunted realm a creature unlike any is born, and must be protected. Diverse young adult epic fantasy with dragons and magic

Memory's Wake Trilogy

A modern girl lost in and hunted in a fairy tale world. An illustrated young adult portal fantasy with Arthurian and Victorian themes.

Empath Chronicles

Teenagers with superpowers fueled by emotions ... what could go wrong? A young adult superhero romance.

Fairy Tale Wishes

Romantic fairy tale retellings with a twist. Young adult, standalone paranormal romance in urban and epic fantasy settings

About the Author

Professional daydreamer, Selina A. Fenech writes "adorably dark" Epic and Urban Fantasy for teens and adults. Filled with sweet and quirky characters, laugh out loud moments, and perilous adventures, her magical worlds are perfect for readers who love daring twists and happily ever afters.

A cancer survivor determined to live life to the fullest, she is an escape room enthusiast, avid gardener, foodie and self-proclaimed geek, residing in Australia.

In addition to literature, Selina applies her unique take on the dichotomy of light and dark as a professional fantasy artist working under the name Selina Fenech and has published many illustrated books, oracle decks, and colouring books.

Find Out more About Selina

OFFICIAL WEBSITE:www.selinafenech.com